Speech Team

SPEECH TEAM

A Novel

TIM MURPHY

Viking

VIKING
An imprint of Penguin Random House LLC
penguinrandomhouse.com

LIBRARY OF CONGRESS CATALOGING-IN-PUBLICATION DATA
Names: Murphy, Timothy, 1969– author.
Title: Speech team: a novel / Tim Murphy.
Description: New York: Viking, [2023]
Identifiers: LCCN 2022037197 (print) | LCCN 2022037198 (ebook) | ISBN 9780593653845 (hardcover) | ISBN 9780593653852 (ebook)
Subjects: LCGFT: Novels.
Classification: LCC PS3563.U76196 S64 2023 (print) | LCC PS3563.U76196 (ebook) | DDC 813/.54—dc23/eng/20220804
LC record available at https://lccn.loc.gov/2022037197
LC ebook record available at https://lccn.loc.gov/2022037198

Printed in the United States of America
1st Printing

Designed by Amanda Dewey
Illustrations by Nada Celsha

To Ellie

Careful the spell you cast,
Not just on children
Sometimes the spell may last
Past what you can see

—Stephen Sondheim,
"Children Will Listen," *Into the Woods*

MENDHEM PUBLIC SCHOOLS

Mendhem High Gazette, Mendhem, Massachusetts, April 22, 1987

Mendhem High Speech Team Warriors Crush "Elite" Private School Rivals in State Finals

Story by Tip Murray '87

Can we *tawk*?

To that inquiry, popularized by supremely mouthy and controversial comedienne Ms. Joan Rivers, the answer would be a resounding *yes*. The last weekend in March—and a frightfully frigid one at that—the silver-tongued minions of Mendhem High's Speech Team, under the skillful tutelage of team coach and Honors English teacher Gary Gold, nabbed gold medals across several categories at the Massachusetts Speech and Debate Society Finals, held at tony, Tudor-style Truscott Academy on the elbow of Cape Cod.

Especially shocking was the fact that, in most categories, Team Mendhem placed higher than participants from so-called "elite," and usually highest-scoring, private schools statewide including Truscott, the Barnes School in posh Wycham, St. George's in rustic Minleyham and, most eyebrow-raising of all, Samuels Farm in horsey Blandford, longtime incubator of the nation's presidents, professors and other cultural pooh-bahs.

Among the Mendhem gold wins were Hampshire College–bound Mr. Peter Stroman, in the original oratory category, for his quirkily uplifting *cri du coeur* "All I Really Need to Know I Learned from

Rush" (the band); University of Massachusetts (Amherst)–bound Ms. Natalie Farb-Miola, in the children's literature (fondly known as "kiddie lit") category, for her artfully bilingual rendition of the Italian youth classic "La Tartaruga Pigra" ("The Lazy Turtle"); New York University–bound Anthony Malouf, in the debate category, for robustly arguing the "pro" side of the question "Is Stress Good for Eighties Teens?"; Yale University–bound Ms. Jennifer Douglas, in the oratory interpretation category, for her stirringly soulful reading of Sojourner Truth's seminal "Ain't I a Woman?"; and finally, this writer, Bard College–bound, in the poetic interpretation category, for his coolly exuberant delivery of selected sections from Walt Whitman's iconic "Song of Myself." (Note: News writers seldom, if ever, refer to themselves by name in their own copy.)

Asked to comment on his team's landslide win, the team's always (sometimes *too*?) candid Coach Gold enthused, "We showed that, with unstinting practice and shrewd guidance, students from your average Massachusetts public school can talk circles around the state's top-ranked teams, bringing home a bevy of ribbons to grace MHS' elegantly refurbished trophy cases in the main hallway." (Note: Mr. Gold signed off on this quote, fashioned by this writer.)

As the Mendhem Speech Team winds down for the year, it looks eagerly toward the 1987–88 competition season, during which one is certain that Mr. Gold's "straight-talk" approach will once again lead "the little team that could" to astounding statewide vindication.

Finally, before this writer decamps for the verdant expanses of the Hudson Valley, just north of the cultural hub that is New York City, he would like to express his unvarnished gratitude to his voluble *confrères* (note: in case you were wondering, foreign terms are often italicized) for the opportunities afforded him by participation on the speech team. The validation and affirmation that this writer could not find on Mendhem's grassy playing fields, or amid its increasingly exclusive social circles (dominated as they are by the ubiquity of Ralph Lauren rugby shirts and frightfully oversized Benetton sweaters), was to be found in spades in the speech team's spirit of exactitude and solidarity.

So, to reiterate the query that commenced this piece—that being, *Can we talk?*—it appears that, when it comes to the Mendhem High School Speech Team of academic year 1986–87, the riposte would be most robustly in the affirmative.

Photo caption: On the bus back from Truscott Academy, the Mendhem gabbers hold aloft their profusion of first-place ribbons. (Photo courtesy Mr. Gold)

FEBRUARY 2013

Sarasota, Florida

On the Ringling Bridge from Longboat Key to the mainland, on the way to find Gold's house—Anthony driving the ridiculously massive Escalade he'd rented at the airport, Jennifer sitting up straight beside him in the passenger seat, Nat slouched beside me in the back, mute—I contemplated the numbing idiocy of Florida. It was a better train of thought than obsessing over what we were about to do. Additionally, it was impossible not to, watching the eternal unfurling of periwinkle sky, cyan water, green palm trees, white boxy homes. How could someone not be rendered utterly imbecilic in this land of relentless sun that bleached away critical thought, frictionless weather that made cynicism a moot point? Was this what you yearned for once you hit your sixties or seventies, to trade the cold and damp of New England, that inclemency that made you cranky and mean but also kept you skeptical and alert, for this mindless blank paradise? Apparently this was what Gold had wanted. No more damp and musty herringbone overcoats, no more ugly rain boots, no more exhaling that final plume from his Vantage cigarette into the frigid gunmetal air of a Reagan-era Saturday morning in January before flicking it into the slush and boarding the bus, his breath sour with carcinogens and his tongue front-loaded with corny competition-day aphorisms, soon to be bestowed on us as the bus groaned its way toward the highway.

"This is the most mind-numbingly monotonous landscape," I said.

Anthony snorted a short, nervous laugh. "I'll take it over New York right now."

"Amen to that," followed Jennifer.

I glanced at Nat beside me, rolled my eyes. I'd picked up on this dynamic the night before, this subtle alignment of Anthony and Jennifer against—or, at very least, in counterpoint to—Nat and me. It had class overtones, Anthony's dazzling success and Jennifer's quieter but still unambiguous good fortune lording itself subtly over my existence as a nonprofit communications drone in a second-tier city, over Nat's near-poverty as a small-plot farmer.

Projection on my part or no, the cleft bonded me more closely to Nat. I wanted her to roll her eyes back at me, at least yield a faint conspiratorial smirk, but instead she just glanced at me, her eyes full of—terror? Was that what I was seeing? I took her hand. It was shaking.

"Are you okay?" I asked her quietly. (Not so quietly, though, that Jennifer, hearing, didn't twist around in her seat with a look of concern, brow furrowed.)

Nat looked straight ahead. "I'm fine." Only then she glanced at me. "I mean, I admit it, I'm nervous. But I'm fine."

Jennifer put a hand on Nat's knee. "I'm nervous, too," she said. "It's understandable, isn't it? We're doing something kind of weird."

Nat, finally laughing briefly, nodded emphatically as though she were relieved and grateful that Jennifer had spelled it out. "It's *really* weird."

"And it's justified." It was Anthony, glancing at Nat in the rearview mirror. "But honey, if you wanna back out, there's still time. You could just wait for us at a Starbucks or something."

Nat didn't answer right away, as though she were seriously considering the offer. But then: "No. I don't want to back out."

As soon as she said it, the tremble in her hand—still lodged in mine—intensified. I squeezed it.

And then Anthony was turning the Escalade off a shopping strip into a network of residential streets, an infinite middlebrow landscape of fairly modest white- or sand-colored single-level ranch homes, landscaping tidy if not lush.

Jennifer pointed at the GPS mounted to the dashboard. "Look," she said. "He is now about nine hundred feet away."

Anthony slowed to a crawl. "This should be it up here on the left," he said. "Sixty-seven fifty-nine, fifty-seven, fifty-five, and here we go."

We were crawling up on the opposite side of the street upon a butter-yellow ranch house, fairly indistinguishable from the rest, a well-tended lawn. First I saw the mailbox.

"Gold!" I exclaimed, reading the name stenciled there.

And then we saw him. Gold, 1987 with the addition of twenty-five years, sitting on the front steps with a mug of coffee at his side, that same tight crown of curls now entirely snowy white, peeking out from under a Red Sox cap. The body still slim but smaller-looking, slightly hunched, in a polo shirt, golf shorts, and flip-flops.

"Oh my God, it's him," Anthony said, hushed.

But Gold had barely had a moment to look up from his newspaper at us before Nat cried out, "Keep driving!"

We all twisted around toward her. "What?" Anthony asked.

She exploded in tears, her hands to her face. "Keep driving, please!"

"Anthony, drive on," said Jennifer sternly.

"But—"

"Just drive *on*, Anthony."

"Okay!"

Which he did, down the street, then a left, then a right, all of us silent while Nat cried and I rubbed her back, until we were back on the main commercial road and he pulled into the parking lot of a Denny's.

"Sweetie," I cooed to Nat. "Shh, it's okay. It's okay."

"It's *totally* okay," Jennifer said, her hand on Nat's knee again.

But, for me, it really wasn't okay. Regardless of what had just snapped in Nat, I was quelling my own private panic. Was this how it was going to end? After all the coming back together, the sharing of notes, reliving that shame, the deliberations about whether this was the right thing to do, and exactly how to go about it—*now* we were reversing course?

I would not. If the others decided to bail, if I had to get out of the Escalade alone and walk back to Gold's, I'd do so. I'd come to believe that I could shake loose something in myself if I confronted him, that some kind of peace or freedom lay on the other side of the reckoning. I had to go through with it. The GPS, still running, told us he was only a quarter mile away—it was, in fact, outlining in emphatic blue the route back to his house. It was time to be brave, I thought, a rare chance to avenge the mortifications of youth.

Avenge? No, no, I thought. This wasn't vengeance. Far too base a word for such a long and considered journey. This was—reckoning! Truth and reconciliation! As Jennifer put it: Restorative justice! Noble ends, unmarred by something as petty, primal, and hurting as vengeance.

Okay. It may have been all those things, but there was a touch of vengeance in it, too. At least for me. I'd felt that the moment I'd seen Gold sitting on that stoop, older and smaller. He was—vulnerable.

Like we'd been.

One

OCTOBER 2012

I walked away from alcohol and cocaine five years ago. *Walked away.* That makes me sound like a staunch and resolute heroine at the end of a film, frightened but brave, doesn't it? Anne Welles leaving Lyon Burke at the end of *Valley of the Dolls* by marching out of her own ancestral New England home and into the snow-blanketed woods—in a mink coat, of course, her bouffant flawless. (That's an ending that always baffled and delighted me in its camp illogic. Who dumps someone by walking out of their own home, leaving them in it?) Or Jill Clayburgh in the final shots of *An Unmarried Woman*, closing the door on her lover, tempestuous artist Saul Kaplan, and signaling to us that she can survive in gritty 1970s New York City without a man by wielding that enormous expressionist canvas *all by herself* through the streets of Soho.

Those analogies not only make me feel somewhat like the glamorous person I've always wanted to be, but conveniently also frame my vices as external bad actors—alluring but seductive men who were coming after innocent old *me*—rather than as extensions of my own internal demons. And I like that. It's always nicer to think that you were just fine—perfectly well-adjusted, going about your business—until you stumbled upon some shiny object, wide-eyed and curious like Snow White confronted by a preternaturally red apple, and consumed it like anybody else would. Who wants to admit they felt like a wreck inside and were looking to get wrecked on the outside?

Because that's really what it was for me. But I still like to say I *walked away* from that affair with amber liquids and white powders, because it has that air of Hollywood denouement to it. And seeing my own life as not quite dully and inconsequentially mine but as something grander, more crafted—scripted, scored, and lit—has always been a huge coping mechanism for me.

So, what I meant to say: Ever since I *walked away*, I've prided myself on staying connected. I know that sounds like a Forsterian start to a story, and in full candor, yes, *Howards End* is one of my favorite novels, and, yes, I've taken its famous edict, "Only connect," to heart. But the truth is, when I was using, I blew off so many people, including my own family and friends, that, these past five years, every time I promptly get back to someone, or—more to the point—reach out to someone to catch up, check in on them, see how they're doing, I consider it a kind of living amends for all the brunch dates, birthday parties, friend-in-need crises, even weddings, that I missed back in those messy years of the late nineties and the aughts. If you saw Aronofsky's *The Wrestler*, you may remember the scene where Mickey Rourke wakes up, after a long night of sex and drugs in a seedy roadhouse, and realizes that he's slept through his date with the daughter he's been desperately trying to rebuild a relationship with. That's the kind of shame that makes you want to die right then and there, and I knew it intimately, over and over again, until I woke up like that on my bathroom floor one Tuesday in 2007 around two p.m., a few days after my thirty-seventh birthday, my wallet and phone gone and my last bit of rebel fight, something I'd nurtured fiercely since I was eleven, depleted.

I sobbed into the tiles for a good ten minutes, then crawled to the landline, called a friend who'd repeatedly offered to take me to an A.A. meeting, and begged him to do so. Once there, slumped in a folding chair, my head pounding, words and phrases I'd long despised—*surrender, powerless, turn over your will*—suddenly seemed like invitations to peace, an armistice of the soul. I became the very twelve-step foot soldier I'd long sneered at, and my relief was total.

And with the exception of a twenty-four-hour binge last year, toward the end of which Marcus was about to call the Providence cops to find me when I walked back into the house stinking of debauchery and shame, I would say that a daily formal practice of mindful humility has managed to help me live with gratitude for all I have rather than with simmering resentment for all I do not. I've always been an acerbic little bitch, mainly for survival reasons, so believe me when I say that gratitude's not a philosophy that came to me easily, or that's easily maintained.

I tell you all of this not to suggest I'm about to embark on yet another dreary once-was-lost-now-I'm-found narrative—haven't we had enough of those?—but to say that, despite my reformed social habits of recent years, I'd fallen woefully out of touch with Nat, our much-revived friendship during my early days of sobriety having dwindled to the occasional call, then a random text here or there, then an occasional Facebook "like" or "Congrats!" then, for the entirety of Obama's first term, basically nothing. I suppose our tapering off coincided with her having moved with her latest boyfriend from Connecticut to New Hampshire, where they rented new land and started a new farm, and my having gotten both a real job and a real boyfriend myself, the aforementioned virtuous Marcus. Prior to that, with me in Providence and her near Hartford, we'd see each other fairly often.

As for why we drifted: Maybe, implicitly, we were giving each other permission to cultivate another primary relationship, one that each of us had been lacking for a while. I hadn't been the only one who'd floundered in my thirties; her entanglements had been not with substances but with cocky Jack and then sullen Julian—one nonstop shitshow of infidelity and screaming recrimination right after the other, each yielding her no lasting happiness except one of her two miraculous kids.

All of which is merely prelude to say that I was mildly surprised to see her show up one morning at the top of my text queue on my phone.

Tippy my love . . . very long time, no speak, I know.
But did you hear about Pete Stroman?

Pete Stroman. I merely stared at the name for a moment, slightly dumbstruck, as though it were an asteroid flying in from the past. Let me tell you something: No crush will imprint itself on your hippocampus like your high-school crush, such that even seeing their name in print years later will make you catch your breath and recall a kind of beauty that has gone unrivaled by all the succeeding beauties. No Hollywood star, no Celtics or Patriots god, no muscled, Speedo-wearing deity of Provincetown or Fire Island, will ever compare, because your first flush of desire, amid the tender years where there is no clear line between the treble notes of infatuation and the bass notes of brute lust, will always be the sharpest and the sweetest.

Such were my feelings upon seeing Pete Stroman's name. He was a small-town hick beauty with the most stick-straight hair and nose I'd ever seen, lips like Jim Morrison's, six feet two inches of lithe cross-country superstardom, huge hands whose machinations on a guitar fretboard melted my closeted seventeen-year-old heart. No article of clothing that wasn't ripped, frayed, faded, or overshrunk ever caressed his lean frame. A vision in three-quarter-sleeve baseball shirts that were billboards for the prog rock he adored, talked about in long, uninflected, unblinking monologues—Rush, Genesis, Yes, King

Crimson. He was too cool and beautiful, too aloof and esoteric, to be bullied, but too weird, folded into himself, to be truly popular. He existed in a high-school genre netherworld, a hybrid of dreamboat and doofus, a heat-seeking missile into my heart. Even the fact that he participated in Speech Team, that apex of geekery, was a testament to his unpindownable mystique. I was searching for some Romantic ideal, some seeker out of the Whitman verse I was so besotted with, and in that football-, beer-, and Van Halen–obsessed New England middle town, he was as close as it got. So I privately worshipped him.

To pass him in an empty hallway was cause for palpitations. I'd have only a moment to arrange my face into some kind of sardonic rictus, to affect an indifferent sashay. Desperate for jocularity, I'd point at his Rush jersey and declare, with mock enthusiasm, "Tom Sawyer, man! Rad!"

Once, absorbing this, he gently but firmly pushed me up against a locker, his breath—intriguingly earthy, like sage—warm in my face. "You know what you are, Murray?" he asked.

"What am I, Stroman?" Could he hear my heart throbbing?

"You're a fucking *pundit.* Do you know what a pundit is?"

His right hand was up against my left shoulder. I had to keep my bearings. "Of course I know what a pundit is. It's a commentator. One who *opines.*" We were thick in the days of SAT tests, gaggle is to geese as pride is to lions, all those words that the average person needs in life about as badly as a real-estate agent needs calculus.

He sneered lightly. "I mean *pundit* in the original sense." Then he released me, swaggered off, pulling his BVDs out from under a bunch-up below the top of his jeans. He did this so unselfconsciously, with such indifference, it only made me love him more.

Later that night on the phone with Nat, I asked, "Did he mean he thinks I'm an ancient Indian wise man? Like, India Indian, not Native American Indian. Because that's actually what a pundit was. A *pahn*-dit, actually."

"You should've just sucked face with him and gotten it over with," she said. "You know you're in love with him."

We had this thing, Nat and I. Nat outright accused me of being gay and I protested extravagantly, even though she didn't really think I was gay and of course I really wasn't, even though she really *did* think I was gay, and in fact I really was. But that third layer down didn't clarify itself until a few years later. Nat said she'd be gay for Janis Joplin, young Grace Slick, or Joan Armatrading on the cover of her *To the Limit* album, but I think she said that just to sound cool, because actually she was obsessed with male endowment. The few times she'd encountered such extreme giftedness, she'd recounted it to me with eyes popping wide, as though she were talking about a good mushroom trip, which she also enjoyed.

So when she said that, I answered "Shut *up*!" with ostentatious offendedness, and then we moved on to other things.

But on this late morning in 2012, when I glanced at my phone while sitting at my desk at work—inside an old retrofitted Providence mill overlooking the power station on the water, office space consumed by university-affiliated research centers and nonprofits with purposes too marginal, or futures too tenuous, to waste on actual campus real estate a mile away—the text from Nat, the first in a very long time, read just that: ***Did you hear about Pete Stroman?***

I picked up my phone. ***No—what?***

He killed himself.

I stared at those three words, blinked, stared again. My first reaction was puzzlement, disconnection. He may have preoccupied me in high school, but he wasn't someone I'd thought much of in the ensuing twenty-five years save occasions, over drinks or a long car trip, when everyone is recounting stories of their high-school crushes. He'd not become one of the dozens of hometown people with whom I'd reestablished some shallow connection over Facebook; I never saw him there. Nor might I have seen him at our twenty-fifth reunion a few months prior. That was an affair I'd long told myself I'd only attend armored in blinding wealth and fame, and that certainly hadn't worked out. The only other way I'd have shown up was as a caustic fly on the wall.

I'd heard through Nat and others that, after dropping out of Hampshire College, Pete had drifted up into Maine and Vermont and become a construction worker, or a restorationist, which made sense to me. He'd never married or had children, as far as I knew.

What? I texted Nat.

Call?

I did.

"Hi." I drew out the *hiiiiiii* that way you do with someone where it's your first *hi* in a long time, the elongation conveying that fact.

And she slow-hi'd me back. "How have you been?" she asked.

"Steady," I said. "I can't complain. I mean, I can, but I won't." I stood at my desk and turned to look at the water and the power station, its three smokestacks vivid against a sky the hard blue enamel of early October. "What about you?"

"We're really good! We're harvesting lettuces. Isn't that riveting?"

"Yummy. Salads!"

"Lots of salads! I miss you!"

"I miss you too," I said, realizing abruptly that I sorely meant it. Just to hear her voice, those old ironic cadences, felt like coming home, in the best way.

"Let's make a plan."

"Totally." We paused, and I continued, "So . . . what the fuck? That's awful."

"Right?"

"What—" I began, *—do you know?* I was going to finish, but it suddenly sounded so crass.

But Nat intuited it. "Did you see his Facebook post?"

"I thought he wasn't on Facebook. I never saw him there."

"I think he went on it to write this last thing."

"I'm on my computer at work."

"I'll DM you the link. Hold on."

In seconds, it popped up in my chatbox. I clicked. In the taxonomy of Facebook profiles, there is a subgenre one might call "I'm never here and I don't give a fuck." No profile photo, or a very outdated one, little to no biographical information, friends that don't exceed the double digits, a few half-hearted reposts of articles about events that occurred four years ago. Such was Peter Stroman's page.

"You have to scroll down through the posthumous tributes," said Nat.

There were a good few dozen of them.

I will miss you, you beautiful man.
I'll always think of you when I look at my back deck.
Uncle Peter, we love you so much!
We hope your [sic] *in heaven now.*
Strobaby, gonna miss you bad. I know life frustrated you.
Hope you're finally at peace.

That sort of thing.

And then I found it, which I reported to Nat before I read.

That's it, folks, I'm out, it began. *tired of trying to connect, tired of trying to find someone to love me and understand me, tired of trying so hard to "read faces" and make sure I respond the right way, tired of this fucking unequal oligarchy of a country (fuck you Wall St.), tired of this planet we've destroyed with our laziness and greed, tired of eeking* [sic] *out a living—just tired of it all. Don't feel bad for me. Seriously. I'm relieved. Sending love and good vibes to everyone. And to Gary Gold, who told me I was a fucking drone robot, go fuck yourself. Seriously. You smelled like a wet dog, too, you fucking creep. Peace, everyone. See ya around. Pete.*

I absorbed it, my eyes widening as I read. An image flew back to me, the first time in twenty-five years—Pete sitting alone in that dark hallway at Barnstable High School, his headphones on, impervious to my entreaties that he come back and join us at the little impromptu dance in the cafeteria.

"Fuck," I finally said into the phone to Nat.

"I know, right? *So tired of trying so hard to read faces,* he wrote. Do you think he was—um—on the spectrum?"

I considered this. "That totally makes sense now."

"All the fucking things we didn't know in the eighties, right?"

"Right," I echoed slowly. Then paused. "Oh, poor Pete Stroman."

"I know. But—"

"I know," I said, predicting her. "The Gary Gold part."

"I know!" she exploded. "Do you really think he said that to Pete?"

"Would you be surprised?" My heart quickened and my brow flushed. "Wasn't that just his delightfully unfiltered style?"

She was silent a moment. I realized my tone had quickly sharpened, unbidden. "Yeah, but—wow. That's rough."

"He *did* smell like a wet dog," I added. "Gold. That damp overcoat."

"Yeah," Nat said uncertainly. "I don't really remember. It's a long time ago."

We were both silent for several seconds.

"Do you know how he did it?" I finally asked.

"You didn't read the obituary?"

I had scrolled right past it, it turned out, as I searched for his final post. "Oh, here it is," I said, clicking it.

"He drowned himself in Lake Winnipesaukee. Off his family's dock. I mean, it wasn't their dock anymore. But he used it anyway."

"Oh, man," I said. "That is just too, like, *A Separate Peace* or something."

"I thought, 'It's so New England Gothic.'"

"Totally!" We both cracked up, relieved to be laughing finally. This was the marrow of our friendship, going all the way back to prepubescence. Nothing was too sacred that we wouldn't seize a pop culture reference to cheapen it with. It's why people in high school called us Statler and Waldorf, after the two old men who sat in the balcony on *The Muppet Show* and shaded everyone. It was why I loved her—because we'd been outsiders together, looking in, taking everyone's measure.

"Do you wanna get together this weekend?" I asked.

"We have to pick all weekend," she moaned.

"I'll help."

"Seriously? Like when we used to work on Molaski's farm together?"

"Totally." We had indeed worked on a farm together one summer in high school—during which she cemented her love of the earth and all things that come out of it, and I, sunburned and devoured by bugs, had resolved never to work outdoors again.

"Then come up! Olivia and Otis are with me this weekend, too. They'll be so excited when I tell them Uncle Tippy's coming."

"I can't believe you let them call me that." The day I left for college, I rechristened myself Thomas, my real name, and had been using it ever since. *I can't believe your childhood nickname was Tippy!* friends in adulthood would shriek.

And I'd roll my eyes extravagantly and say, "Yes, that's the name I was cursed with the first eighteen years of my life." Nat was among the tiny handful of people outside my family I allowed to still use it, because to hear it was to immediately be thrown back into the state of being small, fey, unprotected: a turtle denuded of a shell—a sitting duck, a target.

I beat Marcus home that night, home to the two-bedroom top-floor unit of a Greek Revival in Fox Point we'd bought together a few years ago. Enough time remained for me to slather a chicken with olive oil, sea salt, cracked pepper, rosemary, and thyme, surround it on a cookie sheet with similarly dressed shallots and potatoes, then shove it in the oven. Then I poured a wineglass of Perrier while shedding work garb and donning shorts and a ratty old Bard T-shirt that I cherished as an artifact from a time when I was decadent but hadn't yet totally debased myself. The wineglass of Perrier was what I turned to nearly every evening after work to still feel like a grown-up. If I really needed to feel sophisticated and soigné, I added a lime wedge.

Briefly bereft of something to do, I flipped open the laptop, returned to the Facebook page—hastily constructed, it seemed, to pen a digital goodbye letter to the world, a perfunctory attempt at explanation for one's imminent absence. I scrolled and scrolled through the tributes—some of which, I noticed, were from high-school friends. *I'll miss you, Stromie, you were always an original,* someone with the supremely blandly Massachusetts Irish name of Bill McGibbon had written, someone whose teen face I couldn't even recollect and whose profile I didn't bother clicking on. I didn't need to see photos of him at a soccer tournament with his equally bland wife, some girl named Kerry or Casey, and their pink-faced, prematurely obese spawn.

A certain Jennifer M. had written: "This comes as very sad news. I still remember fondly my days on high-school Speech Team with Pete, all those early-morning bus trips practicing our entries, and I hope he is at peace now. Sending condolences to his loved ones."

Gears in my head turned as I clicked into Jennifer M.'s profile. The lead photo was of a fashionably bespectacled Black woman, tight curls stylishly cropped and faintly dusted in silver, in a large, sweatshirted embrace with a Hispanic-looking man roughly her age and two handsome children, a boy and a girl. What appeared to be the beach houses of Wellfleet or Oak Bluffs rose up in the background.

"Fuck!" I whispered to myself.

Jennifer Douglas-Maldonado.
Lives: Montclair, NJ
Works at: Professor, American Studies, Rutgers University
Grew up: Mendhem, Massachusetts
Studied at: Yale University, BA; University of Michigan, MA, PhD

Jennifer Douglas! I'd heard, years ago, that she'd gone into academia, but I'd not kept up with her—in fact, not since that devastating fall freshman weekend many years ago in New Haven, which still mortified me to think about.

But now here she was! Looking so much more—relaxed? loose?—than I recollected her. Which I suddenly did, with a surprising pang. I recalled her brisk kindness and her tidily packaged intelligence and her game good humor, as though she were always waiting for someone else—like me—to make the naughty crack she would not permit herself, so she could then release herself in delicious laughter upon hearing it. On Speech Team, we'd always gently teased her for her too-perfect elocution; her near-uniform of pearls, Benetton sweaters, long skirts, white stockings, and sensible flats, straightened hair forever pulled back neatly with barrettes or with a headband; her prissy and charming way of responding to our vulgarities, with an "Oh, my!"—a hand raised to the clavicle, as though she were an Edith Wharton dowager. We never thought about what it must have been like for her being one of, if I remember correctly, three or four Black students and no more than a dozen students of color, nearly all of them Asian or Indian, in a high school of about twelve hundred. We'd say to one another, "Jennifer's not really Black," or "Jennifer acts whiter than I do!"

I remembered her intense devotion to Black literature, how she always had in hand a paperback of Toni Morrison or James Baldwin or Gwendolyn Brooks or Langston Hughes, often just for pleasure, how she'd sometimes put it down, spine up, when we approached, her hand lightly over the cover, as though she were embarrassed by it. It had never occurred to me that she was perhaps trying to hold on to her Blackness in a world where we denied her that merely because she defied our stereotypes of what a Black person should be, that perhaps she was dreaming of a future where she and other brainy Black people could discuss Black literature together free from the puzzled gaze of white people whose picture they didn't fit into.

I thought of her standing before a roomful of Speech Team competitors and teacher- or parent-judges, white to a one, straightening herself and folding her hands neatly at her waist, launching into her interpretation of "Ain't I a Woman?" that had won her an oratory interpretation blue ribbon. I suddenly, intensely missed her—beyond reason for someone I'd barely thought of in all the ensuing years since that New Haven weekend, after which I'd determined that she'd more or less decided that whatever friendship we'd had in high school was over.

The key turned in the door. Marcus entered, in his blue nurse scrubs, doffed his backpack onto the bench by the door. I loved catching him in his scrubs, before he traded them for a T-shirt and shorts on his scarecrow frame, cleared his frazzled work head with a short run around the neighborhood while I prepared dinner. I'd picture him at work, inserting a chemo line into a patient's implanted port, deftly focused while still managing soothing small talk about the Red Sox or Governor Chafee.

"He's not edgy, but he's perfect" is how I'd first described him to

Nat, a few months after meeting him in 2009 via Grindr, shortly after the debut of that gay hookup app that digitized desire into neat localized grids of mainly headless torsos. I'd have laughed if you'd told me, in my first months of its use, that amid those tiny *Brady Bunch* squares lay my future domestic partner.

I'd sent Nat a screenshot of Marcus from the app, the mop of brown curls and the wire-frame glasses, the "Obama-Biden '08" T-shirt and the hiking boots, standing on a mountaintop.

To which Nat replied, "He's so Jewily adorable." (She was Jewish on her mom's side.) "Plus, I think you need less edgy for once. And I'm sure he's not perfect."

"No," I'd responded cheerfully. "He is. But there's just enough cynical smartass in there to make him bearable."

It wasn't supposed to be like this. I'd spent so much of my life, since the single digits, growing up in that hateful town, dreaming about or chasing a life of exotica and glamour, interpolating myself into novels and films. I'd be a foreign correspondent based in Paris, a screenwriter in Los Angeles, a film critic for *The Village Voice* who gabbed the night away in Soho with Fran Lebowitz and Michael Musto, never arriving back to my loft before midnight. And in all three scenarios, I was a boldface name, a byline that commanded recognition and respect. Yet except for a brief period when I lived a sordid, failed version of that New York fantasy, none of that had happened. I'd ended up a communications writer for an education-reform nonprofit based at a university I hadn't even gone to, living in a city that, albeit charming in many ways, was of no real global cultural consequence, all but married to a bright, kind, wry, and existentially untroubled oncological nurse, someone whose idea of adventure was one very well-structured week a year in a European capital.

The other thing I couldn't have predicted was that, after an initial period of extreme discomfort and restlessness, culminating with that twenty-four-hour disappearance, I'd be happy with this life. Which I *was*. I was sure of it. Fairly sure. If you saw the two of us together, Saturday mornings at the farmers market or holiday weekends walking Commercial Street in Provincetown hand in hand, you would think that you were looking at a happy couple.

He approached me after kicking off his work Nikes, bent down for a kiss, strafed my cheek lightly with his mild stubble. "What are you making, Tommyboy?" Vestiges of his native New Jersey accent.

"Roast chicken. Basic."

"You know I love that." He'd once told me my roast chicken was as good as his Bubbe's. Then, just in case I'd missed the import of that, he'd told me it was one of the highest compliments he could pay.

He opened the fridge, pulled out his half-finished bottle of rosé.

"You're not running today?"

"I don't have it in me. I just wanna collapse."

I always made a point of looking away when he poured a glass of wine. It was just too poignant, too painful, watching that magic liquid spill into the glass, too much sensory recall. When we first moved in together, he asked if I'd rather he not bring alcohol into the house, and I asked him to keep it to beer (which I hated) and wine (which I . . . didn't hate), because I figured the presence of vodka and tequila would undo me. And for the most part, I'd been okay with that compromise. Except for the moment of the pouring of the wine. Once it was poured, I could cope. But the pouring. Or, worse, the uncorking. All the potential, all the promise, of a freshly uncorked bottle of wine, the snug assurance that there'd be bottles to come . . .

I snuck a look at the poured glass. Translucent pink, crisp, and cold.

He flopped down next to me on the couch. I ran my hand through his curls, a favorite pastime of mine. "How was today?" I asked.

"We were slammed. That's all the energy I have left to say."

"Okay."

"What about you?" He dropped his head back on the couch, submitting to my fingers.

"Fine."

"*Fine.*" He mimicked my lifeless tone. "You have to look for another job."

"Like there are any around here for a failed hack writer."

"You're not a failed hack writer. And you could commute to Boston."

"Yeah." I hated talking about trying to find a more meaningful work life. So, partly to switch the subject, I said, "I did find out someone I went to high school with killed himself."

"Shit." His head was still cantilevered back onto the couch, only politely interested. "Someone you were friends with?"

"I wouldn't say we were exactly friends. We were on Speech Team together. And I was madly in love with him—or lust—even though he was probably on the spectrum. That's what Nat said today and I think she's right, looking back."

Marcus said nothing, his mouth wide open, as though he were asleep. Finally: "That's sad."

"Yeah. Nat texted me to tell me and then we talked. In fact, would you wanna drive up to New Hampshire with me on Saturday to see her? Maybe overnight and do the New England fall thing?"

Now he yanked up his head. "Saturday," he reflected. "I was gonna run a 15K, remember? A charity thing for work."

"Oh, okay. That's cool. You don't mind if I head up—maybe overnight?"

Now it was his turn to grab a thatch of my hair, caress it inexpertly. "Why would I mind?"

"Just—you know—we try to do something, like, meaningful on the weekends."

"Well, we've got Litchfield the weekend after, right?"

"Yeah, that's true."

"So, you know, go see Natalie and catch up."

It had taken us a while to get to this point, this realization that we only needed to be on the same page half the time—okay, honestly, make that about one fifth the time—to make things work.

"Okay then." I rose from the couch.

"How is Natalie, anyway?" His voice trailed behind me as I went back into the kitchen. He always called her by her full name.

"She's good, I think," I called back.

Marcus liked Nat. Raised in an indifferent Jewish Reform home himself, he liked the novelty of my half-Italian, half-Jewish hometown bestie who celebrated Hanukkah and Passover with her maternal grandparents, Christmas and Easter with her paternal ones, and the Fourth of July at the beach with all four of them. He also still delighted in the fact that, one randomly arranged weekend in Maine with Nat and Marcus's brother, Sammy, when Nat was detoxing off Julian and Sammy was coming off his own bitter separation, the two of them had sex in the adjacent bedroom late at night when they thought Marcus and I were sound asleep.

The next morning at breakfast, as Nat and Sammy tried to feign normalcy, Marcus couldn't keep a straight face. After breakfast, alone with Nat, because—I was fairly certain—there was nothing we didn't share, I asked her, "Had fun with Sammy last night?"

She gasped. "You heard us? It was nearly two!"

"We were still up."

She suppressed a scream, hand over her mouth. "I'm mortified!"

"Why? You're both free. Good for you."

Then her hand fell and her eyes narrowed. In her low voice: "Tip, he's so *big*."

I laughed, delighted. "I guess it runs in the family."

Saturday morning, I passed the two-hour drive from Providence to their little farm plot in Stratham, New Hampshire, in a happy haze of caffeine in my bloodstream and Grizzly Bear on my speakers, trying to make the music match the exquisite melancholy of a New England fall. When I pulled up on their land around noon, they were already in the field, picking lettuce—Nat; Aaron, her boyfriend of the past two years; and Olivia and Otis, Nat's kids from cocky Jack and sullen Julian, respectively. Nat must have heard my car, because she was coming out of the crop rows, wiping her hands on her jeans, her bobbed brown hair—that style unchanged since high school—pulled back under a red bandanna. She was tiny. She didn't age. She would forever be sixteen years old to me, in a batik skirt and Converse high-tops, discoursing on the difference between the Grateful Dead and the Velvet Underground while rolling me my first-ever joint.

Her arms outstretched now. I'd never had a sister and I always thought of these reunions with her like the end of *Twelfth Night*, twins Viola and Sebastian finding each other again, collapsing into each other's arms as though they were reclaiming their lost half.

"It's so good to see you."

"It's so good to see *you*."

"It's been too long."

"I know."

My arrival occasioned a lunch break for everyone: sandwiches, pickles, chips, and lemonade on the back deck of the small, slumping three-bedroom Cape they rented along with the land. I loved Otis and Olivia, split variations on Nat, her shrewd, sardonic side embodied in Olivia, fourteen, and her loose, shaggy side in Otis, eleven, whose hair was longer than his mother's or his sister's. I'd only met Aaron once before, briefly, but I liked him, because he was a variation on the kind of boyfriend she always had: a hippie, a left-of-Obama leftie faintly inclined toward anti-corporate conspiracy theories, a pot-loving slacker, the kind of well-educated, low-earning, non-alpha white guy very distinctly native to upper New England and the west coast from Vancouver down to about Santa Barbara, but not farther south. (I only prayed that his sleepy-eyed mensch factor ran deep; I'd had the same first impression of Jack and Julian before Nat told me, as those relationships crumbled, all that had been mere veneer atop two differently hued bedrocks of mindgame-playing asshole.)

"You and my mom were best friends when you were my age, right?" Otis asked. This tendency in kids, to want to know what their parents and older people *were like* when they were *their* age, was one of the ways in which they sometimes stabbed me with pangs of regret that I had none of my own, nor likely would. I could call kids breeder spawn all I wanted, write them off as straight people's way of plugging up the hole of existential dread we all lived with, so they didn't have to think about it—but as soon as I met smart, kind, and sardonic kids like Olivia and Otis, all that crumbled. They reminded me of myself at that age, full of unguarded wonderment, just before I became afraid and vigilant all the time.

Nat and I glanced at each other, doing the math. "Not quite your age," she finally answered, latching Otis's hair out of his face and behind his ears while she spoke. "We became friends in high school, when Tippy was a sophomore and I was a freshman. We went to different schools before that."

"Is that what they called you then?" Olivia deadpanned to me, sympathetically. "Tippy?"

I rolled my eyes. "Yep! Just like Tippy the Turtle. Oh, wait. I'm dating myself. You guys don't know who that is, do you?"

Otis shook his head vigorously, his mane flying about, but Olivia said, in the same underwhelmed drawl, "I know who he is. We had him in a magazine in school when I was little. You're supposed to draw him, right?"

"Right. And send it in to a contest."

"Well," Aaron interjected. "Livy's a potter now, right?"

Olivia frowned at Aaron, but in the affectionate way a teenage girl frowns at the annoyances of her real dad, not the truly resentful way she might frown at some random guy with whom she now had to compete for her mother's attention. Or at least I thought.

"*Aa*ron," she began. "I'm a ce*ram*icist."

Aaron straightened up. "Oh! I'm sorry. A ce*ram*icist."

Nat reached over, scratched the top of my hand. "She actually has something for you."

I looked at Olivia, eyes wide. "You do?"

"It's a bowl. It didn't come out as perfect as I wanted it to. I'll get it for you later."

I think I blushed, moved. "I'm deeply honored." I put my hand to my heart and bowed my head in exaggerated gratitude, which made Olivia roll her eyes and Otis yelp aloud. I always wanted to make them laugh: an extension of always having wanted to make Nat laugh in high school.

That night, after I'd put in a few hours with them in the fields as promised, after we'd set aside some of the day's yield to make a salad to eat along with the pizza we'd had delivered, after the kids drifted away and it was just Nat, Aaron, and me on the back deck in sweatshirts as the sky darkened and the crickets got loud around us, Nat and Aaron passed a joint back and forth while I held a mug of tea between my palms and we again took up the topic of Pete Stroman's suicide.

"Tippy was in love with Pete in high school," Nat explained to Aaron.

"I was not in love with him!" I protested, half-heartedly. "I—" I searched for the words. "I was *intrigued* by him."

But Nat rolled her eyes. "You wanted to get in his pants and you know it. You just couldn't admit it at the time."

I looked sourly from Nat to Aaron, his face a study in careful neutrality, then back to Nat. "Okay, fine, whatever. Yes. He was beautiful. And he was also so weird. I was obsessed. I can say it now!"

Nat cackled, ripely stoned now. "Doesn't that feel good?" She reached out in her chair to Aaron, laced her fingers in his. "He was quite striking, I'll grant you that."

Aaron cocked his head. "I don't feel like I can compete."

"I dunno," she drawled. "You're okay." Then she leaned over and kissed him. I wondered if I should retire to bed soon so the two of them could get on with it.

But then she turned back to me and asked, frankly, "Do you think Gold actually called him that? Called Pete that, I mean? I don't remember him being that nasty."

Gold. My stomach curdled slightly at the sound of his name. I had barely thought of him in many years prior to the news about Pete, but since that news, I'd thought of him often, considered with increasingly sharp outrage how on earth he could have said to *me* what he'd said, that day after school in the empty classroom. It wasn't just that, as the offhand slights of the eighties became the career-ruining capital offenses of the twenty-first century, I couldn't believe he'd said it. It's also that I couldn't believe I'd just taken it, pushed it down in shame, told no one—not the principal, not my parents, not Nat, or anyone—because on some level, I'd felt he was right. I *did* have to change. I even wondered, later, if his catching me alone after school and taking me aside the way he did was a sort of kindness, a looking out for my best interests. He wasn't calling me out in front of others, to bully or humiliate me, which was the way it had usually gone for me. He was talking to me *privately.*

And now it appeared that I wasn't the only one he'd spoken to privately.

So now I answered Nat: "You mean what Pete wrote in his parting words? That Gold told him he was a drone robot? Yeah, I believe it."

She caught something in my tone and her eyes narrowed. "Why?"

I couldn't believe I'd never told her. I remember having *wanted* to tell her that day, to bike from school to her house, but I'd walked out of school too stunned to do so. I remember just biking home in a daze, thinking, *God, I really* do *have a problem, and I'm not even trying to act that way, I can't even control it.* I'd felt so vulnerable, nakedly exposed in my queerness. It was one thing for other kids, from an early age, to call me faggot, homo, and *queeah* (in the regional greater Boston parlance), but it was another to be served the same news, in calm and concerned tones, from an adult.

"I kind of can't believe I never told you this," I began.

Her brows furrowed, her fingers still enlaced in Aaron's, who also regarded me with a keen concern.

"Well," I began. And then I sighed heavily. I was stunned at the intensity of unloading something that hadn't occurred to me, in twenty-five years, to unload. Could its weight really have been that heavy all those years? It had to have been—I'd never forgotten it. Not even in twenty-five years of presumably becoming comfortable, as a matter-of-fact, *integrated* (as they say) into my gayness. Whenever I thought of it, it burned as though it were happening again that very moment.

"It was junior year. In the fall. And I was basically alone in the school, after school, because I was always there after school for one reason or another. If it wasn't Speech Team practice—"

"Tippy ran everything," Nat cut me off, turning to Aaron. "Speech, the newspaper, the yearbook, the literary magazine, student council," she recited.

"I was just really desperate to have a killer resume and get the fuck out of there," I explained. "Not that anything came of it. Certainly not like it did for Anthony Malouf."

"Anthony Malouf!" she howled.

"Anthony Malouf?" Aaron echoed.

Nat again now: "What's going on with Anth— Wait, no, go on with your story, Tip!"

"Anthony Malouf," I said again. "So glamorous."

"We'll get to him. Go *on*."

Where had I been? "Right," I said. "Well, so, I was, I think I was getting my books from my locker to go home, and he—Gold—he stepped out from his fishbowl."

Nat raised a hand, turned to Aaron. "You have to understand, we went to this high school that was built in the early seventies with this thing they called 'open concept' to make it sound all progressive, but basically it just meant that there weren't real walls. There were just, like, these partitions on wheels that separated classrooms, which meant there was no quiet or peace of mind anywhere. The real reason they built it like that is because it was cheap. You save a lot of money when you skip the walls."

"Right," I added, "except at some point they enclosed some areas with these cheap, like, Plexiglas walls, and those rooms were called fishbowls, because everyone could see in."

"Right!" recalled Nat. "And Gold had his own fishbowl, right?"

"Right. He'd insisted on one so he could have a quiet place to coach us for Speech Team. So this one afternoon, he pops out from his fishbowl into the hallway area, and he sees me, and he goes, 'Tip? You got a minute?' And he beckons me into the fishbowl, and so I pack up my backpack and I go in and he closes the door to the fishbowl, which I think is weird, because we're alone anyway, and he tells me to sit down across from his desk."

"Oh my God," Nat interjected. "I'm scared where this is going."

"I'm getting creepy Catholic priest vibes," said Aaron.

"He was Jewish, actually," Nat said. "I'm pretty sure he was the only Jewish teacher in the school. I can just picture him now, with his Jewfro and those square glasses and that brown corduroy suit."

"And those *earth shoes*," I interjected.

"I know!"

"But he was strangely sexy on top of all that," Nat added. "He looked like a slightly shorter Elliott Gould—really intense dark eyes and an amazing nose and a *very* strong jaw."

"It's true," I added. "He was hot under his dorkiness, which made the whole thing even weirder for me, because I had faint daddy feelings toward him—I realize now."

Aaron leaned forward. "So what did he say?"

I inhaled again. "So he folds his hands in front of me and says, 'Murray, what's your deal?' I thought he was going to ask me something about Speech Team. So I said, 'What do you mean?' And in this very calm voice, almost like he's trying to be nice, he goes, 'Why do you sashay around this school all day like a goddamned mincing queen? Like a flaming homosexual?'"

Nat sat up in her chair. "*What?*"

"Fuck," Aaron exhaled. "Seriously?"

"Or he might have said 'like a flaming, mincing drag queen.' I can't remember. But I'll never forget 'mincing queen,' because I'd never even heard the term before and I didn't even know what 'mincing' meant at the time. And then he said, 'Whatever you really are, you'd have a hell of an easier time if you put a lid on it.' Or 'toned it down,' or something like that."

To my great surprise, tears brimmed in my eyes and ran down my cheeks before I could stop them. I'd not felt them coming.

"Tippy!" Nat leapt up and hugged me. "Why didn't you tell me? We told each other everything."

"I don't know." Embarrassed, I smudged away the tears. "I was so stunned. I just remember riding my bike home in a daze and ignoring my mother and going up to my room and closing the door and just lying there on my bed, feeling, like, very exposed. Very unmasked. It was one thing to be called that by kids for years, because I could always say, *Well, they're just stupid Mendhem troglodytes*, but for a teacher to say it—I think I was like *Oh, God, it's true, I really* am *that, and there's nothing I can do about it because I can't even hide it.*"

"But it's pretty weird," said Aaron, "that he used the term 'mincing queen,' isn't it? Kinda like, takes one to know one? What straight dude would say that—especially back then?"

"Yeah," I said. "I've thought about that over the years. It did kind of feel like he was trying to have some kind of inside talk with me, you know, like to warn me?" I turned to Nat: "Do you think he was gay? Or even bi? He did live in Newburyport, right? That's kind of arty."

She was oddly silent for several seconds, staring into space.

"Babe," Aaron finally said.

"I guess he could've been," she answered at length, as though she hadn't disappeared for a moment. "Maybe bi. Possibly." Then: "Did he ever bring it up again?"

"No. We just went on with Speech Team and practice and stuff. And the funny thing is, after the initial shock, I don't even remember really thinking about it that much or feeling weirded out when I saw him. I even asked him to write me a college recommendation and he did, and when I got to Bard, when I worked in admissions, I pulled it out and he'd written this very positive thing. I remember him writing something like *As much as Bard needs a student like him, he needs a school like Bard.*"

Aaron laughed. "Because he knew you so well!"

"Yeah. And like I said, I didn't think about the fucked-up-ness of what he'd done until years later, when there was all this public stuff about bullying and homophobia in schools, and court cases."

"You could've gotten him fired if that had happened today," Nat said, rather sharply.

"I know, right? And I think I realized later on that it bothered me so much because, before he said it, he was one of the only older men in my life who—you know, who loved arts and literature, and he wasn't some kind of macho, sports-obsessed guy like my father and everyone's father in that town."

Nat, seated again, turned back to Aaron. "Most of the male teachers in our high school had gone to high school there and never left town, and they became teachers so they could coach sports." She turned back to me: "Aaron went to the Putney School in Vermont, so he has no idea what we're talking about."

He laughed gamely. "It's true. The only sports there were, like, ultimate Frisbee and jazz dance." He sipped his beer. "So he was like a mentor to you."

"I wouldn't have put it that way at the time," I said, "but yeah. I mean, the man got me into Walt Whitman and Jack Kerouac and fucking Sylvia *Plath* and Anne Sexton."

"Yeah, I get it," Aaron said.

Nat had gone mute again, lost in space.

"Anyway," I finally said, partly to break the silence, "so, yeah, I can totally see Gold lasering in on this issue with Pete's personality—basically what we would now all call being on the spectrum—and pointing it out to him, in this weird mix of wanting to quote-unquote help him, and also because the guy had a nasty side."

"Maybe not a *nasty* side," Nat interjected. "Maybe more like foot-in-mouth syndrome?"

"I dunno," drawled Aaron. "What he said to Tip sounds pretty damn nasty to me."

"Yeah," I said, slightly annoyed at Nat's minimization and grateful for Aaron's correction. "I definitely think there was some nastiness behind it. And even if there wasn't—I mean, look, here I am twenty-five years later remembering it. And so did Pete."

"It was basically the last thing he thought about," said Aaron. "That's fucking sad."

"Tip?" It was Nat, looking right at me now, vaguely—chastened? "I am so, so sorry he said those things to you. I wish you'd told me. I guess I never really thought about what that aspect of high school was like for you. Kind of like being in the closet to yourself."

"Yeah. I guess you could put it that way."

She paused. "Man, the *eighties*, right? We were so backwards."

We fell into silence again. I felt oddly light, unburdened. I half lay back in my chair, my mind wandering slightly.

"Wasn't he totally creepy with you?" I asked Nat at one point.

A pause. "He was?" she finally replied.

And Aaron echoed her: "He was?"

"Yeah," I continued. "I remember you telling me that he was always giving you a sort of gentle rub on the back, or a little quickie shoulder rub on the bus, on the way to a competition. Didn't he?"

I glanced over, caught her squinting at me with what seemed like irritation. But she then glanced away, up at the stars. "Did I really say that?" she finally asked.

"I totally remember you saying that."

"Yeah," she answered slowly. "I guess there were a few instances of inappropriate touch. But that was when I first came on the team, and then I remember they stopped. I remember we found out that his cousin had grown up in Newton with my mother. So maybe that was like a no-no for him. Like, he didn't want something bad about him going through the Greater Boston Jewish grapevine."

"Hmm," I murmured.

The three of us were quiet for a spell, the crickets filling the silence. I was thinking about a bus trip to a competition at Truscott Academy, a series of Tudor-style buildings right on the water on the way to the Cape. On that bus, so early on a November Saturday that there was still frost on the windows, we burrowed deep into our coats and blew on our hands while we rehearsed our entries, breakfasting on the box of Dunkin' Donuts that Anthony's mother, who was serving as a parent-judge, had brought along. Coach Gold up front, the smell of his beloved Vantage cigarettes, the one he'd smoked and stubbed out right before boarding the bus, the cold still clinging to his dark curly hair and his musty herringbone overcoat. He sat alone, leafing through the *Boston Globe* and *New York Times* he'd brought along with him. Nat and I sat together practicing, Anthony and Jennifer sat together practicing, Jennifer in her perfectly modulated schoolteacher voice, Pete Stroman slouched several seats behind all of us, encased in his Walkman, dozing in and out of sleep.

The nearly straight shot south from the North Shore, right through Boston, all the way down to Buzzards Bay, pulling up in front of that sprawling faux-Tudor building that fronted the water, filing into that great hall, its table of coffee and (more) Dunkin' Donuts, the five of us disappearing into the churn of students from other schools—the public-school girls with their high, moussed hair and boys with their bowl cuts and bad sport jackets, and the private-school girls with their messy bobs and vintage overcoats, the boys in their wool navy coats and rep ties. This was as cosmopolitan as it got for us, these Saturday afternoons sprung free from the banal loop of Mendhem High School, this opportunity to mix and mingle and compete with the broader adolescent nerderati of the Bay State. I loved those Saturdays; they were magical and glamorous to me, my first taste of the world beyond.

Finally, I broke our silence. "Guess who left a note on Pete's Facebook page?" I asked.

"Who?" I could tell from Nat's voice that she was falling half-asleep in her chair.

"Jennifer Douglas. She left something very short and sweet, a note about remembering him from Speech Team."

"Jennifer Douglas!" Nat hooted, revived. "The Schoolmarm!"

"I know, the Schoolmarm. But strangely she didn't look so schoolmarmy on Facebook anymore. Her hair was natural and she was actually wearing a sweatshirt and jeans. Looking—relaxed."

"Wow," said Nat. "It's hard to picture her that way, she was always so prim and proper." She paused. "But so sweet."

"So sweet," I echoed. *Maybe not* that *sweet, anymore*, I thought. The

New Haven weekend was coming back to me again, a pinprick of bitterness way back in the nether regions of young adulthood. But I didn't bring it up with Nat. I didn't think I could bear vocalizing another betrayal in the same evening; Nat might wonder if I was nothing but a walking file cabinet of resentments and grudges.

Nat interrupted my thoughts, anyway. "Can you imagine what it was like for her being the only Black person in that school?" she asked. "In that town?"

"But she wasn't," I said. "Remember the Dreamgirls?" They'd been the other three Black girls in the school—Janis, Liz, and Angelica—chorus stars who all lived in the same apartment complex by the highway and were constantly working out harmonies to Whitney Houston songs in the hallways between classes. Privately, Nat and I called them the Dreamgirls.

Both hands flew to Nat's lips. "The *Dream*girls! That's right. Oh, they were sweet!" Then, after a pause: "Was it bad that we called them that?"

I shrugged. "I mean, we had a special shady name for everyone," I countered. "We could have made up a whole glossary of our private nicknames."

She shrugged in turn. "That's true."

"But anyway," I continued, "Jennifer is a very distinguished professor now. At Rutgers in New Jersey."

"That doesn't surprise me at all," Nat said. "She was wicked *smaht*."

I laughed. "Do you think Gold said fucked-up shit to her, too? In the confines of the fishbowl?"

Nat groaned. "Oh, God. I really hope not."

"Yeah, me too."

Aaron rose, bent over, kissed Nat on the forehead. "You two are gonna have to excuse me. I can't keep my eyes open."

Nat reached up to him. "Me too. I'm coming in a second."

Aaron disappeared, leaving just the two of us.

"He's a sweetie, too," I said, gesturing toward the screen door he'd just closed behind him.

Nat sighed. "He is. He's the best. I just hope it lasts this time."

"So do I. But the last two were assholes, right?"

She didn't answer right away—then, finally: "Yeah." It sounded oddly half-hearted, drained of the vitriol that had once spiked her talk of Julian and Jack. "I just can't put the kids through another breakup, that's all," she continued. "Another life upheaval."

"I hear you."

Then, after a pause, she said, "I am still so upset about what Gold said to you."

"Oh, thanks. Yeah, it's weird. Do you think people remember the things they said or did to people that stayed with them their whole lives? Do you think that was their intent?"

She considered. "No," she finally said. "I think they're just like little bombs that people casually drop and then go on their way. My mother once told me that I'd be lucky if I could hold down a job as a waitress when I grew up. I'm sure she doesn't remember saying it, but I sure do."

"Are you serious? Marlene said that to you?" We'd always referred to our parents by their first names: Marlene and Donald for her, Susan and Mitch for me.

"Yeah, she tossed that off once. And I always think of it when I think about the fact that I'm forty and I don't have two nickels to rub together. And why I'd rather try to get by as a farmer than have a real job."

"You do have a real job. You're a farmer."

"Yeah." She sounded unconvinced. "I guess. It's kind of itinerant, though. I've never owned my own land."

"Well, who knows what's to come?"

"Yeah, I guess."

She rose. "I'm falling asleep, Tipster." She bent down, kissed me on the nose. "Sleep in tomorrow."

"I probably won't be out there with you guys as early as seven, I gotta admit. Maybe nine? Nine-thirty?"

"Whenever! I'll leave you pancakes."

"Oh my God!" I laughed. "You are still the pancake princess." She'd always adored pancakes. They'd been her favorite meal, no matter what time of day or night, sometimes tricked out with fruit and whipped cream, nuts, and chocolate chips, sometimes straight up classic style with syrup and butter. They held some kind of talismanic power for her, an assurance of comfort, constancy, the way I'd felt about tequila and coke. If she ever had to choose, pot or pancakes, I wondered which it would be—especially because the two together had always been her happiest place, the stoned one-in-the-morning walk from the car into Denny's or Friendly's or Bob's Big Boy, the loud orgasmic groan upon the first bite that would earn the attention of the entire restaurant and make the rest of us explode into stupid, obnoxious adolescent laughter.

"Damn straight," she laughed now. "I am still a proud pancake princess." She stood over me a moment longer. "I'm so glad you came."

"Yeah, me too. It's been too long."

"Yep." She went inside, turned out the big light in the kitchen in favor of the small one on the table.

The switch bathed the deck in darkness. I lay down on the deckboards, my hands behind my head, looked up at a sky encrusted in gaudy stars. I felt oddly vulnerable having shared that story about Gold, as though I'd ripped off a scab. But I hadn't told them the coda, which was that, after Gold said that to me, I was assailed by fantasies about the two of us, in the very room where he'd said it, after hours, when nobody else was in the school. At that time, all my fantasies and desires of men went unspoken, obviously. I barely acknowledged them myself. I'd simply indulge them briefly, then push them back down, as though they'd never happened, or as though they were something I'd grow out of.

Gold had never figured in them—until he said those words to me. After that, the sheer fact that someone knew me, saw me, identified me that way, was brazen enough to say it to my very face, was so powerful that it made me want to turn myself over to him completely, to show him just what an eager little homosexual I could be. In group settings, I'd search his face, waiting for that connection, that knowing glance, that wink. I'd wanted it so badly. But it never came. He'd proceeded as though he'd never said a word.

TWO

The protocols of competing on Speech Team were truly weird, a 1980s throwback to some antique age of elocution and comportment, when well-heeled young ladies might rise from their seat in the parlor after dinner and recite poetry to impress callers and lure offers of betrothal. Whether you were competing in poetry, kiddie lit, original oratory (a speech you wrote), oratorical interpretation (reading someone else's speech), or perhaps some other categories I've forgotten, you were not expected to deliver your fare in a manner that felt natural, conversational, or unrehearsed, but rather polished to a fare-thee-well, right down to the glance and the gesture. Your speech was supposed to sound elevated, magisterial, im*por*tant. Most of the girls who did Speech Team—and speech teams were made up mostly of girls—were prissy, headband-and-long-skirt types, and most of the boys were either proto-gays like myself or hopeless nerds with bad skin, polyester navy coats, and tenuous social skills, the kind who thrilled to the latest Weird Al Yankovic parody song or spent most of their free time glued to Super Mario Brothers or Castlevania via their Nintendo consoles.

This prissy fakeness was best embodied by the introductions we would give before launching into a piece. The point of these introductions was to set the piece up, "tease" the audience, give context, and then—*voilà!*—finally name the piece and its author. That meant intros with spectacularly cheesy crescendos, such as: "As we listen with increasing terror, we finally learn the true meaning of"—and here there'd always be a dramatic pause—"'The Lottery,' by Shirley Jackson."

Or: "It all adds up to yet another day of antics and adventures, in one of the world's most iconic hotels, on the part of our heroine . . . *Eloise*, by Kay Thompson."

Or my own intro, if I remember it correctly: "Join me now, on a journey through the universality of man and the divinity of the everyday, as, together, we sing a"—dramatic pause—"'Song of Myself,' a selection of the groundbreaking verse of Walt Whitman."

So cheesy. Even just thinking about it now, I cringe (with, admittedly, a touch of nostalgia for how highbrow we thought we were).

Then, of course, there was that magical moment between the intro and the entry, when—across categories—everyone knew, as though it was some unwritten rule that traced back through the annals of Speech-Teamhood, you were supposed to gravely bow your head, leave your audience in a state of delicious anticipation, then suddenly snap your head back up again and launch into your entry with an alacrity that bordered on adolescent mania, grabbing your audience by the throat from Minute One and not releasing your grip until you uttered your final line and bowed your head again, with mock humility, to signal that the magical journey you'd taken your listeners on had finally wafted gently to a close.

Then, polite applause from your narrow-eyed, cutthroat competitors and the volunteer parent-judges or teacher-judges in their Fair Isle sweaters or tweed blazers, likely salivating for their coffee, cigarette, or donut break, thinking about the latest videotaped episode of *Cagney & Lacey* or *Hill Street Blues* they were going to curl up with that night, their yearly or twice-yearly custodial obligation dispatched with.

Between the opening and closing bow of the head, every unbearably phony device was employed—the "natural" hand gestures (open palm, double open palm, lightly shaken fist, thoughtful index finger and thumb to chin), the "casual" stroll across the front of the room while elucidating a new point, the "searching" gaze into the eyes of your listeners, that all-important effort to "connect," "engage," "compel." I forget exactly how winners of rounds were scored, but you were judged across, if I remember, four categories—something like the quality of your material (particularly if it was your own), diction (bite those consonants and bring fullness to those vowels!), physicality (the ability to make all that gesturing and strolling look "fresh" and "spontaneous," although it never was), and then something like "emotional connection" or "audience rapport" (here, once again, we go back to that all-important mandate of periodically locking eyes with individual listeners, as though a certain line or point were being delivered *just for them*).

It was all so phony. Many an evening in the years since high school, Nat and I had entertained other friends with our imitations of the mannered excesses we'd been pushed to.

"All she has left," Nat would intone, "is her memories . . . her regrets . . . her . . . *Pentimento*, by Lillian Hellman." Boom, head down.

"Only when Mathilde has lost everything will she learn the devastating truth about . . . *The Necklace*, by Guy de Maupassant," I'd join in.

When we got stoned, we'd make up intros to amuse ourselves.

"Lost in a world of hard drugs and cheap sex, these privileged young people eventually learn that they are less than mature . . . less than kind . . . *Less Than Zero*, by Bret Easton Ellis," I'd venture.

"Join us," Nat would join in, "as our narrator realizes that she is experiencing not only a total meltdown of the mind . . . but . . . a 'Total Eclipse of the Heart,' by Bonnie Tyler."

Then there was the accent gap. If you're from, or have ever spent time in, Massachusetts, you know that there is no brighter class divide—between Brahmin and Masshole, between the Brooklines and the Brocktons, between the private and public schools—than the Boston accent. The elite lacked it and the great unwashed had it in spades. I'm not talking the special Jack and Jackie Kennedy, Gore Vidal, or William F. Buckley upper-crust subset of the accent, rich and affected-sounding. I'm talking your garden variety, nails-on-chalkboard "Mass accent," emanating from high up in the nasal passage, a minefield of dropped *r*'s. The great curse of the Mass accent, of course, is that—almost like virginity or body odor—you don't really know you have it, and that you should lose it, until someone tells you. And, for me, that person was Gold.

"Listen, Tip," he interrupted me once, exasperated, while I was rehearsing in front of him in the fishbowl. "It's not *ahmies*. It's *arrrrmies*. Can you hear the difference?"

He'd stopped me on the line, "The armies of those I love engirth me and I engirth them," from "I Sing the Body Electric." I was having a hard enough time finessing the word *engirth*.

"That's what I said," I answered. "*Ahmies.*"

He shook his head, laughed. "For some reason, Tip, you're the only one on the team with such a strong Mass accent. We have to tone it down."

My face went hot with shame. I hadn't even known this!

"When you see an *r*," Gold continued, "you gotta hit it. Unless you wanna sound like one of the barflies on *Cheers* for the rest of your life. Is that what you want?"

I shook my head no, mortified.

"Say *arrrrmy*. When you say it, you should feel your chin tighten a little."

"*Arrrrrmy.*" It hurt to say it.

"Don't overdo it."

"Arr*my*."

"Good! I want you to mark all the *r*'s in your script from now on and pay special attention to them when you practice."

I became obsessed with *r*'s. Not just on Speech Team, but everywhere, always. My parents and my little brother asked what was wrong with me. Haughtily, I told them I was "talking *correctly* from now on." It wasn't easy. It made the ordinarily unselfconscious act of speech itself a chore. But by the time I went to college, I'd subjugated my Mass accent so thoroughly that my freshman roommate told me, the day we met, that I sounded like I was from Southern California.

He had no idea how happy that made me. I vowed that my voice would never again betray my point of origin. And it didn't—unless I was drunk, tired, angry, or all of the above. But for the most part, the era of dropped *r*'s was behind me. I had Gold's rude interjection to thank.

I suppose I had him to thank, as well, for a piece of happiness at the time. It's hard to overstate how profoundly uncool it was to be on Speech Team. Unlike the other provinces of the nerderati—Drama Club, Newspaper, Yearbook, Literary Magazine, Student Council, all of which I also participated in—there was no manifestation of our labor before the rest of the school. You might be a lowly drama fag until everyone came to see the play, at which point you were given some grudging respect for your talent, or at least your nerve. You might be a Yearbook or Lit Mag drone until the actual book or mag was distributed, at which point you might be thanked for your labor. Student Council carried its own prestige; you were one of the leaders, the decision makers. But there were no Speech Team performances for one's own school; the focus was outward, elsewhere, away. You were merely some dork whom other students, lingering after school, might spy inside the fishbowl, emoting soundlessly with a folder in your hands as you stood before Gold, who flouted school policy after hours and chain-smoked his beloved Vantages, the arm with the cigarette crooked outside the open window, while he leaned back in his chair and appraised you, the smoke accumulating in the confines of the fishbowl and smarting your eyes.

I knew it was the uncoolest club to be in—with the possible exception of the Math Team and Science Squad—but I still loved the feeling of standing up before an audience and presenting. It was a chance to show off, to sculpt and polish something to within an inch of its life, to strive for perfection in a drab and indifferent world.

After the weekend with Nat, I could not stop thinking about Jennifer Douglas. Her unflagging punctiliousness of comportment and scholarship, her frequent use of "My *good*ness!" with a palm brought to her chest, her navy or beige Pappagallo flats with a contrasting opaque stocking. I don't understand the chemistry by which you can barely think of someone for nearly twenty-five years, then suddenly find yourself thinking of them several times a day, hungry to talk to them. But there it was, as I updated website copy and refined press releases by day and devoured *Game of Thrones* alongside Marcus at night.

Jennifer and I had been friends in high school—hadn't we? We'd been in all the same classes since her arrival in Mendhem in seventh grade, "smart-track" classes, in all the same clubs, part of an afterschool and occasional weekend clique, nights in finished basements watching movies we considered "highbrow"—*A Room with a View*, *Amadeus*, *A Sunday in the Country*, the latter partly because it conferred us extra credit for French class. True, I was considerably closer with Nat, while Jennifer was subtly closer with Anthony, but we were still a foursome of sorts—capable of giving the impression of being out on a double date together if you squinted really hard and tuned out Anthony's screeches.

So when, my freshman fall at Bard, a new friend with her own car, Jodi Lewin, had asked if I wanted to road-trip one weekend to

New Haven, where she wanted to visit a high-school friend at Yale, I jumped. I'd visit Jennifer! I called Yale, got her dorm-room extension, left an excited message. No reply. Left another message the morning before we left. No reply.

"Did you get in touch with your friend?" Jodi asked me on the way down, leaves in smears of flaming color flying by us on both sides.

"I didn't hear back. I guess she's really busy and I'll just find her once we're there."

Yale's campus was so much grander than Bard's; even the freshmen had the air of America's future CEOs and court justices, as opposed to scruffy Bard's future poets and postmodern dancers. I was already feeling cowed, inferior, by the time I knocked, alone, on the door of Jennifer's dorm room. No answer. I knocked again, called her name.

A girl stuck her head out the door across the hall. "She's in Commons eating dinner with her friends. Just go over and find her."

I found her, in fact, on the pathway to the dining hall, spotting her face in the evening gloom among a group of four Black girls walking in tight formation, laughing, book bags slung over shoulders. She looked the same save that she now wore cooler glasses, the round gold-rimmed John Lennon kind, rather than the larger oval plastic ones she'd worn in high school.

"Jennifer!" I cried. I was so excited to see her in this new, adult setting that I inadvertently bumped one of her friends slightly off the path as I dove in for a hug. "I found you!"

"Tippy!" she cried back, startled.

"Tippy?" one of the friends echoed instantly, followed by a short sharp shock of laughter. "Like the turtle?"

"Yep, like the turtle," I replied. (Such had been the story of my life until I left Mendhem.) I pulled back, held Jennifer by both elbows. "It's so good to see you! I love your new glasses! Did you get my messages? I said I was coming down."

She regarded me, her mouth open. She seemed not eager to see me, I slowly registered, and—well, if not exactly unhappy about it, then at least uncomfortable.

"I did!" she replied. "I'm sorry, I meant to get back—I've been swamped." By this point, her friends had stepped back a few paces, forming a kind of silent, three-point dragnet around us. "Uh—" She struggled for words. "How are you? How's Bard?"

"It's great! It's not quite as opulent as this!" I gestured broadly at the immense quadrangle. "Do you like it here?"

"Uh—" She glanced nervously at her friends, then back at me. "I *do*. Yes. It's a lot to—process."

"Totally! We're definitely not in Mendhem anymore, right?" Suddenly, I was desperate to remind her we had a past in common, because she seemed to be looking at me as though she barely remembered.

"No!" She laughed mechanically. "We're not."

The three friends stood by, politely silent. Jennifer glanced at them. "We have a meeting we're rushing to," she told me.

"Oh!" I nearly shouted. "Oh, okay. Uh—do you want to hang out later tonight?"

"We're going to a movie," one of the friends said. I looked at her. She was ridiculously stylish. I only remember her enormous spray of hair tied up messily, Janet Jackson–style, in a cobalt scarf, her pointy black boots with silver buckles. She had Denise Huxtable Black boho written all over her. She had to be a New Yorker. I'd come to know the look already, in just a few weeks at Bard.

"Oh!" I exclaimed, feeling more embarrassingly exclamatory by the second, in contrast to the girls' aloofness. "Okay, no problem!" I turned back to Jennifer. "Would you have any other time?"

I caught behind her glasses what I thought was a kind of pleading look, before she drew in breath, as though she were thinking.

"Take him to the Doodle," said the Denise Huxtable one.

"When are you going back?" Jennifer asked me.

"Tomorrow late afternoon. Jodi wants to get back for a party. Oh! I'm sorry—that's who I came with. My friend."

"Can you meet me at the Doodle tomorrow for breakfast? At eleven?"

"The Doodle?"

"Oh, yeah, I'm sorry. We all call it that. The Yankee Doodle Coffee Shop. On Elm Street. It's, like, a local legend."

"It's a greasy spoon but it's cute," said one of the other friends.

"Yeah!" I exploded. "Sure!" I thought I might cry from relief, I'd been so certain she was about to blow me off completely.

"Okay, Tip." She hugged me cursorily. "I'll see you there tomorrow."

"I actually love your name," the greasy spoon friend said to me.

"I like Tippy better," said the hyperstylish one. She'd been the one who'd said "Tippy" in the first place, I realized. But now she sounded not derisive but—vaguely friendly?

"I hate it," I said. "I don't let anyone call me that anymore."

"I'm sorry, it just slipped out," Jennifer said. "Habit."

"You can still call me that," I said. "You're grandfathered in." To which the other girls said, "Awwww" and "That's sweet!"

"Bye, Tip." Jennifer rubbed my arm. "Have fun tonight."

"See you tomorrow!" Could I have sounded any squeakier?

They moved on down the path. I stood there, watching them go, suddenly bereft of a next step. I wasn't even entirely sure where the building was where Jodi had told me to meet her later, assuming I'd get dinner with Jennifer. I hadn't thought to ask Jennifer and her friends, and I didn't even know where to get something to eat.

To my surprise, Jennifer glanced back, once, briefly at me, before turning. Only when she and her friends were yards down the path, out of earshot, I heard their laughter resume. By now, the quadrangle was almost entirely dark, vague shapes of trees and august old buildings, endless rows of windows, some squares of yellow light, some dark.

I found pizza, then found Jodi, went on with her, her friend, and her friend's friends, to a bar, then a party in a dorm room, Prince's *Sign o' the Times* loud on the stereo. Nervous, I drank faster than usual, got in a loud, drunk conversation with a cute boy and a chubby girl, names I can't remember, although I do recall that the conversation was a sort of debate about whether Prince or Madonna was better at deconstructing gender—the kind of debate I was suddenly having a lot my freshman year, when I learned that everything I had simply thought existed naturally in the world was actually a *construct* that begged to be *de*constructed, whatever that meant exactly. I still wasn't entirely sure.

The boy and the girl and I left the party, walked across quadrangles that were alien to me, ended up at another party, drank more, until the boy and I left, ended up in his dorm room with Sade's "Sweetest Taboo" on his stereo. I had my first gay sex, nothing too major-league in the era of rampant AIDS hysteria, but it was my first time both kissing and lying naked with another man, although sadly I was too drunk to remember much of it the next morning, upon waking at 10:45 with a headache royale, the room spinning, the boy—I think his name was Robert or Robinson—passed out beside me facedown in the pillow.

Then a second look at the clock radio by the bed, the sudden onset of panic. I leapt up, threw on my clothes, slipped out of the dorm room, found a bathroom where I splashed water on my face, tried to tame my hair, took the great liberty of squeezing a dollop of toothpaste from a tube left on the sink and smearing it over my teeth and tongue before swishing it all around and rinsing it out. Out into the crisp October morning, the sunlight an assault on my eyes, students crisscrossing the quad hauling backpacks. I hailed one, asked directions to—what was it called again?

"It's like a kind of weird patriotic name," I told the girl, who stopped for me at a safe remove from what I imagined was my sour-smelling disarray. "Like, old-fashioned?"

"The Yankee Doodle?"

"That's it! The Doodle, right?"

"Right."

Jennifer would judge me, frown, when she saw my dishevelment, smell my liquor breath, I worried as a speed-walked to the aforementioned corner, Elm and York. I arrived at 11:02. The place was an unprepossessing hole in the wall, a small crowd of students standing outside, waiting for seats. I shouldered my way through, past scattered protests of my effrontery, to enter and scan the room, no more than a line of stools against a counter, the air thick with the smell of griddle grease. No Jennifer. I'd arrived before her, which gave me some measure of relief. I exited, stood to one side of the crowd of students, desperate for aspirin but not wanting to venture away in search of a nearby drugstore, for fear of missing her arrival.

But she never came. At ten past eleven, then a quarter past, I assumed she was merely late, as I'd nearly been. This was a different time, when a blow-off arrived not with a shoddy last-minute cellphone call or text but amid a thundering abyss of silence, no presence and no words. You might be left to distract or soothe yourself with the outlier possibility that the other person had been kidnapped or struck by a car or lightning, or had perhaps inadvertently fallen into a giant hole in the ground on their way to you. But mostly you would just be thrown back on yourself, left with the extra-ness of your own anticipation, time, and energy that suddenly had no container. The moment felt existential, as though all your life you'd been showing up to find people who weren't there and had never had any intention of being there.

I found a payphone, called her dorm room. Just the answering machine.

"Hey!" It was that high, overexcited register of mine again. "Uh—I'm here. At the Doodle. Are you okay? Uh—okay, well, I'll wait a few more minutes. I hope everything's okay."

At twenty to noon, I went inside by myself, took the one empty stool at the far end of the counter, ordered bacon and eggs rich in grease, rancid coffee, and put it all away, grateful for the absorption despite intermittent sour waves of nausea. Exiting, feeling as though I might cry from shame and disappointment, I reentered the campus, began the headachey task of finding Jodi Lewin. I did, finally, in her friend's dorm, the name of which I'd managed to retain from the night before. Jodi was hungover, too, curled up alongside her friend on her friend's twin bed.

"Where'd you go last night?" she asked me.

"Can we just head back?" I sat on the edge of the opposite bed, whose rumpledness suggested it had been recently vacated. I desperately wanted to leave the campus before I inadvertently ran into Jennifer, toward whom I suddenly felt such a startling wave of rage that I burst into hungover tears, in turn startling Jodi, who sat up in bed and assured that, yes, yes, of course we could head back, just let me pull myself together and get a coffee.

Back at Bard, my hangover having faded to mere exhaustion, I thought maybe there'd be a message on my own machine from Jennifer, some kind of apology, a manufactured excuse about a forgotten morning obligation. There was nothing. I nearly called her, keen to leave some icily scathing message, some kind of acid commentary on how she had a long way to go before she looked even a fraction as chic as her new friends, but I managed to calculate that it would only further debase me.

For an entire year, I'd not speak to anyone of the humiliating incident, which burned into the tenderest part of my brain, and then when I finally did, to some college friends, it was with a ferocity and bitterness that continued to surprise me. My friend of youth, one of my few compadres in square-pegdom, had rejected me, unambiguously and without remorse. It had never occurred to me that she might not want to stay friends after high school, which was why her blow-off not only hurt but, in fact, shocked me. It was probably not for another decade, until my early thirties, that I even allowed myself to briefly consider that perhaps, that freshman fall of 1987, something had been going on with her.

Finally, after that farm weekend with Nat, in a lull at work one supremely dreary Providence afternoon—a thin sheet of rain falling into the Seekonk River outside my window—I found Jennifer's Rutgers email and began composing:

Subject: Remember your speech team confrère after all these years?

My dearest Professor Douglas,
I know many, many years have passed since we last spoke, but I was visiting our old partner in crime Natalie Farb-Miola this past weekend and you were much on our minds. Especially after we learned the news about Pete Stroman and noted that you had left some kind words on his Facebook page . . . All weekend, Nat and I were reminiscing about the inanities of the Speech Team era and of course not only Pete but you and Anthony were among our thoughts. I am not surprised at all to find that you have become a most distinguished professor and hope that life has treated you well.

(I determined that it would be creepy, borderline stalker, to note that, based on Facebook pictures, life seemed to have blessed her with a beautiful family.)

Then I was compelled to fabricate:

I currently live in Providence but need to visit a friend in New Jersey very soon who is going through a rough spell health-wise . . . and wondered if perhaps you might spare an hour for a coffee or a drink. Would be so lovely to catch up for a moment and hear your most Edwardian "Heavens!" again after all these years.

In high school, I had affectionately called her, and her sedate mannerisms, "Edwardian." But now, twenty-five years on, I thought better of that last line—would she find it sad, pathetic even, that I remembered such details from high school? Would she even be offended? I deleted it.

My very best to you,
Thomas (Tip)

Before I hit "send," I paused. Twenty-five years prior, I'd sought her out and she'd rebuffed me. Why did I think now would be any different? Was I a masochist, programmed to set myself up to be ignored? Was I an optimist, too confident in the belief that others spent half their inner lives in the past as well?

I sent the email.

Over the following week, I told myself stories to absorb the wound of her non-reply. She could be on some sort of vacation or leave, I told myself, checking emails only periodically. She might have read it, charmed, and set it aside, fully intending to write back, only to have life intervene. She had children; I'd long ago realized, not without hurt, that friends with children edited out much of the world outside their home, not out of cruelty, but merely an inability to process a surplus of information. After all, how were you supposed to think deeply and critically about human rights abuses in Myanmar when little Aiden or Brittany refused to take their ADHD meds?

Over the second week, I let myself wallow in what by then seemed the inevitability of her silence, the pathetic desperation of my overture. Of course she'd put me off, as she'd done before. Really, what outcome had I expected?

And then one morning, exactly seventeen days after I'd reached out, I found in my inbox, to my genuine surprise bordering on incredulity, her reply.

Tippy Murray! it began.

> *How delighted I was to hear from you! Please forgive the delay in getting back; I've actually just come out of the tenure review process here at Rutgers—successfully, thankfully—which has totally consumed me in the worst way and made me a less-than-exemplary spouse and mother for several months, never mind friend. I've just begun trying to reclaim a semblance of normalcy, which includes finding a moment to write back to old friends!*

How delighted she was to hear from me, an old friend? Were my eyes deceiving me? I was worthy of her time?

Her voice, even in writing, was so utterly familiar that I could almost hear her old cadences.

It's so funny, she continued, *that you and Natalie were recently reminiscing about Speech Team, as I find that since I learned the unhappy news about Pete, it's been much on my mind as well, despite the interval of 25 years. (I can't believe I just wrote that. Boggles the mind.) Those freezing morning bus rides to all those different schools and all the silly hand gestures and of course all the afternoons rehearsing for Gold and suffering through his inappropriate-isms. (I fear I may have just invented that word.) A different era, indeed!*

This piqued my interest. What had been Gold's inappropriate-isms with her? I shuddered to think.

Well, she went on, *how funny to hear that you are living in Providence—I was there only last May for a conference and would have loved to have seen you. But in that you are coming to NJ—sorry to hear about your infirm friend—I would very much like to have that reunion! So do please let me know when you'll be here so we can make a plan. I would love to have you to lunch or dinner so you can meet my partner and kids. And I *very much* hope that* *happiness has found you as well in the years since our escape from that grim land of walls on wheels!*

My very best,
Jennifer

I hope that happiness has found you, she'd written. Not the reverse: *I hope that you have found happiness.* It was a queer yet striking image, the idea of happiness rushing up behind one's hangdog self, tapping one on the shoulder, and announcing: "I'm here!"

I picked up my phone, texted Nat: *You are not going to believe who actually just got back to me. Professor Jennifer Douglas herself!*

The rest of the afternoon, I was nearly giddy over her reply, rain outside my window be damned. I commended myself: I'd not mentioned the Yale blowoff, perhaps giving the impression that I didn't even recall it, and neither had she. We were adults now, past the awkwardness of Mendhem caterpillars squirming to become worldly butterflies. We could be friends again—maybe.

Once more, I asked Marcus if he wanted to hit the road with me—this time, to New Jersey—and once again, he said he was scheduled to work the weekend.

"You're going away on weekends an awful lot these days," he noted that night, uncorking wine as I plated our broiled halibut and broccoli rabe.

"She really wanted me—*us*—to come out and meet her husband and kids," I said, in another lie. "I think Pete's death really upset her."

"Whose?"

"Pete's. The guy from high school who killed himself. I told you about him."

"Oh, right." He took his first bite. "This is good."

"Thanks."

"You're in a high-school retro phase," he observed.

I gave him a *huh?* look.

"First visiting Natalie."

"She's my oldest friend."

"Yeah, and now—um—"

"Jennifer."

"Right." He chewed thoughtfully. "Just feels like you're in some kind of a backward reflection period."

"I hadn't thought of it that way."

He regarded me with what felt, uncomfortably, like equal parts tenderness and concern. He put his fork down, took my hand on the table. "Are you happy with us? In the here and now?"

"Of course!"

"And can I ask you something else?"

My stomach flopped a bit. "What?"

"Are you—okay?"

"What do you mean, okay?" Even though I was fairly sure I knew what he meant.

"I mean—are you going into a space like you did last year before—"

"No!" I interjected. "Absolutely not. If anything, I feel kind of—I dunno, perked up by getting back in touch with people. What's wrong with that?"

"Nothing." He picked up his water glass, sipped, put it down. "Have you been going to meetings?"

"Yes! Faithfully." But not in nearly a month, I failed to add.

He considered this, perhaps a little chastised. "Can you make this your last weekend away until after the holidays? I hate coming home from work to an empty house on a Saturday night."

I leaned over and kissed him. "Of course."

"I need you."

It was sweet of him to say that. I didn't think he really needed me. He was far too self-contained, reliably functional. I was the needy one—the emotional vortex, the broken thing repaired with Scotch tape, what shrinks call "the identified patient" in a relationship. I hated that role, but I'd certainly earned it.

"And I need you," I replied dutifully.

No sooner had he left the table than I picked up my phone, texted Nat if she wanted to come with me to visit Jennifer. No answer until the morning: ***Yes! My kids are with my mom next weekend. Let's do it!***

It was a leaf-peeping trip, blazes of gold, orange, and red all the way down the long, dull stretch of I-95 out of Rhode Island and along the Connecticut coast, cutting into Westchester and over the Hudson River, then south into New Jersey. Sunroof down, we played the Velvet Underground's *1969* album, sang "What Goes On" and "Rock and Roll" together. With my Ray-Bans on, my oldest and best friend beside me in the passenger seat, both of us hopped up on cappuccinos, our hair blowing around, I felt young again, sixteen, light as a feather, the open road laid out before us, limitless.

"What's Aaron up to this weekend?"

"I'm not sure. He's a free man this weekend. I think he might see one of his girlfriends."

"What?" I lowered the music.

"Yeah," she said, with studied casualness. "We have an open relationship."

"You're—" I searched for the word I'd heard. "Polyamorous? Poly?"

"Yeah." She pulled her hair back in a scrunchie she fished from her jacket pocket. "We have been almost the whole time we've been together."

"Oh, wow. How do you feel about that?"

She laughed. "It was my idea. I was scared I was going to want to have sex with other guys, or women, at some point anyway. You know, feel trapped in the typical way? So I decided that this time around, instead of cheating and feeling guilty and ruining the relationship like I did with Jack and Julian, I'd be honest about it this time."

I was silent a moment. She had indeed done this before, with Jack and then Julian. I'd been slightly baffled, because I assumed it stemmed from sexual insatiability, a trait I associated more with guys, particularly gay guys. But then she'd assured me that her wandering was merely a symptom, consequence, of the real reason the relationships had ended—Jack's verbal abusiveness and Julian's emotional iciness. I believed her. What else could I do? She was one of my best friends and I was supposed to take her side in these matters.

So now I asked of Aaron: "How'd he take it?"

"I think he was kinda freaked out at first and said no. But then I made him read *The Ethical Slut* and we joined this New England poly group online and now I think he likes it and realizes its advantages. He has, like, two secondaries, I think. Maybe three."

"What about you?"

"Right now, I have this couple in Maine I might see every six weeks. They're farmers, too."

"Wow." I processed this. "Well, good for you for finding something that works for you."

"I just think that it's dangerous to give all of yourself to one person," she added matter-of-factly. "You do that, and one day you wake up and you don't know who you are."

I was silent for a moment, considering that. I'd never thought of relationships quite that way. Wasn't the point to give all of yourself to one person, to commit that wholly? Did that not prove one's love? I thought back to a year ago, to my twenty-four-hour AWOL status I'd subjected Marcus to. In the weeks leading up to it, I remembered now, I'd felt like a caged animal in the apartment, desperate to break out and behave like someone responsible to nobody but themself. I'd done just that—with a vengeance. But once it was over, in my guilt and shame, all I wanted to be was the good boyfriend again, to disavow the little demons that had urged me to flee. Did I live in a world of unhealthy extremes? Maybe I could learn something from Nat.

"Marcus and I have a very limited don't-ask-don't-tell thing," I ventured. "Kind of a when-we're-in-separate-cities deal. But the few times I've acted on it, it's always been with a guy ten, fifteen years older than me."

She laughed. "Daddy issues!"

"Except once you're past forty, you're becoming the daddy."

"This is true."

A few hours later, in Montclair, we were cruising down a wide, tree-lined boulevard, passing one stately early-twentieth-century home after another, wraparound porches and wide lawns blanketed in leaves, a ubiquity of *Obama–Biden 2012* signs, fat pumpkins sitting beside front doors, and European cars parked in driveways.

"Whoa," said Nat, gazing out. "This town makes Mendhem look trashy."

"I know," said. "I guess Jennifer did okay."

"No surprise there." Nat nodded down at her jeans and sneakers. "Do you think we're underdressed?"

"Too late to worry now."

The GPS deposited us in front of a blue neocolonial with white trim, maybe not as grand as its neighbors, but gracious nonetheless. We were barely out of the car when she—Jennifer Douglas—stepped out the front door, walked down the path toward us in her own sneakers, jeans, and sweatshirt, a dishtowel clutched absentmindedly in one hand as though she'd dashed out of the kitchen. I'd glimpsed her face the first moments she'd set out the door—resolute, businesslike—but by the time she was within steps of us, she'd applied a smile.

Life seldom asks you to contemplate the mesmerizing, terrifying passage of time as it does when it presents you with someone you have not seen in twenty-five years. You may, beneath your polite veneer, be stunned by how the years have ravaged someone, or you may in turn be stunned by how lightly they seem to have intervened. In the case of Jennifer Douglas, it was definitely the latter. I could barely find clues that a quarter-century had nibbled at the edges of her adolescence, except for her Saturday at-home garb, a level of slouchiness she would never have allowed herself at Mendhem High. And her hair. As in the Facebook picture, it was short and natural now, tight corkscrew curls. In high school, it had always been immaculately pressed, pulled back snugly in a headband or a barrette.

She let out a hoot, extended both arms as she approached us. "This is crazy!" she called. "Talk about a time capsule!"

We embraced. "You look seventeen!" I exclaimed.

"You really do!" Nat echoed.

She stepped back a pace. "*Y'all* look amazing! Look at you!" She paused again, her face now a (reassuring) picture of wonderment. "Come in, come in! I have lunch for us."

Nat and I followed her up the path, glanced at each other. *"Y'all?" Is it just me, or does her voice sound different?* I yearned to ask Nat, but of course I could not.

We followed her into the house, where I ticked off its fulfillments of my predictions: Comfortably tasteful and a bit farmy-antique-y in its appointments, Shaker sideboards, and wool plaid blankets thrown over invitingly overstuffed couches? Check. Lots of interesting Black

American art and photography on the walls? Check. Enough books to bury Leonard Bast alive several times over? Absolutely check. One long wall in the living room, ceiling to floor, was nothing but books. Propped up against the lower shelves was a poster, still on a stick as though it had been brandished at a protest: Trayvon Martin, that cherubic face framed in a white hoodie, with the word *JUSTICE* right above it.

"Your place is beautiful," Nat remarked.

"I'm sorry it's a slight disaster." Jennifer waved us into the kitchen, nearly the size of my entire apartment, and perfectly orderly, despite her apologies. "Weekends around here are a little bit crazy. And this is Chloe. And Dudley."

Perched on a stool at the kitchen island, glued to an iPad, was a little girl, about nine, spectacles the echo of her mother's, but in red. At her feet dozed a caramel-colored labradoodle.

"Chloe, this is Mister Tip and Miss Natalie, my friends from high school, who I told you were coming."

Nat and I, simultaneously, laughed, embarrassed. "Please just call me Tip," I said. "Or Thomas."

Jennifer's hand flew to her mouth. "Oh, I'm so sorry, Thomas! You did use *Thomas* in your email, I forgot."

I smiled, shrugged. "It's okay. A few people like you are grandfathered in with Tip."

Nat turned back to Chloe. "And please just call me Nat. Anything with a Miss or a Missus in front of it makes me feel so old."

Chloe straightened herself, smiled. "Okay. It's very nice to meet you, Thomas and Nat."

I smiled. "It's nice to meet you, too." Her politeness, just faintly as prim as her mother had been in high school, was endearing.

"You have an iPad!" Nat exclaimed. "So cool. My daughter wants one."

"I'm addicted to it," Chloe allowed.

"You don't get to meet the male half of the family for another hour or so," Jennifer announced. "They're at soccer. Meanwhile, you must be hungry after that drive. What is it, three hours?"

"About four," I said.

"Do you think it's still warm enough to have lunch on the back porch?"

It was, and we did. She'd made two quiches and a large salad, as well as banana bread, whose scent I'd caught the moment we'd stepped inside. We were seated outside shortly, with a view of an expansive yard where Dudley chased and fetched a red ball, slimy with drool, that Chloe repeatedly flung into the yard from the porch.

"Chloe, don't play fetch with Dudley while you eat. It's not hygienic."

"I'm not eating with my hands," Chloe replied calmly. "I have a fork."

"Still. Please."

I ate my quiche and salad while forever stealing glances at Jennifer, careful not to hold them so long that she would feel scrutinized. But it's hard to carry on casually with someone you haven't seen in eons while you're still processing them, parsing what's old from what's new. Jennifer's face certainly looked the same, exactly the same, and she'd not gained the weight that sometimes distinguishes someone's adult self from their adolescent self. But the jeans, the sweatshirt, the natural hair, the new bodily looseness and subtle *drawl* in her voice, for lack of a better word, all signaled that, in the intervening quarter-century, she'd changed, or perhaps had willed herself to change. Her lips remained always slightly pursed, though—I remembered that from high school—and I couldn't help but notice that she smoothed her napkin in her lap obsessively.

Chloe's presence while we ate shaped our conversation, the chatter about her schoolwork and her judo lessons, about the family's big summer trip to Colombia a few months prior, to see aunties and cousins on Chloe's dad's side they hadn't yet met, Chloe's pronouncement that she preferred Medellín over Cartagena because "Cartagena is for tourists." She pronounced both cities perfectly, inserting the *j* into Medellín. She was exactly the daughter that I would have expected Jennifer Douglas to have had, luminous with intelligence and maturity.

"It's true," I said. Marcus and I had been to Cartagena two years prior. "Cartagena doesn't feel like a real city, does it?"

Chloe rolled her eyes. "Hardly." I suppressed my smile, amused at her discernment.

Upon her last bite, she turned to her mother. "May I be excused?"

"Yes. Bring your plate and cup to the sink."

The three of us watched her go back inside, then I turned back to Jennifer. "She is the spitting image of you," I said.

She smiled, apparently pleased by this observation. "I know it's a gender cliché, but it's true, and Raffy is the mirror image of Andres. You'll see. Nat, how old are yours?"

"Olivia's fourteen and Otis is eleven."

"How is fourteen going?"

"She hates me about three days a week and she's my best friend the other four days."

Jennifer laughed. "I guess I have that to look forward to."

"It's not that bad, really."

I smiled. It was one of those moments—not frequent, but regular—when my childlessness was thrown onto me, my bafflement that I would likely never know this kind of exquisite ambivalence about my progeny, this tangle of feelings that bonded parents.

Almost as though she sensed my exclusion, Jennifer turned to me. "And how long have you been with . . ."

"Marcus. Going on three years now."

She nodded. "And he's a—"

"An oncological nurse. At Miriam Hospital."

"That's terrific. And isn't Providence the sweetest city?"

"That's a good word to describe it," I said. "Sweet. With a bit of an H. P. Lovecraft Gothic vibe to make it interesting."

She smiled at me, with what felt like an indulgent fondness, and turned back to Nat. "That's exactly the kind of Tip Murray reference I remember from high school."

I laughed. "I'm still that pretentious, name-dropping little dweeb," I said.

"Oh, no!" Jennifer leaned over in her chair and rubbed my shoulder. "You were adorable. You both were. We had fun. Thank God for Speech Team in that sports-obsessed town."

So there. She'd signaled she was ready to go back—a moment I'd not been sure would occur. As she shook her head slowly, remembering, conflicting traces of fondness and dismay in her face (or so I read), I wanted to ask her what had been much on my mind, which was, simply, what had it been like for her being nearly the only Black student in that entire school? How had her family even ended up in Mendhem instead of somewhere a bit more cosmopolitan, like Boston or Cambridge? But I didn't know how to ask it, and I didn't want it to seem as though that was the reason we'd come.

Why *had* we come?

As though she read my mind, she turned back to me. "Have you seen your friend yet?"

I drew a blank. "What friend?"

"Your friend you mentioned here in New Jersey who you said was sick."

"Oh!" I had completely forgotten this pretext for the trip. "Oh, he's hanging in there. He actually texted this morning saying that he wasn't up for a visit today, but Nat was already on her way to Providence, so I figured, let's just do the trip anyway!" My cheeks flushed crimson as I spun this reversal.

Nat's brow furrowed. "You didn't mention that."

"We just got so caught up in the car talking about other things!"

A vaguely awkward silence briefly ensued. "Well," Jennifer finally said, "we're having this lovely catch-up of our own, so I hope you think the trip was still worth it. And it's a gorgeous weekend to be out on the road."

"It's stunning out there," I said, to which Nat heartily agreed, before we all fell back in yet more uneasy seconds of silence.

Which Jennifer broke. "I did mean to ask you both, have either of you stayed in touch with Anthony Malouf?" When she said his name, her eyes widened a bit in anticipation.

Nat and I both shook our heads. "I do know," I said, "that he's a very successful menswear designer in New York. For Pietro Cuccino. Like, suits."

Jennifer gasped. "You're kidding me! Andres's favorite suit that I picked out for him is a Pietro Cuccino."

"They're beautiful," I agreed. They also started at around $2,500. "But I haven't stayed in touch with him."

There was a bit more to the story than that, but I didn't share it. I'd long ago told Nat that Anthony had cut me off, but I'd never told her of the precipitating event.

"Well," said Jennifer, "I'm not surprised he's done so well. He was always very—" She paused, then laughed. "*Aspirational.* He would pass me in the hall and point at my sweater, skirt, and shoes and say, 'Benetton, Limited, Capezio,'" she said. "And he was right every time!" She shook her head. "My God—I was such a Miss Priss back then."

"You were very preppy," I ventured.

She laughed curtly. "One did what one had to in Mendhem."

"Anthony would call me 'dirty little hippie,'" Nat said. "DLH."

"You were not!" cried Jennifer. "He was awful! But so funny." She paused, dabbing her eyes. "You know, I remember now, I reached out to him once after high school. But I never heard back. I guess he'd already moved on to more fabulous pastures."

I merely raised an eyebrow, then glanced away. *As we're wont to do*, part of me wanted to say. But I didn't. After all, she'd gotten back to me this time—and was serving me quiche in her home, no less.

"And that is just so heartbreaking about Pete Stroman," she continued. "That truly upset me to hear."

Nat and I nodded gravely. "Very sad," I said.

"Do you know anything more about it?"

I shook my head. "Not really. Just that final note." And then I took the plunge. "Did you see what he wrote about Gold? *Coach* Gold?"

"I *did*. Wasn't that heartbreaking that he hadn't forgotten it in all those years?"

"Well," I began, "as I was telling Nat last week, I also never forgot what he said to me once when nobody else was around."

Jennifer's hand flew to her lips. "Oh, no. What—" Treading carefully. "Do you mind—?"

I repeated the mincing queen story. I thought it might be easier to tell than the last time, that it might have lost some of its sting, but in fact, it hadn't. Again, I had to hold back a catch in my voice and a welling in my eyes as I told it, especially the damning words themselves. Perhaps, I thought, because I'd only begun vocalizing it recently, after an interval of a quarter-century.

Jennifer was properly horrified. "He would be *fired* for that today! Oh Tip, I'm so sorry! That's just—shitty that he said that to you."

Had Jennifer Douglas actually just said the word *shitty*? Apparently.

Then she added: "The eighties!"

Nat and I glanced at each other and erupted in laughter. "That's exactly what Tip said a few weeks ago," Nat marveled.

I nodded. "Yeah. It was a different time."

Then I caught Nat glancing at me knowingly, as though sensing why I'd retold the story.

She was right—and apparently I'd succeeded, because, after a thoughtful, inward moment smoothing her napkin in her lap, Jennifer looked at us both squarely and said, with what appeared to be some reluctance: "I have a very unpleasant Gold memory myself."

Nat and I both remained silent a moment. "What's that?" I finally dared.

She sat up straight, sighed. "So, for my senior year entry for oratory interpretation—"

"I remember it!" Strangely, it was important to me that she knew I remembered. "'Ain't I a Woman?,' right? Sojourner Truth."

She drew back a moment. "*Very* impressive. What a memory, Tip Murray."

"Believe me," said Nat, an eye roll in her voice, "he doesn't forget a thing. Whether you want him to or not."

I side-eyed Nat, with mock approbation, while Jennifer continued. "Well, yes, that's what it was. And he—" She paused, cocked her head slightly, her eyes narrowing. Nat and I stared at her, Nat's mouth slightly agape, both of us waiting. Then I was taken aback to see a glassy sheen come over her eyes, before she closed them for a moment, firmly, then reopened them. "Let's just say he did not understand where I was coming from with that material. Which was to *honor* her, *not* make a mockery of her." She looked at us both briefly, keenly, then looked down. "And I remember thinking, 'I am getting out of this town in a few months and *never* looking back.'"

There was a new bite in her voice. Nat and I glanced at each other, then back at Jennifer, said nothing.

"But as you said," Jennifer continued, now in a brighter register, "it was the eighties! Much was still left to be—interrogated. And thankfully it has been."

That word—that academic word, a piece of her trade language—seemed to signal she was ready to put the moment aside, despite my burning curiosity.

"He didn't think before he spoke," Nat said softly.

And then, more sharply, from Jennifer: "But maybe he did."

So I then dared it. "I never really thought," I began, "about how hard it must have been for you to be basically the only Black student in the whole school."

"Don't forget the chorus girls!" Jennifer said instantly.

"Oh, that's right!" I said. The Dreamgirls, she meant. I'd be mortified now, I realized, if she knew we'd called them that. But I did venture: "I remember their three-part harmony to 'I Wanna Dance with Somebody.'"

"Bless them," she added, then: "Let's just say I saved being Black for college. Then I was probably *too* Black, for a few years at least. And then I became a professional Black person, meaning I studied it and taught it, so it all kind of evened out in the end."

We were all quiet a moment. *Too* Black in college. I remembered the moment on the Yale quad, bumping into her with her three friends, seeing her surrounded by more Blackness in one random moment than she'd known in a decade in Mendhem.

"There's a lot of things in life you don't think about, or see clearly, until you're older," I finally said.

She looked at me significantly. "I can only imagine being a gay kid must be easier today than it was back then."

"I can't believe the high school has a gay-straight alliance now," I said. "I can't even conceive of having been out in high school. It was so confusing, because kids would be like, 'You're a fag,' as though that was the worst thing somebody would be, and then some other kids would defend me and be like, 'No, you're not, you're just *different*—you're an *individual*.' And I wanted to be like: 'But I *am*! But, wait, I'm *not*! But wait, I actually *am*!' It was mentally exhausting."

Jennifer briefly put her hand over mine on the table. "Oh, honey. Well, I feel terrible thinking back on it because I was madly in love with Anthony—"

Nat and I both sat up. "You were?" we chorused.

Jennifer laughed, delighted. "Oh my God, *yes*! I thought he was *so* handsome and *so* sophisticated and just a touch mysterious. For one thing, he wasn't quite white, like Mendhem white, which I must have latched on to in some way. What was he? Palestinian?"

"I think he was Lebanese on one side, and Italian on his mom's," Nat said.

"Right! And, I mean, that thick head of hair and those big brown eyes and those lips—and the *wardrobe*. I mean, he had more clothes than I did! I don't think I ever saw him wear the same thing twice."

Nat and I were convulsing with laughter by this point. "It's so true!" Nat and I both cried.

Jennifer had laughed so hard that she was smudging tears from her eyes. "And I remember we were at a graduation party together and I got a bit drunk and basically threw myself at him. I was like, 'Can I come see you in New York in the fall?' And he just gave me a look of *death* and said"—and here she dropped into a kind of bored deadpan—"'not if you're wearing that eye shadow.'"

Nat howled. "Oh my God, I remember that voice! It was so gravelly."

"Very Bea Arthur," I said.

We were still laughing, dredging up various Anthony memories, when a boy of about seven, a mop of black curly hair and a soiled soccer jersey, charged onto the porch and headed right for the plate of banana bread.

Jennifer caught his wrist. "Raphael Maldonado, go wash your hands before you touch that food. And say hello to Mommy's friends—Thomas and Natalie."

"Hello," he echoed boredly as he marched back inside the house. He was replaced by a man, truly a grown version of Raphael, yet half a head shorter than Jennifer, whose forehead he kissed as he approached. Briefly, almost imperceptibly, Jennifer's eyes closed, then opened—a nanosecond of married bliss.

"I told him to go wash his hands before eating. But did he listen?"

He looked at Nat and me, smiled and shook his head, as though he assumed we'd already been woven into the family dynamic. Then he reached out a hand to both of us.

"Andy," he said. "Nice to meet you." He sat down with us, helping himself to lunch, soon joined by Raphael—with clean hands. A brief conversation about the soccer game ensued.

"Nat has a boy," Jennifer informed Andres. "You said eleven?"

Nat nodded. "But he's a swimmer."

Raphael's face lit up. "I can swim!"

Jennifer leaned over and scrunched a hand through his hair. "Raffy's an *excellent* swimmer, it's true."

"And I dive, too."

I smiled. He was adorable. "What's your favorite dive?" I asked. "You like doing the Meatball?"

His face scrunched up skeptically. "What's that?"

"When you jump and you wrap your arms around your knees and you hit the water like a meatball."

"That's not a real dive!" he protested. "But yeah, I like that."

"You're a fish once you're in there, right?" It was Andres. "You don't wanna come out."

"Yep!"

He gobbled his food, wriggled in his seat a moment, asked to be excused, then began to race away.

"Raffy!" Jennifer called back, forcing a stop and a turnaround from him. "What do you say to our guests before you leave?"

"Nice to meet you!"

"Nice to meet you, too!" Nat and I chimed back. Then he vanished and we fell into the expected pleasantries and information-sharing, now that we had a new element at the table in the form of Andres. I found myself stealing glances at his handsome, alert face. Jennifer Douglas, an image of virginal primness in high school, married only to her books, had not only found her other half but had also made new human beings with him, small blended versions of themselves. It was so banal in a way, part of the expected human cycle, and yet I found it remarkable, fascinating.

At one point, the briefest silence fell over the table, as though we'd all simultaneously acknowledged we'd exhausted our avenues of conversation. Jennifer took to smoothing her napkin in her lap again. I felt a wave of mortification, paralysis. Why had I brought Nat and myself here? How would we wrap this up graciously? Surely this family, busy all week, had a Saturday afternoon and evening to get on with.

I was about to turn gingerly to Nat, suggest that we let the Douglas-Maldonados do just that—go do a crunchy-leaved October hike at a nature preserve not far away—when Andres, perhaps himself groping for the next skein of conversation, asked: "So you three were all on the . . . debate team together?"

"The *speech* team," Jennifer corrected, with mock approbation. "*Not* just debate."

"It offered many avenues to total nerd-dom," I said.

And then we were back on the topic, which led to my inevitable capsule retelling of my tale of private humiliation at the hands of Gary Gold.

And Andres's inevitable reaction: "That is *fucked up*. He'd be fired for that today." He turned to Jennifer, massaged her shoulder: "Babe, did he say fucked-up shit to you, too? Because if he did, I'll go and find him and take care of him for you."

His faux machismo was funny. I laughed, then glanced at Nat. Maybe now we'd get the full story. But Jennifer, after a moment's consideration, merely sighed. "It was a different time, as we've been discussing. The word *microaggression* didn't exist."

"That's for sure," I added.

"If I'd made an issue out of every little casually racist slight—"

she added, then trailed off. Then she turned to Nat, who'd long been quiet. "Did he ever say anything inappropriate to you?"

Nat opened her mouth as though to speak, then paused. "Not *really*," she finally said. "He'd say Jewish things to me."

Jennifer's eyes widened. "Jewish things?"

"Well, you know, he was, I think, the only Jewish teacher in the school. I think he was originally from here—New Jersey—and came up to Massachusetts for college and never left. And so he'd, like, he'd use Yiddish words with me and make jokes about us being the chosen people—because he knew I was Jewish, or at least that my mother was Jewish. I remember once he said something about the two of us being stuck in a town full of dumb goyim. And I'd go *ha-ha-ha* and laugh along for his sake. I mean, there *weren't* many Jewish families in Mendhem—I can count them on one hand."

She was right about that. The nearest synagogue was two towns over.

"But," Nat continued, "I don't think I felt as alienated as he did, because alongside the big Jewish holidays, we'd also have a Christmas tree like everybody else. But having another Jew to bond with seemed so important to him."

We were all quiet a moment. "Hmm," Jennifer finally allowed. "That's interesting."

"But other than *that*," Nat added, "no. I don't remember him being weird with me."

More quiet all around, punctuated by the chatter of birds in the woods beyond the yard. Then Andres suggested: "You guys should reach out to him. Seriously. Tell him you remember the things he said after all these years."

Jennifer turned, startled, laughed. "What, call him?"

"Find his email and email him. Or look for him on Facebook."

"I already did once," I said, slightly embarrassed. "Looked on Facebook. I couldn't find him."

"Did you Google?" Andres asked.

"No."

Andres rose swiftly and exited the porch.

"Oh, no," Jennifer lamented. "He's getting his laptop."

She was right. He returned with it, pushed some plates aside on the table, then set it down and popped it open, pulled up Google. "What should I type in?" he asked.

I rose, came around behind his chair, as Nat followed and Jennifer nudged herself closer to him, so that finally we were all looking at the blank search field.

"Type in 'Gary Gold,' in parentheses," I began. "Then 'Mendhem High School' and 'Massachusetts.'"

And so Andres did, then scrolled slowly. There were several links with a "Gary Gold" attached—not surprising for a relatively basic name—and several links with a "Mendhem High School," but none that seemed to connect the two.

"He might've left before the Internet really took off," noted Nat.

But then I noticed the name "Gary Gold" attached to a link for "Sarasota Senior Golf Club Dinner, 2007." I pointed to it. "Click that."

It was a page of photos from the self-said event, what appeared to be a golf club for seniors in Sarasota, Florida, which I knew to be a retirement mecca. Image after image of vaguely prosperous Baby Boomers, mainly in their sixties and seventies, in their version of sporty evening wear, pastel print dresses on the women and jackets without ties on the men, wineglasses in hand. Andres scrolled his way down.

"That's him!" Nat suddenly cried.

Jennifer peered in. "Where?"

"Right there." She pointed at an image of a couple, arm in arm, the man, still reed-thin, with a mop of tight salt-and-pepper curls, forcing a photo smile, slightly cockeyed behind round tortoiseshell glasses, traces of that Elliott Gould handsomeness still in his face, the jaw still square, and the eyes still darkly piercing. One hand was holding a glass, the other wrapped around the waist of a tiny, birdlike woman, looking about a decade his junior, hair a highlighted wispy nimbus around her face, clutching her own glass, looking—what was the word?

"That woman looks absolutely terrified," Jennifer supplied.

That was the word.

"But," she added, "that's definitely him. That same little curly hairdo he had, just gray now."

"And that same squinty sort of smirk," said Nat, transfixed by the image.

And the caption confirmed it: *Gary Gold and Janet Milken-Gold, members since 2004.*

We all just stared at the image for a few seconds, as though we'd discovered the Rosetta stone with alarming, almost implausible ease, mere moments after determining to look for it.

"I think he had that same brown corduroy jacket in high school," Nat noted.

Andres peered forward. "He looks so mild-mannered. Like a dweeby professor at a small college somewhere."

"That's exactly what he was like," I said. "But I don't remember that woman. Do you guys?"

"I remember he brought a girlfriend on the bus with him to some meets once or twice," said Nat. "This really mousy girl with long, stringy hair who looked like she was in high school herself."

"That's right!" interjected Jennifer. "I remember her now."

"But I don't think her name was Janet. I think it was, like, Myra or Meerna or something."

"Well," I said. "Janet sure looks thrilled to be at the golf dinner."

We all laughed a moment, then fell back into silence. Jennifer sighed that kind of time-marking sigh and absently massaged Andres's shoulder. And it was Andres, once again, who broke the silence.

"Hey! You guys should go see him!"

Jennifer broke out laughing. "Oh, stop!"

"Seriously! Go down this winter for some fun, but drop in on him and tell him you remember the things he said. That'll give him a kick in the butt." Andres seemed to say this with some bite, as though perhaps he could think of a person or two he'd like to do the same to.

Jennifer regarded Andres, equal parts annoyed and amused. "Why are you always trying to get me to go away without you?"

"Because you need to learn to detach from your children for two seconds," he answered instantly. "Especially the puppy. That's why, mi amor." Then a peck on her cheek.

Jennifer looked at Nat and me, shook her head. "He means Raffy, not the actual dog. This is an ongoing theme of his, as you can see." But then, thoughtfully, "I have to admit, the idea of having the opportunity to ask him if he remembers what he said to me gives me chills." She paused. "But in fairness, I'd also tell him that I loved Speech Team. Because I did. It gave me a lot of confidence. Especially once I started winning!"

Nat nodded. "I loved Speech Team, too. I'm not too cool to admit it."

They both looked at me now. "We had fun," I allowed. And I wasn't lying. It had been a loser's sanctuary and a nerd's paradise.

Andres looked up at Jennifer. "Go on your January break. You'll have some fun either way. I'll take care of the kids." Pause. "Because you know we have to practice at that!" He turned to Nat and me. "She's a very doting momma."

"I'm a neurotic momma," Jennifer corrected. "Just come on out and say it, Andres." But then, back to Nat and me, eyes widening: "Do you think Anthony would come? Wouldn't that be wild?" She looked absolutely giddy now, at the thought of reuniting with her bitchy gay high-school love object.

I shrugged. "I guess I could track him down and say hello as a start," I said, although the thought made me vaguely queasy.

But Nat stood there with a sort of awkward half smile. "It might be hard for me logistically," she finally said. "This is a crazy school year for the kids."

This seemed to deflate Jennifer somewhat. "Well—why don't we bookmark the idea and keep talking about it? It's only October, after all."

Andres sat up straight. "I think you guys would have a *blast*."

Nat nodded. "Well—sure, let's keep talking about it."

Jennifer clapped her hands together. "Why not?" A smile curled at her lips. "You know—I'm awfully glad you two visited. You're honestly the first two people from high school I've seen since then."

Nat raised her eyebrows. "Seriously? I mean, I haven't seen a lot, but—"

"I thought I'd closed that door firmly behind me a long time ago," Jennifer continued. Then she gestured with her open palms at Nat and me. "And now it's open again."

She said it with a kind of wonderment. If she hadn't just said she was glad to see us, I might not have known how to take it.

Moments later, after the usual round of parting pleasantries and affirmations, Nat and I were back in my car, waving to Jennifer and Andres on their front portico as I pulled away, slices of banana bread wrapped in foil by Jennifer on the center console between us, the Velvet Underground back on the speaker.

I had not yet turned onto the next street before I erupted. "Oh my *God*. She changed, right?"

"She *changed*. Absolutely. I mean, I saw lots of traces of the old Jennifer, but she was so much—"

"Looser, right?"

"Exactly. *So* much looser."

"I mean, the hair alone."

"The hair had a lot to do with it. Definitely."

"And just—" I continued. "I dunno—so much more."

"You mean Blacker, right? Not, like, in some overdone way. But subtly. Even how she talked."

"Yes! All those *y'alls.* But I still sensed something there," I added. "Some tightness. She was, like, constantly smoothing her napkin. Especially when she was talking about Gold."

"Yeah, I noticed that."

Approaching the highway, I saw the sign for the nature preserve. "You wanna do a quick hike?"

"Sure."

I looked over my shoulder, maneuvered across lanes for the exit. "It's weird she wouldn't tell us what Gold said to her, isn't it?"

"Totally. I wanted to ask so badly, but I got a distinct 'Let's move on' vibe from her."

"Me too. What do you think it was? He obviously said something disparaging about Sojourner Truth. Some dumbass white guy thing."

"He probably didn't mean to upset her."

I glanced at Nat. She'd have had to have been jabbed by him to know where Jennifer and I were coming from, I thought. "I'm not totally sure about that," I countered. "I think he had a perverse side."

To which she merely shrugged, finally said: "Maybe so." Then, as I was edging into the trail preserve, slowing to find a parking space past a long column of cars, suburbanites in their ubiquitous quilted jackets unloading children and dogs, she asked: "Oh, hey. Why didn't you tell me about your friend?"

"What friend?"

"Your friend in New Jersey who's sick who you were supposed to see today."

"Oh, right! Oh, well, they told me not to come before I invited you." The illogic of that then struck me. "I mean, after I invited you. And I figured, let's go anyway!"

I glanced rightward at her. She was eyeing me curiously.

"Which friend?"

"A friend from college. My friend Ben." I did, in fact, have a college friend Ben from New Jersey, but he wasn't sick. At least I certainly hoped he wasn't.

"Oh," she said, still eyeing me, I noticed, as I glanced her way again. "Okay. Well, whatever. It's still a fun day."

"It is, right?" We parked, walked past the gated dog run, up onto a less-landscaped ridge, then onto a trail that rose a long, slow grade into an oil portrait of flaming colors. We were soon truly alone, the closest people a quarter mile ahead of us.

I asked her then, with a preemptive note of sarcasm to suggest I wasn't invested in the idea: "You think we'll all be sunbathing on the Gulf Coast together in January?"

"Oh, God. I don't know if I can pull that off."

"I know." I wanted my tone to telegraph that I'd not taken Andres's idea too seriously in the first place, as much as it had appeared to have animated Jennifer—at least once the thought of Anthony came into it. "It does feel a bit like a very special one-hour episode of a sitcom or something, doesn't it? Like when *The Facts of Life* went to Europe."

She laughed, but mirthlessly, it seemed to me.

In a moment, she spoke again: "The truth is, I can't afford it."

I glanced at her, reddened. That much hadn't occurred to me. "Oh," I said. "I get that."

But she shook her head, as though to signal that, in fact, I did *not* get it. "We're not doing well," she said. "This rental farming thing isn't working out, as much as we've given it the best go possible. We're probably both going to have to get job-jobs soon and break the lease on that land and just find the cheapest apartment we can possibly find in Bedford to put the kids in school there, 'cause the schools are good. I think this is our last harvest season."

She hadn't shared this with me prior, and I sensed the reluctance to do so in her voice. "Oh, hon. That sucks. I didn't know that."

When I glanced at her again, I saw she was smudging a tear out of her eye. "I can't make anything work, Tip."

"That's not true!" I protested, putting an arm around her. "You have the best two kids! I'd kill to have those kids."

She glanced up at me, brightening vaguely. "Really, you would?"

"Yes! They're the best. And you have a hot boyfriend who's not an asshole—for once."

"Who I forced into polyamory."

I laughed, unsure how to reply. So instead I continued: "Look. I can help you out if you guys really need it. Like, with the up-front on an apartment or whatever. You would let me know, right?"

"Yeah." She laced an arm around my waist. "That means a lot, thanks."

"And I'll front your trip to Florida if you wanna go."

"Well—let's just put a pin in that for now." Then, after a moment: "But let's just say we did go. Do you really think the punishment would fit the crime?"

"What do you mean?" A large fallen branch lay in our path, and I stooped down to break it cleanly over my knee, handing half to her as a walking stick, retaining the other half for my own.

"This idea of confronting Gold. I mean, it's not like he *abused* us. You and Jennifer, I mean. He just said some stupid things. It was just—*speech.*"

"Speech from the speech coach," I said." Yeah, I've thought of that, too. I wouldn't call it full-on abuse either. Like, physical or sexual abuse, or sustained psychological torture. But I have thought: Do people ever think that the things they just toss off are going to stay with someone for the rest of their lives? What's wrong with telling someone that they did? Aren't we entitled to?"

"Yeah." She sounded vaguely skeptical. Then, after a long pause: "Would you say you're happy in your life these days?"

She'd caught me off guard. "Happy in my life?"

"Yeah. We haven't really talked in a long time. I know you had that—like, slip in your life last year. With your recovery."

I'd forgotten I'd told her, but she was right. We'd texted lengthily after that. I always felt overly confessional after a relapse, as though if I just told enough people, talked it out, I'd expunge it completely from my being and it would never happen again. Hadn't that been the point of my mother dragging my brother and me to confession every six months when we were young, going into the dark booth with the faceless priest on the other side of the screen, dredging up a half-year's worth of tantrums, backtalk, and small lies and deceptions so that one could emerge with, in my mother's words, "a clean slate"? Eventually, my brother and I, who dreaded the whole affair, had protested and our mother had stopped making us go, even eventually ceased going herself, as though our pushback had slowly undone her Irish Catholic girlhood's sense of duty. But the urge to purge, to reclaim that elusive clean slate, followed me, secularized, into adulthood. With alcohol and drugs, though, it never worked. Even as I told and retold friends just how my wheels had come off, how and why and *what I'd learned* and all that boilerplate, I knew deep down that that particular slate wasn't ever getting clean. What felt good about those detours, what chronic low-grade unease they delivered me from, always lived more powerfully in my memory than how they derailed me and hurt others.

So now, approaching the crest of the trail, I glanced Nat's way. "Am I happy right now? Yeah. I think so. I've been doing okay since then. I like my job enough. I write for a living, even if it's boring some of the time. Okay, most of the time, but whatever. And Marcus is great."

"He is." She truly liked Marcus. And unlike some friends, or so-called friends, she'd never suggested that I didn't deserve him.

"I do feel like there's this—*gap*—between us," I admitted.

"Sexually?"

"No, that's okay. Not, like, *edgy*, but okay. Adequate. More like this part of me I don't want him to see. A very, *very dirty bad* boy."

I laughed at my own overemphasis, it sounded so camp, but she was silent before saying: "Yeah, I feel that way with Aaron, too. Like, if he only knew—"

"Exactly! That's it. Except I don't even know what it is that I wish he only knew, you know?"

To our great surprise, at the crest of trail, amid a clearing, emerged a very dim vista, miles away, of the skyline of Manhattan—site of my failed experiment in cosmopolitan living, The Big Dream Botched, some fifteen years before.

"Look!" exclaimed Nat, rushing forward a bit for the better view. "I didn't even know we were so close!"

I caught up to her. I wasn't going to spoil the moment for her by mentioning how that particular view always stung me for a moment.

Instead, surprising myself after a spell of silence, I said, "You know, there wasn't any sick New Jersey friend Ben I meant to see today."

She laughed a little, ruefully. "I figured as much. I think Jennifer did, too, honestly. You just wanted to see her. Right?"

I nodded.

"Why?" Her tone made it clear she hadn't shared my quest, as happy as she'd been to come along.

I wouldn't go so far as to tell her about the long-ago visit to Yale—it was still too humiliating, to have longed to see Jennifer that badly and to have met far less than the same sentiment, if not in fact its opposite.

But I still answered honestly. "I just needed her to look me in the eye and call me Tip again, and to just acknowledge that we had been in that time and place together and shared something."

"But why? Can't you do that with me?"

"I don't really know why. I feel like that time in our lives is a hole in the ground. Like a deep, Baby Jessica hole—"

"Baby *Jessica*?" Nat hooted. "Oh my God—I'd forgotten all about that."

"Right? Like a Baby Jessica hole in the ground. And I can't get out of it, but I would really, *really* like to, because I think if I could, then things would be different."

THREE

It's maybe not saying much, but I grew up in a more open-minded town than I realized at the time. When I was thirteen, fourteen, fifteen, because I'd not been anywhere else, I believed steadfastly that there could be no place in the entire world more backward than Mendhem, with its sports-obsessed Yankee and Catholic families, its theater and arts programs that felt anemic, small-fry, compared to the glut of private schools in the area or even the nearby better public schools, the rich suburbs west of Boston like Newton, Wellesley, Weston. In Mendhem, everybody's parents were former Kennedy fanatics who'd gone Republican for Reagan, and everybody thought that a regional Catholic college like B.C. or Holy Cross was the last word in an elite higher education. It was a white-flight town, full of families like mine and Anthony's who'd fled the nearby defunct mill city, Lawton, when it began filling up with Puerto Ricans and Dominicans in the 1970s and '80s.

Mendhem was full of everyday, garden-variety racism, full of outrage and protest when the local Catholic archdiocese announced that, out of moral obligation, it was going to build affordable apartments on land it owned next to the highway on the Lawton border, far from the heart of town. Everyone knew what that meant: Hispanics would be crossing the border, coming to live there, invading the schools and the stores. There was a huge fuss, blatantly bigoted in nature, but the development ultimately was built and ever after referred to as Mendhem's "ghetto," even though I went there a few times in high school for parties and it was just like any other suburban apartment complex—buildings, lawns, and parking lots arrayed around a club house with a pool and tennis and basketball courts.

Many kids think they grow up in hell, then only come to realize that the meaning of hell is relative once they learn a bit about the rest of the world. In college and after, I realized that hell would have been growing up in actual poverty, in a neighborhood blighted by segregation and crime, where every walk to school risked making you a victim of a drive-by shooting and where you were lucky if you finished high school. Or hell would have been growing up in the Deep South or smack in the middle of the country, where religion was fanatical, evolution was doubted, and gayness was cause for horror and being sent off to a "pray the gay away" conversion camp.

In Mendhem, with the exception of the enthusiastically liberal Unitarians, religion was ignored by Yankees or practiced dutifully, passionlessly, by Catholics. Like most other families, mine went to mass on Saturday late afternoons because Father Pete got us out in under thirty minutes so we could then proceed to pizza, the movies, or the mall. This was greater Boston, after all, where, in the 1980s, not one but two popular congressmen, Gerry Studds and then Barney Frank, were outed in gay sex scandals with younger men but went on to be reelected multiple times because they delivered for their districts. Nobody was really that invested in crushing gay people; everyone was much more concerned about whether the Red Sox would ever win the World Series again.

At the time, I didn't appreciate the teachers who introduced us to Herman Melville and Walt Whitman with the casual notations that both were gay—and so what?—or the teacher who made us read *The Color*

Purple, and who, in a 1980s version of a trigger warning, told us matter-of-factly, "If a certain part bothers you, turn the page and move on."

I didn't appreciate my piano teacher, a sweet older woman in a peeling Victorian on Main Street, who, when she was teaching me some Cole Porter, told me offhandedly that he'd probably written many of his love songs with men in mind. Amid the untoppled cultural bigotries of the Reagan era, they were trying to tell me something, I now realize—that it was okay to be gay, that I was fine the way I was, that there was a place for me out there, that I wouldn't always be so miserable and angry and knotted up inside. But let's face it, teenagers are often stupid and unobservant, told and shown a lot of things whose import and subtext they'll never understand until later in life.

Twenty minutes away was Boston and Cambridge, and even closer were the arty sea towns of Newburyport and Rockport and Portsmouth, New Hampshire, access to a wealth of culture and subculture, more European magazine racks and used bookstores and record stores and clothing stores, more arthouse cinemas and experimental theaters than we could tunnel our way through in an entire weekend, though Nat and I certainly tried. But at the time I thought I was growing up in a cultural wasteland, a million miles from New York City, the only place that really mattered. It never occurred to me I could actually be growing up in West Texas, or outside Wichita, Kansas, or in Laramie, Wyoming, where a decade later a young gay man would be strung up on a fence and left to die.

I guess all this was obscured for me by the fact that, from my first day of school upon moving to Mendhem in fifth grade until the middle of junior year in high school, when my underclass pariah status magically morphed into the senior class cachet of being "an individual" and "marching to my own drummer," I lived a daily nightmare of abuse. I had no self-awareness coming into the situation, could not have anticipated the sheer loathing I inspired in boys my age for traits—voice, walk, hand gestures—I did not even understand as gay. But life became a kind of physical and psychic obstacle course, a decade-long unnatural surge of adrenaline and cortisol, from the moment I left the house in the morning until the moment I was back home. If I took Route A to school, then I would likely encounter Bully A, who would throw both me and my bookbag into a mudslick on the side of the road, meaning that I would go through the school day smeared in what looked like shit, but if I rode my bike to school via Route B, then I would encounter Bully B, who would stand in my path, shove me off my bike, then stomp on both tires until they were mangled, leaving me to somehow walk the twisted mess to school, whereupon I would be late for homeroom, sometimes disciplined for it, too mortified to explain my tardiness.

These memories probably wouldn't be seared onto my adult brain if they'd happened once or twice, but the grim fact of my life at the time was that they happened every day, turning junior high school and at least the first half of high school into one long migraine that would pound behind my right eye every day upon arriving home, at which point I would knock back Tylenol, lock myself in my room, and cry, ashamed my parents would hear me. I felt like a raw wound, an open target churning with nausea, walking into that dreaded, low-slung mid-century brick and glass building every day, the American flag billowing atop a thirty-foot pole on the front lawn. Eventually, I found it easier to just accept that I would be flogged and flayed, rather than to scream and thrash about in resistance or try to run away, to know I would come out of it with my underwear pulled up well above my waistline, or soaked from the melting snowbank I'd been shoved into, but having survived to live another day.

The apex of this dissociation came on a frigid January afternoon my freshman year in high school, when, as I left the building, three seniors on the football team literally picked me up like a sack of potatoes, put me in the trunk of their car, drove off with Bruce Springsteen's "Born in the U.S.A." blaring from the speaker, opened the trunk on a deserted forest road about eight miles away on the rural outskirts of Mendhem, told me to get out, and then, laughing in chorus, drove away. I remember pausing not even for a moment, but, as though this had simply been my routine humiliation of the day, turning around and beginning the freezing trudge home. After about twenty minutes, a random acquaintance from school pulled up alongside me in his mother's Chrysler.

The heat in the car was a godsend. When he asked me what I was doing out on the edge of town, I told him, flatly, removed from my own duress, what had happened. He said not a word and drove me up to my own house, whereupon I thanked him for the ride. We never spoke of it again.

Leaving that town, going to a college full of brilliant freaks and sexual outlaws, then eventually moving to Manhattan in its last decade of pre-gentrified nocturnal euphoria, was my proof that I'd survived, that I'd come out unscathed. But I was woefully out of touch with the rage and desperation boiling inside me, didn't understand why I wanted to take the partying, the drugs and sex, further than my friends, why I yearned to be in situations that felt edgy and unsafe, why I loved walking the streets at three in the morning in unfamiliar neighborhoods, itching for some kind of trouble, some kind of encounter with a less-than-nice guy that felt a bit degrading and predatory.

Riding on that energy, I managed to torch my Manhattan life to the ground in less than five years—lost job, lost apartment, lost friendships, lost pride. I was that unreformable mess, breath sulfurous with last night's liquor and mood rotten with the chemical hangover of last night's eight ball, whom nobody wanted to hire, or hire back; to be around when I got drunk, high, and nasty; to invite to the birthday party, go on a second date with, or depend on in any way. Wrecked nights bled into mornings of nausea and self-loathing, into afternoons of tearful private vows of reform, into evenings of bitter craving amid withdrawal, then back into the sweet oblivion of wrecked nights. Somewhere in the middle of all this, I flipped through newspapers and magazines in order to curse New Yorkers who were successful, telling myself it was clear they'd whored themselves in various ways, sold out, when really it just galled me that they had that much focus, drive.

I evacuated the East Village on a perfect June afternoon with the contents of my studio in a rented U-Haul, burning with shame, saving face by calling it a fresh start. In Providence—do you love the cloying poetry of my escaping to a town called Providence?—it would take twelve-step meetings and therapy, attended with diminishing resentment over a period of many months, for me to realize much later that my cortisol and adrenaline had been primed and pumped my whole adolescence, that they didn't want to simmer down, that I didn't know what safety or normality felt like, that I actually had to learn it with someone like Marcus, which was no easy feat, because in the first year of that relationship, I felt like the safety and normality—the shocking fact that Marcus didn't want to hurt me or throw me abusive curveballs—was going to suffocate me. It took a long, long time for me to learn to appreciate them.

And now, I'm happy to report, I wouldn't want it any other way.

I'm pretty sure.

So I tell you all this as a prelude to saying that, amid this adolescent misery, anything having to do with art, literature, or culture was an oasis, an escape. A novel, assigned or picked up on a whim, was an escape, something I could immerse myself in for hours, never wanting to leave. Writing melancholy poetry for the literary magazine, or a scathing social commentary for the school paper, was an escape.

A day in Boston, coming back with an armload of new books, magazines, records—a fortress of new ideas, images, and sounds I could bury myself in for weeks to come—was an escape. And certainly Speech Team was an escape, because not only did it take place in the company of other weirdos and brainiacs who had no desire to shove me in a filthy puddle or try to stuff me into my own locker, but also because, in a school where sports were the only competition that seemed to matter, it was a different kind of competition, an arena where the winners were those who could best create, or if not make from scratch then at least skillfully interpret, language.

The first time I competed in poetic interpretation, the winter of my sophomore year, I read a self-selected collection of Robert Frost's winter poems, culminating, of course, with "Stopping by Woods on a Snowy Evening," which has become a parody of the kind of poem one is forced to memorize in school, but which I found absolutely healing in its desolation, in the idea of walking so deep into a forest that no aggressor lurked behind a tree, that you were safe and finally at peace in your solitude. The collection was my first venture in curation, of sifting out a mere few options among many, of sequencing them in a way that felt like I was making of several small stories a new, larger story.

This little collection, whose delivery I polished obsessively in rehearsals with Coach Gold—himself an admitted lover of Frost—I doted over, recited with such love and infinite emotional inflection and meaning, because I had chosen it. It was all mine, a little universe I entranced listeners into inhabiting for exactly nine minutes and thirty-five seconds, because ten minutes was the limit for entries in the poetic interpretation category. That January at the winter tournament at snobby little Samuels Farm School in Blandford, I took first place, besting a Samuels girl in a Fair Isle sweater and plaid wool skirt who recited Amy Lowell's "Patterns" followed by Maya Angelou's "Phenomenal Woman," thinking that juxtaposing the two poems was her shortcut to the blue ribbon. She was wrong. I triumphed.

It was Gold, of all people, who, after I won the first time, suggested that I read Whitman for the next tournament, telling me to hunker down with "Song of Myself" and figure out which part, or parts, I thought would best work in the ten-minute window. I was staggered once I sat down with it, a whopping sixteen thousand words in one poem, an overwhelming fifty-two sections, a torrent of language and ideas the likes of which I'd never seen, so overabundant and lush—almost unbearable—compared to the laconic spareness of Frost. Why had Gold tasked me with this?

And yet I literally found my heart racing and my eyes welling as I read it, over and over again, because it seemed to encompass all of human life, and felt so bracingly vivid and clear and modern for something that had been written a hundred and thirty years ago. It was full of depictions of men, in all their brawn and sweat, that aroused me and embarrassed me. But mostly it freed me; it was as though wings lifted me high above the miserable confines of Mendhem and showed me the rest of the world, promised me it was all out there waiting for me if I could just hold on.

Ultimately, I decided to bookend my selections with sections 1 and 52, the beginning ("I celebrate myself, and sing myself . . .") and the end ("Failing to fetch me at first keep encouraged . . ."), and about a half dozen sections in between. One of which, I dared to include, feeling emboldened by the sheer bravura of the entire work itself, was section 5:

> I mind how once we lay such a transparent summer
> morning,
> How you settled your head athwart my hips and gently
> turn'd over upon me,
> And parted the shirt from my bosom-bone, and plunged
> your tongue to my bare-stript heart,
> And reach'd till you felt my beard, and reach'd till you held
> my feet.

My heart pounded while I read these lines alone to Gold in the fishbowl. I remember our eyes met—they had to; in every category, you were instructed to ruthlessly hold eye contact with your listeners—and he seemed to smirk slightly, his lips vaguely upturned, before looking down at the pad where he scratched notes while we practiced.

In a moment, I was on to the next section, relieved. But also victorious. "Song of Myself" contained an excess of homoerotica—a word I didn't even know at the time—so to choose one fragment (whose "you," after all, could have been a man *or* a woman, though I highly doubted it was a woman) felt, to me, not just justified but perhaps necessary to get across one of the main themes of the work. More to the point, I felt as though Gold, while suggesting the work and leaving it to me to figure out what parts to read, was almost giving me permission. And though, after I read in rehearsals, he would give me detailed notes on every section—how to adjust a cadence, extend a pause, tweak a pronunciation so that my Boston accent, which I still struggled to suppress, was less obvious—he never said a word about section 5.

The first time I read the selection in competition, at Dover-Sherborn High School in October, the first tournament of my junior year, I took first place. I and Pete Stroman, who'd won the blue ribbon for his original oratory about how much the band Rush meant to him, were the stars of our bus ride back to Mendhem that Saturday night, after which we'd all gone to McDonald's to celebrate, Coach Gold even joining us briefly for a Filet-O-Fish sandwich and a black coffee before hopping in his sporty little white Ford Capri, tuning to the classical station, sparking up one of his beloved Vantages, and driving back to coastal Newburyport, fifteen minutes away, where he lived. Even Pete was, by his own measure, extroverted that night, victory having coaxed some discernible pride and joy out of his mumbling affectlessness.

It was actually during the following week, when maybe I was a little bit puffed up with my triumph, perhaps more in unselfconscious sashay mode than usual, that Gold took me aside well after final bell, amid an empty hallway, and asked me, in that infinitely patient and bemused voice, as though he were gently trying to help me, why I flounced around like some kind of mincing homosexual. And that regardless of what I actually *was*—almost as though he were giving me an out, accusing me merely of demeanor and not of act or essence—perhaps I try to tone myself down.

So that's largely why I walked out of that exchange as though reeling from a body blow, too stunned to say anything back to him or tell anyone else. I'd thought I was safe with him. I'd thought he'd signaled to me that *it*—that I—was okay, that there was a place for me.

Yet it wasn't what he'd been signaling at all. Part of my unspeakable shame was that I'd been so stupid, so unvigilant, as to have misread him. As I discomfited and even sickened others, often to the point of violence, I apparently did the same to him. That he was so mild-mannered, even *friendly*, about it, only made it worse.

It felt like he was speaking in proxy for my father—who, stoic and athletic himself, the father of the most embarrassingly bad player on every team he'd ever coached, had never directly condemned my flamboyance. He would merely frown and shake his head, as though what I'd turned out to be even amused him slightly, in a shrugging gallows humor kind of way, as much as it disappointed him. But Gold's remarks made plain what I knew, which was that I was a source of acute discomfort and a target of disdain among grown straight men, which had to include my father. Which maybe explains the confusing yearning I felt for Gold after he took me aside, as though I wanted to say to him, *Okay, sir, so you see who I really am, now please love me, hold me, protect me, anyway.*

I was on my lunch break a few days after getting back from New Jersey with Nat, scanning the magazine rack at CVS while I waited for the pharmacy to fill Marcus's Propecia prescription, when a familiar name peeped out at me from the top half of an oversize glossy called *Hey Mister*—one of those rarified men's fashion magazines, well beyond the mainstream purview of *GQ* or *Esquire*, that always made me wonder who financed them or how they stayed in business.

Anthony Malouf read the start of the coverline, the rest obscured by the tops of the magazines the next rack down.

I pulled up the magazine.

Anthony Malouf Wants You to Live This Well Too.

I laughed out loud. I couldn't help it. The idea that Anthony Malouf, who had grown up in a tiny 1950s Cape house with a Virgin Mary–on-the-half-shell in the front yard, whose father drove a truck lettered *Malouf General Contracting* and whose mother ran her errands in a parachute-fabric salmon tracksuit with teal stripes down the legs, was now such a lifestyle leader that he wished his own good taste on the poor unenlightened general public—it was too hilarious.

But I'll admit that an edge of awe accompanied my laugh—because Anthony, with his relentless immigrant work ethic, had always wanted to be on the covers of the magazines he so worshipped throughout high school—*Interview*, *The Face*, *i-D*—and now here he was. He'd certainly had more career focus and drive than I'd had.

I opened the magazine, flipped until I found his feature. I admit I gasped a bit. There he was, in a beautiful midnight-blue suit that I assumed was Pietro Cuccino, the jacket and pants fashionably fitted and short, but feet bare and chest bare, revealing a perfectly manicured pelt atop of which lay an impossibly thin silver chain and saint pendant (I couldn't tell which one. St. Anthony?), beneath the suit jacket. He reclined on a sleek charcoal gray couch, one hand reaching down to a blindingly white fluffy midsize dog on the floor of a blindingly white, minimal apartment, broken up by massive white pots of fiddle-leaf fig plants. Floor-to-ceiling windowed walls gave out onto a stunning view of the Manhattan Bridge. Anthony stared directly into the camera—unsmiling, aloof, even bored-looking.

The caption read: "Chillin': Malouf and Alexis, his Eskimo dog, relax at home in Dumbo."

Alexis! I laughed out loud. In high school, Anthony and I had both been obsessed with *Dynasty*, particularly the resident diva bitch, Alexis Carrington Colby, so much so that too-cool-for-school Anthony could usually be persuaded to recite Alexis's best lines from the night before.

"Take this junk—and your blonde tramp," Anthony would intone for us on the Speech Team bus, accent British and clipped, pretending to throw Krystle's furs over the balustrade of the Carrington mansion, "and get out of my home."

Or, as we Speech Teamers huddled at our nerd table at lunch over cardboard pizza and tater tots: "The reason that I am *who* I am and *where* I am is because I make everything my business."

Or, his very favorite, perhaps from the driver's seat of his mother's 1979 Chevy Nova, which he'd inherited: "I have a reputation for being unpredictable, devious, and manipulative. And I *cherish* that reputation because it keeps my enemies off guard."

And now he'd gone and named his dog Alexis. I shook my head, smiled. He'd built up an edifice of wealth and glamour around him, but the dog's name was a hint that that aspirational small-town kid was still there. I missed him despite his having cast me aside. We'd been gay together before we even knew or dared to say we were gay—to ourselves even, never mind to each other. But our friendship was crypto-gay: endless dissections of *Dynasty*, Grace Jones, and Madonna, mall trips to buy WilliWear, Generra, and Girbaud.

I skimmed the story, which of course contained more photos of him—at work, poring over fabrics alongside his stylish minions, shopping at the Union Square farmer's market with a canvas bag loaded with greens on his shoulder, a close-up of him and Alexis, their resting bitch faces side by side. He still had the massive brown eyes and full lips that had so enchanted Jennifer, now framed by a short beard, impeccably groomed. Most of the quotes were dumb anodyne fashion quotes—"Men are finally putting more work into their bodies, and I'm committed to making a suit that reflects that in a way that's sensual and fluid but still nods to the haberdasher tradition"—but there was one part that particularly caught me.

"Malouf has always lived alone, with a succession of dogs, the most recent being Alexis, whom he calls his baby girls. 'I've worked hard to curate a life that's just to my liking,' he says, 'and anytime someone's come into it, they've thrown off the composition, no matter where I tried to place them.'"

A few Thanksgiving holidays after college ended, probably 1992 or 1993, I was back at my parents' house in Mendhem, in my old bedroom, propped up on pillows and reading shortly after midnight, when I heard a *plink* on the window. I disregarded it until, seconds later, I heard another. I rose and pulled up the shade to find Anthony waving up at me from the backyard with one hand, the other hand shoved into the pocket of his black leather car coat, which clearly was too thin for the frigid night.

I pulled on jeans and a sweatshirt, padded downstairs barefoot, and opened the back door, blasted in the face by the cold.

He threw his arm around me. "Tipster!" he croaked. He was actually smiling, sloppily, his breath offensive.

"You're so drunk," I observed.

He joggled something bulky under his jacket. "I have tequila."

I put my finger to my lips, opened the door wider. "Come inside."

I led him down to the basement, which was semi-finished, with a disused couch and TV set—a place where my father often disappeared to watch the Red Sox or the Celtics—and, thankfully, a large space heater, which I turned on. We sat down on the couch and he pulled out a bottle of tequila and offered me a sip, which I took.

He pulled Camels from his coat pocket. "Can you smoke down

here?" He'd started smoking his senior year of high school, as soon as he knew he was off to NYU, as though he were preparing for his new demimonde existence.

"Not really, but go ahead." Which he did. "I called you yesterday."

He looked at me with slightly glassy eyes. "I'm sorry, it's been so crazy. My sister is pregnant."

"Gina? Isn't she still—"

"She's one year out of high school. It's not a good thing. It's her Dominican boyfriend from Lawton and my mother is mortified and doesn't want her to have the baby, but my mother is *tragically* pro-life, too, so of course she's having a total nervous breakdown."

"It all sounds very *Moonstruck*," I said, swigging more tequila, settling into that happy burn in the back of the throat.

He cracked up. "Gina isn't exactly Cher, sweetie. But she's trying with her horrible crimped hair." He was still smiling, cockeyed, and I have to admit it was fun to see him too drunk to be aloof.

Then he put a hand on my knee and gasped dramatically. "I have to tell you who I saw in New York!" He'd stayed there after NYU, of course, and was working as a junior buyer for Saks. (He'd go to Parsons two years later to actually learn how to become a designer.) "In the food basement at Macy's."

"Macy's!" I teased him. "That sounds very middlebrow for you."

"They have these Danish butter cookies my mother likes. She thinks they're classy."

I laughed. He'd always been merciless about his mother, whom he nonetheless worshipped. "Who?" I asked.

"Bonnie Boni*fa*ce!" he shrieked.

My jaw dropped. "*What?* What was she doing there?"

"She said she was on a trip with her girlfriends from UConn. Tippy, her *hair*."

"What? Was it still huge?"

"No, listen." He inhaled a puff, exhaled. "Now it's like—she's trying to be, I dunno, up-to-date or something. So it falls straight down like a kind of bob, except in the front, there's like this little moussed *pouf* thing that looks like a—" He paused. "You know those things in science class?"

"What things?"

"Those things—like, the models with the neutrons or whatever in them."

"Like, a model of an atom?"

"Exactly! So, she had the front moussed so it looked like an atom. Like—you know the word I'm looking for."

"Like, sculptural?"

"Yes!" He slapped my knee again. "Like, im*mo*bile. It was *so* tragic!"

I laughed. "You are still such a bitch. So what did you say to her?"

"She starts screaming to her girlfriends"—and he switched into a high nasal register—'Oh my god you guyyyyys. This is *Eyannn*thon*eeee*. From high schoooooool.'"

"Did you totally ice her?"

He swigged again from the bottle. "I wanted to. Then I thought, *Anthony, why be like that?* So you know what I did? I took them to the Coffee Shop." He paused, as though awaiting my reaction.

"What coffee shop?"

He stared at me dully, rolled his eyes. "*Tho*mas. You really haven't heard of the Coffee Shop? I know you don't live in the city"—I hadn't moved there yet—"but come on. Don't you pick up a magazine?"

He'd always had this unique power to shame me on these matters. There was nothing worse than being told by Anthony that you didn't know something you were really supposed to know.

"No, Anthony. I really haven't heard of *the* Coffee Shop. I'm sorry."

He petted my knee again. He was being awfully handsy. "It's okay," he said seriously, as though I'd really sought the absolution. "It's *the* place right now. Where all the musicians and the models go. On Union Square." He paused. "You *have* heard of Union Square, haven't you?"

"I don't *live* there!"

He sighed, drank more. "You better come down so you can pop your New York cherry."

"Okay." I tried to sound casual about it, but the idea of a weekend in New York with him actually sounded wildly fun—perhaps a portal to my future, one as potentially fabulous as his. "So, what happened at *the* Coffee Shop?"

"They thought it was *amazing*, of course. And you know something, Tipster?"

"What?"

"I thought I'd be embarrassed to be seen with them there. But I actually felt—" He paused again, searching for the word, before finally settling on an emphatic: "*Good*. Like, I could've been a little bitch, but I actually did a nice thing. I showed them something they wouldn't have known about. They probably would've gone to—oh, I don't know, *Carnegie Deli* for dinner, thinking it was cool, just because they didn't know any better. But I stepped in."

I was getting drunk now, too, amused by his regard for his own munificence. He hadn't changed at all. "You really deserve some kind of award for that," I said.

He cracked up. "I'm a good person, right?"

"You are a fucking *saint*."

This doubly tickled him, setting off a convulsion of cackles until he was bent over, clutching his stomach. "That little *atom*." He made a kind of *poof* gesture with his fingers in front of his forehead.

"Atom Ant!

"Atom *Ant*!"

He collapsed onto me, his gelled head inert on my shoulder. "Tipster," he drawled.

"*An*tho*neeee*."

We started making out. It was a shocker to me, at first, incestuous and wrong, then it suddenly felt absolutely right, as though we'd both been waiting to do it since we were thirteen. It went on and on, in a plume of tequila and cigarette smoke, and then we were ripping each other's shirts off, the pelt of fur on his chest bracing and irresistible against my own bare chest.

"This is insane," I managed to say at one point. Would my parents awaken, swing open the door at the top of the stairs, erupt in horror?

"Shhh. You know it's nice."

"It is. And you're fucking huge."

"Haha! You're not the first to say it."

We didn't go so far that we needed a condom; no way was I going there with my parents sleeping upstairs. But we did go far enough that we each saw the other, for a moment, in a state of raw, vulnerable pleasure and relief, every single posture and feint that had gotten us both through high school abandoned. We lay there, awkwardly side by side, arms and legs enlaced, on the old couch, our chests rising and falling in near-tandem. Then he started cracking up again.

"I know," I said.

"In-*sane*!"

"I'll get a towel."

Which I found in the corner by the laundry, bringing it back to him. It felt strange to be naked except for bunched-down jeans and boxers in my cold childhood basement.

He started to pull himself together, busily, more or less ignoring me as I did the same, then pulled me back down onto the couch. "I've wanted to do that for a long time," he said. His grin was wide; he was still clearly bombed.

"You really did?"

He nodded. "But I didn't realize it until senior year. Did you want to?"

Had I wanted to? Anthony's eyes were irresistible, that much was certain. He'd been voted "Best Eyes" in the senior poll, and they were: brown and enormous, long-lashed, the skin faintly smudged beneath them, setting them off. Taken alone, his eyes made up a Platonic ideal, but in the context of the rest of him, his grating voice and hippish walk, their sensual beauty was lost. Mostly I thought of him as a matryoshka-doll inset of his shrill, bossy mother; Nat and I called him, between ourselves, "mini-Marie."

"It definitely crossed my mind," I said.

My head spinning, I padded quietly up the stairs behind him, through the kitchen to the back door as he shrugged back into his coat.

"Come to New York," he said, then, the air cold on our faces, kissed me and disappeared around the corner of the house, hands thrust in his pockets.

He'd zapped me. I was only just barely coming out of the closet at that point, just a few timid trips to Boston gay bars and only about two tentative and awkward, anonymous, AIDS-phobic hookups behind me. It had felt cozy and familiar being with Anthony, and I'd also been cowed, in the best way, by what he'd been hiding away all those years in his Girbaud jeans; it suddenly explained a lot of his adolescent bravura and cockiness. I went back to Boston in a kind of swoon, thinking about the life we could have together, dying for more of that Anthony Malouf secret weapon. I found myself looking at pictures of him in our high-school yearbook in a new light, as though I'd never really seen his beauty and his magnetism, the actual man that lurked behind the mini-Marie. I dared to fantasize about a life with him in Manhattan, the fashion maven and the society scribe, out together every night with all the best people.

I gave it a week, then called him, got his answering machine, asked him how things were, suggested I come down to New York two weekends before Christmas.

Five days passed. No reply. Had the machine failed?

Anthoneee! Another try, carefully teasing and indifferent. *I left you a message. Call me!*

I never heard from him again—not even after I moved to New York the following year, too angry at his blow-off to ever call him again yet certain, via our mothers' supermarket chat, he knew I was in the city. Twice in my four years there, I saw him, to my horror, on the other side of a bar or club—yakking away, cigarette in one hand and drink in the other, with a bunch of gelled fashion gays—but I actually beelined out the door and cut short my own evening before having to face the exquisite awkwardness of bumping right into him.

In the years to follow, after my own New York stint imploded and I started over in Providence, I'd catch him popping up in *Spy*, *Details*, *The Village Voice*, those itty-bitty pieces in the front or the back about who was out on the nightlife scene, who was an up-and-comer, who from Parsons or SVA or FIT to "look out for." Then, somewhere around 1999 or 2000, when he was a junior designer at Ralph Lauren menswear, I saw him on a little segment on Cindy Crawford's MTV *House of Style* about young designers who might very likely take over the big luxury labels in the coming decade.

I remember catching the segment, gasping when I saw him, so much slimmer and more toned now, wearing black from head to toe, hair in a Caesar cut, voice deeper, carefully modulated, scrubbed of any trace of a Boston accent, showing off his mood board while the camera occasionally cut to shots of him looking busy as he ran his index finger down the length of a bolt of dark gray wool, apparently explaining a cut to a seamstress.

I watched, equal parts resentful and fascinated. By the age of thirty, he'd transformed himself—become everything he'd ever wanted to be. And apparently that didn't include someone who associated with me.

I ended up buying that copy of *Hello Mister* at the pharmacy counter when I paid for Marcus's Propecia, then, en route to the car, texted Marcus to tell him I'd be home soon with a pizza and a salad. Waiting for my margherita with sausage at Fellini on Wickenden Street, I watched a group of campus kids dive-bomb their own pizza at a table inside, then surreptitiously pour a bottle of red wine into the small plastic cups the restaurant gave out for water and Coke. My face flushed and my heart fluttered. The image brought back such a rush of sense-memory of that age, those same kind of impromptu and rumpled pizza nights in Rhinebeck or Poughkeepsie, that blissful, time-bomb vacuum of self-awareness before things go wrong and you're then forced to learn why they went wrong, that window when you're running on hormones and impulse, your brain incomplete and your reflexes raw and unfiltered. I watched one of them, a gorgeous girl with a caramel face and an explosion of black curls and a thrift-store plaid hunting coat, laugh out loud, then put her little plastic cup to her lips, savor and swallow before she laughed again and socked the arm of the boy sitting next to her—clearly the group jester, its provocateur, maybe her boyfriend.

"Shut *up*!" she declared, beaming. "You're so *stupid*."

I stopped at the small grocery next door after that and bought a bottle of Pellegrino.

Marcus and I ate in front of the nightly news, a depressing segment about how Obama might have just won his second term but very likely would pass nothing his next four years in office because of an obstructionist Republican Congress. This then segued into a far more enjoyable segment on the sudden rise of Channing Tatum.

"Your boyfriend's on TV," I called to Marcus, who'd taken the plates into the kitchen.

"Who?" he called back.

"Magic Mike."

He let out what passed for a shriek by his standards (he wasn't the shrieking type), hurried back before the TV, dish towel in hand, his tongue nearly lolling.

"He's *People*'s Sexiest Man Alive for 2012."

Marcus snorted. "I could've told them that."

"They said that, actually. Before you came in. They said that Marcus Berman, RN, of Providence, Rhode Island, cast the crucial deciding vote."

He looked at me sidelong. "You're just jealous of what Channing and I have together."

"I promise that if you ever have the chance with Channing Tatum, I'll clear out for the night. I'll get a room at La Quinta."

"Good. You better."

I regarded him a moment. I'd caught him in a kind of signature look—mock-injured, mock-fussy—that always made me laugh, re-sparked in me a delight I could easily forget about for days, even weeks, before something he said or did sparked it in me again.

"Come here," I said.

"What?"

"Just come here."

He did, close enough for me to grab a belt loop on his jeans and pull him down toward me.

"Thomas!"

I bear-hugged him, pressed my lips to his. "I love you," I said. I always seemed to forget I loved him when I was away from him, squirming in my own selfhood as though it were a hated prickly sweater, reminded of it—overwhelmed by the feeling, even—only when he was flat-out in front of me, being Marcus Berman.

He indulged me a moment, then pulled himself up. "You're insane," he said, but he was smiling a grudging smile.

"I know."

He headed back toward the kitchen, a moment before I wandered into the bedroom, picked back up the copy of *Hello Mister*, flopped down on the bed, and kept reading the story on Anthony.

> A 2005 trip to Lebanon, the birthplace of his paternal grandfather, was pivotal for him; it's where he became obsessed with Middle Eastern tile work, a subtle version of which found its way into the linings of his second collection for Cuccino.

> "I love the colors, I love the discipline, and I love the stylization," he says. "I think it's the greatest gift the Middle East gave to the rest of the world. That, and hummus, which I live on," he laughs. "And I say this as someone who really didn't think of himself as very Arab growing up, because we were Catholic like everyone else. But then a teacher I had in high school said something incredibly ugly to me, and it actually had the reverse effect of setting me on a journey that's really shaped me for the better."
>
> Precisely what was said that proved so pivotal? Malouf, shrugging, declined to elaborate. "It's the kind of thing I could destroy him with if it happened today," he merely said.

I read the line again: . . . *a teacher I had in high school said something incredibly ugly to me* . . . What? Who? Could it be—?

I picked up my phone, snapped a picture of that paragraph, and sent it, along with the main photo of Anthony lounging in his Cuccino suit on his couch with his fluffy white dog, to Nat and Jennifer. *From a story today on Anthony I found in a fashion mag*, I texted.

A minute later, Jennifer texted back the Munch "scream" emoji—three times. *OMG! Do you think he means Gold? (I should also add he looks amazing.)*

That made me laugh. Her crush was still strong.

Then again from Jennifer: *The kind of thing he could destroy him with today!??! Wowza.*

And then a moment later, Nat: *Tipster, reach out and ask him!*

Me: *Seriously?*

Jennifer: *It can't hurt.*

It could *hurt*, I thought. It brought up the same queasy feeling I'd had when I reached out to Jennifer recently, when I'd first not heard back, that awful feeling that even full-on adulthood could not stop me from setting myself up for another dismissal, that I must be some kind of glutton for shunning.

And yet, I considered, Jennifer *had* gotten back—had even welcomed us with open arms. People changed, I told myself. The insecurities of young adulthood faded and people became nicer, comfortable in their skins. Did they not? Perhaps it was worth a try. Besides, I figured, by this point—having elicited from Jennifer at least a fragment about Gold that had mightily vindicated my own long-archived hurt—perhaps I was onto something, assembling some kind of puzzle unearthed from a dusty closet.

I had no idea how to reach Anthony except through Pietro Cuccino, whose luxe website—at the very bottom—discreetly read "Contact Us." There was an email address for media queries, what turned out to be a PR firm for high-end fashion labels.

Hello there. I wrote. *Would you please be kind enough to forward this to Anthony Malouf? This is Thomas "Tip" Murray, a friend from high school. I and two other old friends, Natalie Farb-Miola and Jennifer Douglas, were reminiscing about him recently and wanted to reach out to him.*

I'd named Nat and Jennifer pointedly. It made me feel less exposed than reaching out "alone," and perhaps mentioning Jennifer in particular might serve as catnip, because he'd always held her in high—almost worshipful—regard, despite her come-ons. "I respect her drive," he'd said to me more than once. "I share that."

I left my cell number. *Thank you so much.* And then hit "send," resolving to think of it no more.

Marcus came into the bedroom, pulled up alongside me on the bed, asked what I'd been doing.

I handed him the magazine. "Just reached out to this old friend from high school."

He leafed through the feature on Anthony. "You really went to high school with this queen?"

"Yep."

"Fancy."

"He wasn't in high school. Well, he was—in his head."

He handed the magazine back, regarded me keenly. "You're in an intense reconnection phase with high school."

I detected a note of disapproval, bristled slightly. "Not really. It's just how you get back in touch with one person, and that leads to another, and so on. It's not, like, a *project*."

He held me. "I have no desire to be in touch with anyone from high school."

I pulled him in closer. "I don't blame you. You're from Tampa."

Four days later, I got a text from a number I'd not seen before.

You heard about Pete Stroman, right?

Could it be? *Sorry, can I ask who this is?*

The reply, about fifteen minutes later: *It's Anthony.*

I was fairly shocked. *You got my email?* I texted.

Indeed.

How have you been?

Muddling through, he replied.

You looked better than that in Hello Mister, I wanted to reply—but did not. I couldn't give him the satisfaction of knowing that I'd seen the issue, let alone bought it and devoured the story. So I merely wrote back: *Glad to hear it. Same.*

Two hours later from him: *Are your parents still in Mendhem?*

This time I willed myself to wait an hour: *My dad died but my mom's in West Mendhem now.*

Surprisingly, a quick reply: ***Sorry to hear about your dad. Mine are still in Mendhem. Are you going up Thanksgiving to see your mom?***

Because he'd earned it, a quick reply back from me: ***Yeah, I'll drive up from Providence, where I live now.*** Was he rolling his eyes on his end over the decidedly noncosmopolitan city I'd ended up living in?

About five minutes later: ***You wanna have a drink that night and catch up?***

I stared at the overture in mild amazement. After having blown me off for twenty years, after our having never spoken again of our one-time hookup, after his making no effort to reach out the four years he knew I was in New York—now he was asking if I wanted to have a drink?

Of course I did.

But I still savored each of the forty-five minutes I made myself wait before replying: ***I think I could do that.*** How else could I project only middling interest? ***Let's text that day and see what's up.***

Right back at me: ***Let's just meet at Happy Panda at 7pm TG night. It's still there.***

Happy Panda! Was he really going to take us right back into the belly of the high-school beast? He may as well show up wearing Willi Smith, with the Cocteau Twins in his Walkman, and a copy of *Less Than Zero* in his backpack.

And then he texted me a snapshot of a snapshot. It was the five of us—me, him, Nat, Jennifer, and Pete—in front of the minibus, our trophies aloft, before the ride back to Mendhem from the competition at Truscott Academy, the spring of '87. Everyone's arms were casually around one another, and standing behind the five of us, one hand on Nat's shoulder and the other on Jennifer's, was Gary Gold, beaming with pride over his elocution kids.

Wow! I texted. ***You kept this all these years? Did your mom take this?***

He just sent back the emoji of the smiling purple devil. And ***See you on TG.***

FOUR

Happy Panda was that staple of the white-bread American suburb, the Chinese restaurant, run by one of the handful of Asian families in town, with a buffet full of fried foods, a cocktail menu heavy on neon-colored drinks with tiny umbrellas, and decor that screamed Oriental exotica transposed to the chrome, glass, and orange-rust carpeting of the 1970s. It was an immense restaurant inside an ugly, blocky, low-slung building surrounded on three sides by a parking lot, and it had been *the* place to be seen when we were in high school—so much so that, amid our little island of Speech Team misfit toys, we would mock it as the epitome of all things townie and mainstream and yet still patronize it, the five of us huddled in a booth, drinking virgin daiquiris we would spike with our own smuggled-in liquor, desperate to be accepted but essentially shunned by everyone else—perhaps grateful if one of the popular kids, resplendent in feathered hair and a crimson-and-white Mendhem High football jersey, nodded a munificent hello in our direction on their way to the bathroom.

When I texted Nat and Jennifer that Anthony had suggested meeting up there, they were agog.

Happy Panda? replied Jennifer. *It's still there?*

Yep.

Then Nat: *I'm slightly dumbfounded.*

Me too.

Jennifer: *Are you going to ask him about the comment in the magazine?*

I'll keep you posted.

I didn't want Marcus to come along to the Panda. That was tricky because, overnight on Thanksgiving, we were sharing the guest room in the condo, one town over, my mom had moved into after my father died. I considered telling a white lie, an *I'm going to see my eighty-seven-year-old aunt fifteen minutes away,* then asked myself what I was doing, entertaining the idea of lying to my partner of three years.

We were on the bed in the guest room, zombified after much turkey, watching reruns of *The Golden Girls.* "You're okay if I head out for an hour or so to see an old high-school friend?"

"Of course." His eyes were half-closed. "I can't move anyway."

"Tryptophan coma. My favorite kind." Shortly I'd make myself rise, pull myself together.

"Who with?" he asked, still sedated.

"His name's Anthony Malouf."

No reply. I thought he might have fallen properly asleep. Then: "Isn't that the one in the magazine? The fancy designer?"

"Yep. His parents are still in town."

"Didn't you two fool around a long time ago?"

I turned my head toward him. "I told you that?"

He laughed dimly. "Yep."

"Oh." I was always forgetting what I'd told him, always retelling stories I'd already told. He called it my early senility. "Yeah. Well that was a very long time ago, and it just happened once. And then he never spoke to me again."

"Maybe he's ready for an encore."

He was still staring straight at the TV, eyes heavy-lidded. I pivoted toward him, held him, buried my face in the back of his neck. "I think a seltzer will suffice. Maybe a Diet Coke."

I'd parked the car in the nearly empty lot in front of Happy Panda, was walking toward the entrance as my breath expelled plumes into the frigid night, when a black Audi with New York plates pulled into the lot. It had to be him. I stood and watched as an impossibly thin figure, clad in black from head to toe—black fitted wool overcoat, black skinny jeans, black Nikes, black leather baseball cap—emerged from the car and stalked my way, head bent down, glued to his phone.

"Anthony!"

He looked up, seemingly startled.

"It's me. Tip."

He just stood there for a second, frozen, regarding me almost like a deer in headlights, before his face—its angular thinness jarringly at odds with my memory of his slight adolescent pudginess—softened into a smile and he came forward, embracing me.

"Tip Murray. I can't believe it." His voice jarred me as well. It was deep, masculine, velvety—a far cry from the nasal Boston screech of his teen years. He'd utterly remade himself.

He pulled back from me, his fingertips still at my elbows. "Look at you. You look amazing."

"*You* look amazing. You're so . . . sleek."

He laughed in a carefully offhand way, as though he'd learned how to absorb this compliment in later life. "I have a very brutal trainer." He glanced down at his phone again. "I'm sorry, just let me complete this sentence. I got an email I'd rather not have seen until Monday."

"Of course." I stood there while he typed rapidly, with both thumbs. I studied him—half in awe, half in distaste, at his metamorphosis. *Anthony Malouf, are you somewhere inside that glossy package?* I wanted to ask.

He slipped the phone into the inner breast pocket of his overcoat.

"Okay, there we go." He smiled tautly, lightly applied a palm to my shoulder. "Let's get a drink."

With the exception of a massive flat-screen TV hung over the bar area, where a group of couples, looking about a decade our juniors, were watching the football game, Happy Panda looked like it hadn't changed in twenty-five years. It even had the same smell, of freshly vacuumed wall-to-wall carpeting mingled with fried food. We stood in the foyer, next to the same gurgling rock-garden fountain we'd thrown pennies into in high school, looked about.

I stated the obvious: "It looks totally the same."

"Oh, yes." He seemed pleased by that fact. "I track it year to year. This is always where I come for my post-Thanksgiving martini. The years I'm able to come up."

I smiled. "Are you serious? You're the last person I'd expect to still come here."

"I love the kitsch." He gestured at the rock-garden fountain. "It makes me nostalgic."

I shook my head, still smiling. "I really wouldn't have thought."

The hostess—Asian, too young to be a face we'd remember—approached us.

"Can we have that booth over there?" Anthony pointed in the far corner of the restaurant, a booth by the window overlooking the parking lot. No sooner were we seated than he asked the young woman to bring him a martini with Hendrick's gin, dry on the vermouth, shaken, three olives.

They didn't have Hendrick's, the young woman answered.

A tiny, aggrieved frown and sigh. "Bombay Sapphire?"

She nodded, then turned to me.

"I'll just have a Diet Coke, please." Being sober usually didn't bother me, but there were times, social times, when I had to grit my teeth and could almost feel my face flush with embarrassment when I asked for a seltzer or a Diet Coke, and this was one of them. Why had I so spectacularly mishandled my drinking that now, at the tender age of forty-two, I was consigned to a life of fizzy water and soft drinks? It was like being made to put on Mickey Mouse ears and sit at the kiddie table at an otherwise glittering and sophisticated party.

"You don't drink?" he asked once she'd walked away.

"I just don't like to drink if I'm driving." We'd only just reconnected; I wasn't up for telling him my whole bottoming-out sob story, especially as it involved my New York years, during which I'd never heard from him.

"That's sensible," he said. He was striking a neutral tone, pleasant and conversational but not warm, as though this could be merely a business drink. "How was your Thanksgiving?"

"Just us and my mom and my brother."

I thought he might ask who *us* was, but instead: "I'm sorry to hear about your dad. He coached our peewee soccer team, remember?"

"All too well," I replied. "What *didn't* he coach? Anyway—your parents are still with you, right?"

He nodded. "They're hanging in there. Same old house."

"I remember that house." It was both difficult and amusing to picture him, so sleek now, sitting in that little Cape, his mom's fussy shelves of Hummel and Lladró figurines within, very likely the red-and-yellow swing set rusting and drooping out back.

"Last year, they came to New York, but my dad had surgery in late September, so they weren't up to it this year."

I nodded. Our drinks came. He raised his martini glass, clinked it lightly against my Diet Coke, whose big, bright red straw I found especially embarrassing. "Cheers. To reuniting."

"To reuniting," I repeated. *After you ghosted me twenty years ago*, I wanted to add. But I said instead: "And to your success! Tell me again the label you design for. Sorry," and I pointed to my puffy H&M jacket, "you can see I'm not the most fashion-savvy." I simply could not give him the satisfaction of letting him know that I'd just read a whole article about him and knew several details of his life, including where he worked.

"Please, you look fine," he dispatched hastily. "It's called Pietro Cuccino. It's an Italian luxury menswear legacy brand."

"Ah." I chose not to ask him exactly what a legacy brand was. "But you're based in New York?"

He nodded. "But I'm in Milan four times a year to choose fabrics and that kind of thing."

"Nice."

"What about you? You ended up a writer, right? No surprise there."

"Well, of a sort." I told him about the marginal university think tank I worked for, cranking out their press releases, website copy, and executive director's conference remarks.

He nodded. "Gorgeous. And you live in Providence, right?"

"Right. With my boyfriend, Marcus. He's a cancer nurse. He's back at my mom's."

It was the first time either of us had touched on gayness, that great unspoken weight we'd both carried in high school. I wondered if he'd nod to that.

But instead he merely said: "You should've brought him."

"He was in a turkey coma in front of *The Golden Girls*."

"Ah. Okay."

"What about you?" I felt vaguely cruel asking him something that *Hello Mister* had already answered for me, but once you commit to pretending you know next to nothing about someone's life, you have to stick with it.

He shook his head lightly. "It's just me. And my little bow-wow." I wondered if he'd say her name. If he uttered "Alexis," he'd unleash the adolescent floodgates. Maybe he'd even start doing his Alexis Colby imitations again. Maybe we could laugh again.

But he didn't. "I would kind of pity that person anyway, if they existed," he continued, "because I'm never home."

I nodded and he shrugged, carefully lifted his martini to his lips. Then we fell abruptly into a pit of silence. I panicked inwardly. I thought back on having reached out first, felt foolish, dumpy, and unremarkable next to him. He'd shot well past me in life and we had nothing in common anymore. I was almost certain I could read the disinterest in his stare, gazing past me at the parking lot, calculating how long he had to stick around to appear polite.

But then, out of nowhere, and with the same vaguely detached tone, he finally said: "I can't believe that about Pete Stroman. Well, maybe I can believe it."

We locked eyes. I was so grateful he'd finally opened the door to the past. I hadn't been able to bring myself to do it, yet if nobody had, surely we'd be heading for a conversational cliff.

"I know," I said. "It's incredibly sad."

"Were you in touch with him?"

"Not at all. I wouldn't even have known if Nat hadn't texted me."

He looked at me quizzically for a moment, then his entire face popped open. "Natalie!" he exclaimed, and for the first time I heard a trace of the old adolescent screech. "Natalie Farb-Miola?"

"Yeah! We're still very good friends. She runs a little farm with her boyfriend and two kids in New Hampshire."

He laughed openly now—as though he'd finally decided to set aside impeccable Anthony Malouf, creative director for Pietro Cuccino who traveled to Milan four times a year. "I can *totally* see that, she was such a hippie chick! And she has two kids?"

"Yeah. Olivia and Otis. They're great. Super smart."

"I'm not surprised. She was super smart. So funny. Almost as smart as Jennifer Douglas."

"Yeah! In fact, Jennifer and Nat and I got together recently. Jennifer's a professor in New Jersey and she's got two kids, too."

He clasped his hands together earnestly in front of him. "My *goodness*!"

He was imitating high-school Jennifer. "Actually," I said, grateful for intel to share with him, as though perhaps it raised my value, "she's really loosened up. Like, still just as obviously smart, just not so prim."

He seemed to absorb this with genuine interest. "Fascinating."

"Yeah. I guess adulthood and success and getting married and having kids—like, she grew into herself." Then I decided to be a bit cheeky. "She did in fact mention being madly in love with you in high school."

He actually blushed, sheepish, then smiled and shook his head. "I knew that. And I was super bitchy to her because I didn't know how to deal with it."

I laughed. "Well, I think she understands why now, so don't worry about it."

He glanced at me, a flash of sympatico, a quicksilver acknowledgment of what those years had been like for us.

"You look great," he said. He'd already said it, but it felt in a different register, sweeter, this time. "It's really good to see you."

"You too." I raised my palms toward him. "Look, you became everything you ever wanted to be."

He smiled, shook his head. "I was insufferable in high school, wasn't I?"

I laughed again. "No, you were funny. You just knew what you wanted."

He looked down, shook his head again. "I still just can't believe that about Pete Stroman."

"How'd you find out?"

"My mother read it in the *Tribune* and told me. And I can't stop thinking about it for some reason."

"Why?"

He was drinking his martini faster now, nearly gulps, as though he wanted to loosen his tongue. "Because I just remember ignoring him, avoiding him, because I found him so nerdy and bizarre. Even though he had an incredibly striking face—like, runway-level striking. But difficult to connect with in a normal fashion. And now I feel badly about that."

"I actually thought he was incredibly hot and had a huge secret crush on him."

"You *did*?"

I nodded. "And I think his weirdness just added to the hotness. Nat and I were saying we're pretty sure he was on the spectrum—like, the autism spectrum. Not that anybody knew anything about that then. Certain people were just *weird*, you know?"

He shook his head slowly. "The eighties. They seem like the Dark Ages now in so many ways."

"Right? He even said something in his suicide note about being tired of trying to fit in, tired of people not understanding him."

He sipped again. "That is heartbreaking."

"I know."

Then I decided it was finally time to see what I could coax out of Anthony.

"He actually wrote something in that note about Coach Gold," I ventured.

Anthony gave me that studied quizzical look again. Clearly he was determined to perform a moment of nonrecognition every time I brought someone up from the past, so I indulged him. "Gary Gold, remember? Our Speech Team coach."

Then he performed recognition: "Oh my God! Coach Gold. Of course. Oh my God, Speech Team. How weird was that?"

"So weird. But kind of fun, too, Nat and Jennifer and I were remembering."

This drew a blank stare.

"So anyway," I continued, "he wrote—I mean Pete, in his suicide note—he wrote that he'd never forgotten that Coach Gold had called him, like, a drone. A drone robot. That stuck with him so badly all these years that it was, like, the last thing he wrote before he killed himself."

But Anthony didn't appear to be breaking on this point. "That is so painful," he remarked.

I decided to go for broke. "I have to admit I wasn't entirely surprised to hear that," I pushed ahead, "because he'd said something pretty awful to me, too, that I'd more or less forgotten about. I mean, not completely forgotten about—kind of half-repressed."

He shot me a wary look now. "What did he say?"

This time, I steeled myself before saying the words, to betray no quaver in my voice or glassiness in my eyes. To do that in front of Nat was one thing; I would not let it happen in front of Anthony.

But the shock he registered seemed real. "He actually *said* that to you?"

I nodded. "I was so . . . stunned that I just walked out, never told a soul. And then Jennifer, when we were having lunch with her a few weeks ago, *she* alluded to something he'd said to her, all alone, when they were practicing. Something offensive about her speech entry, about Sojourner Truth."

His face drew a blank. "About what?"

"Sojourner Truth. She was a slave who became, like, an activist, and abolitionist. And she gave a very famous speech that Jennifer did."

He absorbed this. "Oh. I think I remember that now." He drained his martini, instantly flagged the waitress for another. "What did Gold say to her?"

"She wouldn't say. Almost like it was too painful to say it out loud. So we didn't want to press her on it."

"Really?" He seemed deeply intrigued now. "I'm sure whatever he said, she could destroy him if he said it today—if she wanted to."

Destroy him. There it was again. Perhaps he genuinely did share Alexis Colby's cold-blooded appetite for revenge. "But Jennifer told nobody, apparently," I said.

"And you didn't either."

"No, I didn't." I shook my head. "I didn't want to have to repeat what he'd said to me to anyone. Especially my parents."

The waitress brought his second martini, which he instantly lifted to his lips. "That's totally understandable," he allowed.

It was time to press further, I decided. "We actually looked him up and found out that he's retired and living in Florida and is part of some Baby Boomer golf club. We actually talked," and I said this with a careful laugh, to suggest we hadn't been *too* serious, "about taking a trip down there to find him and ask if he remembers the things he said to us."

Anthony lifted his drink again, sipped copiously, set it back down. He swallowed and then pursed his lips remorsefully.

"I actually remember him quite clearly."

Aha! "You didn't seem to."

"Well, I do. And he actually said something very fucked up to me as well once. When I was practicing with him. In that weird glassed-in room."

"The fishbowl."

"Right, that fishbowl, that's what we called it. That's where he said it." His eyes narrowed, focused away from me and out toward the parking lot. He sipped again—close to a gulp, actually. I felt like I was watching a kind of slow-motion unraveling of Sleek Anthony, seeing someone more raw, interesting, and tender emerge.

"What did he say?"

He refixed his gaze on me. "He called me a hairy terrorist." Then, somewhat alarming me, he emitted a short, high laugh.

"What? What did he say exactly?"

"I remember I was practicing, and he just flat-out interrupts me and asks, 'Anthony, what kind of name is Malouf? Pale-*stin*-ian?' That's how he said it. With that tone."

"Are you serious?"

"Yes. So I said, 'It's my dad's name. It's Lebanese.' And he says, 'Ah, that's what I thought—a hairy terrorist name.'"

Before I could speak, he shocked me by choking out a kind of short, strangled cry. Both his eyes pooled. Smiling, embarrassed, he raised his fingertips to them, dabbed them dry, wiped them on his jeans, then picked up his martini again and took a big gulp. All this in a matter of only seconds. His gaze flickered from me to the parking lot and back again, as though he couldn't hold my stare. He drummed his fingers rapidly on the table.

"That is the most fucked-up thing," I managed to say, before he rose abruptly.

"Excuse me," he said, then stalked across the restaurant carpet toward the restrooms. I sat there, briefly paralyzed. I wanted to text Nat but was still too shaken by his sudden devolution. He'd drained his martini, I noticed, before getting up. My feelings were a riot; I'd shown up cautiously excited to see him, still simmering over the slight of many years ago, feeling a bit inferior, then found myself a bit in awe of his crisp new self, and now suddenly I just felt a kind of pity, as well as a tenderness and an identification. Gold had given it good to him, as well. Beneath his curated veneer, he was a mess.

Two minutes later, he strode back across the carpet in an imperfect line, tailed by the waitress who carried another martini on a tray, placed it before him after he sat. His face looked scrubbed but his eyes were ringed red. "One more," he said, businesslike. "That's it."

"Okay." I was already thinking about how to offer him a ride home without offending him.

He sipped. "That's Islamophobia," he said matter-of-factly, and I realized in a moment he was still talking about Gold. "Or Arabophobia. Whatever you want to call it. And I've even thought about reaching out to him and telling him so. But then I thought, no, don't give him the satisfaction of knowing it stuck with you all these years."

I pondered that a moment. "I don't know," I then said. "I've often thought about what a wallop it might give him to let him know I've remembered what he said after all these years." Then I dared ask: "What if we all did it together?"

He laughed derisively. "Go to Florida and confront him on the golf course?"

"Why not? It'd be a fun trip. And wouldn't you love to see the look on his face?" Then I decided to blink first. "It'd be very season cliffhanger from *Dynasty.*"

He cackled, so loudly that the couples at the bar briefly looked our way. "Oh my God, that would be *soooo Dynasty*. What would we wear?"

"I think we should all wear white. Like, matching pantsuits."

"Yes! Or maybe all black. With broad-brimmed hats with net veils. Something that'll really pop against the green as we're coming toward him."

So there was the old Anthony. After that, we took flight, free to laugh. It was aided, of course, by the fact that he was drunk by that point. Being sober amid people who slowly get drunk is, in addition to a depressing exercise in being left out, a sometimes fascinating thing. You're utterly clearheaded and clear-eyed, so you notice minutely how their demeanor changes, their voice, their body language and mood. With some people, you note a marked turn for the worse, a release of hostility or bitterness, and with others it's the opposite, a noticing of how they bloom from guarded and flat to warm, funny, confiding, admiring of you and others, sentimental—happier, in a word. Anthony was definitely in the latter category. Adult Anthony plus three very strong martinis apparently equaled adolescent Anthony, exuberantly obsessed with over-the-top wealth and glamour, rather than someone carefully, boringly set on embodying such traits himself. Out came all the bitchy, funny stories about people I'd only ever read about or seen on TV, how this one had made a spectacle of himself at a premiere party, how that one had had so much work done that she couldn't move her face, how this one was notorious for bringing paid escorts to galas. He was in his element, shedding tales of a life he'd never imagined he'd have and likely didn't feel completely comfortable in, and I was happy to be his sounding board, all wide eyes and iterations of "Are you *kidding*?"

"Yes!" he'd reply. "She's a *total mess* and everyone in town knows it!"

Somewhere in there, remarkably, he ordered his fourth martini.

"I'm driving you home," I announced once it arrived. "We'll tell them we're leaving your car in the parking lot and you can come get it tomorrow."

"Nooo," he protested slurrily. "I'm fine."

"No." I said it firmly. "I'm driving you home. That would be so tragic if you had, like, a Mothers Against Drunk Driving tragedy right here in your hometown. So go ahead and drink up, you fucking lush."

He surrendered, smiling dopily. "Tipp*eeeeee*," he drawled.

Tippy. So now he was returning to his high-school nickname for me.

"Anthon*eeeeee*!"

He dissolved in drunk giggles, much to my delight. But as he drank martini number four, even amid stories told with increasing difficulty and slowness, he literally started falling asleep right in front of me, his eyelids drooping, then his head bowing forward.

"Come on." I gently pulled his martini away from him, regarded it briefly—pungent, glassy, irresistible—before nudging it into the far corner of the table. "Let's go."

"Tipp*eeeee,*" he protested.

"Anthon*eeeee*!" I stood, offered my hand. "Come on."

"So embarrassing," he muttered, rising, fumbling into his coat. He stumbled across the now-empty dining room, past the now-empty bar, extracting from his wallet his AmEx card, which he waved toward the waitress.

"Here you go, honey," he slurred.

I met her eyes. "Is it okay if he leaves his car out there tonight so I can drive him home? He'll get it in the morning."

She smiled and nodded indulgently, taking his card. When she brought back the card and the check, I peered over his shoulder as he signed it, making sure he was at least lucid enough to leave a proper tip. Which he did—25 percent. To leave such a sum was probably a reflex for him by now, I imagined.

Passing the rock-garden fountain, he grabbed my arm. "Wait." He reached into his back pocket, pulled out a handful of change, half of which he spilled sloppily into my palm. "What are you gonna wish for?"

I threw in my change. "A Pietro Cuccino suit," I said.

This cracked him up. "I can get you a fucking suit!" he brayed. Then he threw in his own change.

"What did you wish for?"

He suddenly got all coy, grabbing my elbow and pulling me out the door. "You're not supposed to say!"

The cold blasted us in the face as we crossed the parking lot. In my car, which immediately erupted with heat and the radio with Bing Crosby and David Bowie's version of "The Little Drummer Boy"—already? Thanksgiving was barely over—he promptly passed out, his chin on his chest. I drove past the convenience store, the middle school, the library, the town common, into the modest part of town where we'd both grown up, far from the lake and the country club and the sprawling estates. It was the network of maple-lined streets with closely standing Cape Cod houses, Dutch colonials, then single-floor ranches, that had sprung up when Mendhem evolved from a New England farm town to a more conventional suburb. I pulled up in front of his family's Cape, a tiny affair with electric candles already in every window and, on the front yard, the stalwart Virgin Mary now sharing space with a full-on nativity scene, including a cradle empty save some hay, enjoying its own grass-mounted spotlight.

"Your mom still does her nativity," I remarked. But he was still passed out. I shook his shoulder. "Wake up. We're at your place."

He came to, looked up, over at me, eyes widening as though he was surprised to see me. "Tippy *Mur*ray," he drawled, with a kind of Bette Davis cadence to it.

"Anthony Ma*louf*."

He giggled again, leaned over and pressed his lips, coated with gin and vermouth, on mine. I was shocked for a moment, then gave in, licking up that sensational liquory taste. At one point, just to get back at him for years of dismissal, I bit his lower lip briefly.

"Oh, wow!" he exclaimed. "So frisky." Then: "I'm so glad to see you."

I pushed him back slightly by the shoulder. "Then why did you never call me again after we hooked up twenty fucking years ago? Even when you knew I was in New York. That really sucked of you."

He gave me an aggrieved look. "Oh, Tippy," he whined. "I was so con*fus*ed."

"Please. You were drunk and you were just too embarrassed to even talk to me after. Probably just like you'll be tomorrow, when you decide again that I don't fit your fancy life."

His face twisted into a lugubrious offendedness. "Stop that! That's not true. I *missed* you."

I regarded him, lips pursed. "If you want, I'll drive you to your car tomorrow before I head back to Prov."

He grinned, triumphant in having mollified me. "I *want*," he said.

"Okay. Oh, look. There's Marie."

Sure enough, the lamp above the front door had gone on, followed by the door opening, Mrs. Malouf, grayer and smaller with age, in her bathrobe, framed in the doorway. Anthony opened the passenger door, wove his way up the little stone path that bisected the front lawn.

"Anthony, you always do this!" Mrs. Malouf's voice was the same nasal Massachusetts shriek I remembered from high school.

"Come on, Ma!" Anthony whined. Then he turned back toward me. "Look who it is! Tippy Murray!"

Mrs. Malouf peered out, clutching her robe at her neck against the cold. "Tip?" she called. "That's you?"

I was leaning awkwardly out the still-open passenger door, the car in park. "Hi, Mrs. Malouf. Yes, it's me. How are you?"

She was cheery now despite the cold. "We'h good! How's ya mutha?"

"She's good, thanks."

"I'm so sorry about ya fatha, hun."

"Thank you."

"Wheah you livin' now?"

"Providence. Rhode Island."

"Oh, nice!" She said it with the forced brightness of someone—which was nearly everyone—who had not a single reference for Providence, perhaps didn't even know exactly where it was, often confused it for Provincetown. "Well, thanks fa bringin' *this one* home. He does this every time."

"It's no problem," I called. "I love your nativity scene."

"Oh, thank you! We'h savin' the baby Jesus for Christmas Day, like we always do."

"Of course."

"Ma, he wasn't even born on December twenty-fifth," Anthony said. "Nobody even knows the real date."

She grabbed his arm. "Get in the house." Then back to me in a lighter register: "Bye, Tip. Get home safe. Say hi to ya mutha."

I waved and drove off, grateful I was sober even though the taste of gin and vermouth lingered seductively on my lips. I didn't envy Anthony the hangover he'd likely have in the morning.

Which he did. When I texted him around eleven the next day, he texted back: *I wanna die.*

I'm not surprised. You don't want a ride to your car?

I think I'm gonna stay here one more night.

Probably a good idea. Okay. It was great seeing you.

It was great seeing you. Then: *Were you serious about Florida?*

I stared at the text, surprised he even remembered last night's conversation, let alone his interest. *Let's talk in a few days. I can loop you in with Nat and Jennifer and we can discuss. I'm sure they'd love to hear from you.*

I think it could be cathartic, he wrote back.

Very possibly so. Get some rest now.
And go easy on the martinis.

He was probably still a little drunk, I figured. I wouldn't be surprised if, the next time I texted, I didn't hear back at all.

And yet I was still glad we'd met. It occurred to me now that both Jennifer and Anthony—two people, however different, whose success I regarded in counterpoint to my own mediocrity—had broken slightly, choked up and rasped, when recounting what Gold had said. I no longer felt so alone in my memories of that afternoon in the fishbowl, after some twenty-five years of his words smarting in my head intermittently, especially on occasions where I felt I might have betrayed myself as too gay (too *mincing*) in a mixed, public space—as though, even in adulthood, I'd not gotten ahold of my own comportment.

And then I thought of Gold, in happy golf-club retirement these past many years. He likely never spent a day thinking about what he'd said to us. He likely did not remember at all. How profoundly unfair that the three of us, the recipients, should live on with those remarks, but not him, their author.

I could destroy him, Anthony had said.

Did I want to *destroy* Gold? Is that what I was out for?

And then I leveled with myself: Gold was the least of it. I wanted to destroy all of them. For every *faggot* spat in my direction, every slap upside the head, every trip-up in the hallway, every load of books and notebooks pushed out from under my arm, every classroom crack about sucking dick or taking it up the butt that teachers had only clucked over (but never really put a stop to), every terrified sprint home from school only to round the bend and be cornered, every snowdrift or mudslick I was made acquainted with, every dreaded, stomach-in-knots Sunday night or last day of summer—for nearly a decade. Then, once it was ostensibly "all over," being left with that churning pit of fear, panic, and rage underneath a thin veneer of adult self-possession. Then falling apart.

I couldn't find all those boys. Most of them, I didn't even remember their names. They were a blur of harsh Mass accents, flannel shirts that smelled like cigarettes and pot, mullet haircuts and workboots, Iron Maiden and Judas Priest blaring out of their car radios, ragged laughter that faded as they drove off, me still on the ground, playing dead until I knew they were gone.

I couldn't find them all, but I could find Gold. Certainly not to *destroy* him. That was going too far. But I realized that I'd like to at least watch his eyes glass over, as ours had, to perhaps see one tear well and drop, as it dawned on him that his words had stayed with us for life.

And I wouldn't leave until I heard the words I wanted to hear: *I am so sorry.*

And even then, I resolved, I might not fully forgive. That was my—our—prerogative. And we could lord it over him as long as we chose, casting the same shadow over his golden years Sunshine State idyll that he'd cast over our tenderest years.

FIVE

Nat and Jennifer were incredulous when I told them, over a text thread, that not only, yes, I'd coaxed out of Anthony that Gold had called him a hairy terrorist, but that he'd expressed an interest in going to Florida to find Gold.

As a half-Jew, wrote Nat, *I'm mortified that he said that to Anthony.*

Whom did Gold NOT offend? Jennifer wrote. *Seems like whatever our sore thumb factor was, he found it!* And then she wrote: *He really said he wanted to go to Florida?*

So he said. But he was also v drunk.

Follow up with him! wrote Jennifer. *Andres says I need to practice getting away! :)*

I couldn't help noticing, with a twinge of annoyance, that her interest in Florida had sharpened upon news of Anthony's possible participation.

I'd rather let him follow up, I replied, *which I don't think he will.*

And then life got busy—work ramped up, pinning me down with one deadline after another, then a visit to Providence from Marcus's sister and kids, and then the holidays, and then my mother needing knee replacement surgery, and then before I knew it, it was the frigid, gray, post-yuletide winter of 2013, the sidewalks of Providence a mess of filthy slush and the gulls loud and stark above the Seekonk River. In the fall, I'd slipped back into the past—the chain of visits with Nat, Jennifer, and Anthony, each one building on the other. But the present, as it has a way of doing, reasserted itself, and some of the pain as well as the sweetness of exhuming those memories evaporated, and I felt like myself again—an adult, an early fortysomething, competent and pulled together, not a banged-up kid in a man's body, preoccupied with knotty recollections.

I had almost completely forgotten about our vague talk of Florida when, in mid-January, came an email, its subject line an eye-popping: *Florida plans from Anthony Malouf.*

Dear Mr. Murray: read the email.

> *I am Susan Wessel, Mr. Malouf's personal assistant and travel/schedule coordinator. Mr. Malouf has asked me to arrange a four-night stay for you, him, and your two other high-school friends over Presidents' Day weekend in Sarasota. He asked me to choose the accommodations, and I've chosen the Resort at Longboat Key Club, if that's okay with all of you.*

She then dropped a link, which I clicked on. The photos were bonkers. It was a luxury resort on a small island off the coast of Sarasota proper, an oasis of chic rooms, massive swimming pools, white sand, turquoise water—and, I couldn't help but notice, impeccable cocktails, brilliant in their jewel tones.

> *Would you kindly reach out to your other friends and ask if the nights of February 14-18 work for them, as well as you, then get back to me with everyone's contact information in order for me to book the trip? Mr. Malouf said he will cover all expenses including flights, resort, rental car, and meals taken at the resort. You will all have your own rooms, of course.*

I laughed out loud in astonishment. AWOL for twenty-five years, Anthony had suddenly become the fairy godfather of our super-luxe reunion? What had changed him?

I texted him: *Hey! I just got an email from your assistant. That is too generous! Are you absolutely sure?*

Much to my surprise, he replied within seconds: *Can Nat and Jennifer come?*

I haven't even told them yet.

Convince them to come and set it all up with Susan, she's great. See you in Sarasota. Get ready, Gold!

I forwarded the email to Nat and Jennifer with a note atop it: *Yes, this is for real. A. and I texted. He really wants to do it. You two in? Think of it as a super high-end, all-expenses-paid high-school reunion.*

Nat got back first: *This doesn't really involve seeing Gold, does it?*

To which I replied: *A. mentioned it over text, but I'm not sure how serious he was.*

Then Jennifer got back an hour later: *How crazy is this? I say we get a little wild and do it! Who cares if we've barely spoken the past 25 years? Plus, four days at that resort sounds absolutely heavenly.*

That particular line of hers stuck out for me: *Who cares if we've barely spoken the past 25 years?* It seemed a little snarky—very unlike her, especially after what I'd considered a successful if intermittently awkward reunion at her home. Weren't most reunions after a long period of detachment slightly awkward? Perhaps, I thought, this was her way of making light of the obvious and I was merely misreading the tone. I decided to ignore it.

Me: *Well, I'm in if everyone else is.*

Which left it in the hands of Nat, who—after a strange interval of overnight and half of the next day—replied: ***Okay, what the hell, let's do it.***

That night at home, I told Marcus, who seemed to inadvertently wince as he took in the news.

"He really said he'd pay for the whole thing?"

"It's crazy, right? But, I mean, he is the head of a luxury brand. He must pull in a huge salary."

Marcus rolled his eyes slightly. "This is the guy you used to hook up with?"

I rolled mine back. "I told you already, *once*. When we were babies, like twenty years ago."

"And then you never heard from him again?"

"Until recently."

"Thanksgiving night when he got wasted and you had to drive him home."

"Right."

Now he shook his head slightly, slowly.

"What is it?" I asked.

"Nothing," he said sharply. "Go. Have fun. I just think it's kind of weird, that's all."

"It's a reunion! What's weird about it?" I'd never told him we'd all batted around the idea of finding Gold. *That* he likely would have found even weirder.

"I just think the whole high-school revisitation thing you've been exploring the past few months is odd. I'd thought it was over."

"What is wrong with getting together with old friends?"

"Who you haven't been in touch with in, what, twenty-five years, except for Natalie?"

He had, unwittingly perhaps, a kind of smug, insufferable look on his face, as though he were determined to embarrass me.

"Why are you being so weird about this?" I asked.

The look persisted. Then he asked: "Did you even remember that we talked last year about going to Paris in February or March? On a cheap flight?"

Oh, I thought. *Yes, in fact, we had—briefly. Vaguely.* "We can still do it! In March! We can look for tickets tonight."

He didn't answer, just looked down.

"What?" I insisted.

"Are you with me?" he asked.

"What?"

"Are you *with* me? Really with me, in the here and now. In the *present* of your life."

His words took me aback. "Of course I am. I'm with you right now. In our house."

"I know." Then he got up and came to sit beside me on the couch, looking like he was going to cry. "It's hard to explain, but I feel like you're somewhere else most of the time." Then he actually started crying, which shocked and dismayed me. "I feel like our life together is getting boring for you again. Like you're phoning it in."

"Boring for me *again*? What is that supposed to mean?"

"I don't know if you remember, but this is how you were last year before you relapsed and disappeared. Like, you were drifting away from me for days before that."

"What?" I held him, weakly feigning bafflement—but in fact I knew exactly what he meant. I distinctly remembered feeling this profound restlessness with him the week leading up to that relapse. Suffocation, even. It was an awful feeling that I wanted to go away, but would not—until I bolted to a certain gay bar downtown, knocked back half a dozen tequila shots, then hoovered up coke I bought from the bar's resident dealer, who said he was happy to see me after so long.

But now, holding him, I tried to reassure him: "I'm *here*, Marcus."

"You're not. You're not. I can feel it."

"I *am*."

We ended up having sex, the first time in a long time. It was the only way I felt I could convince him that I was in fact *there*, as though I were trying to make up for what he saw as weeks—months? years?—of detachment with one concentrated burst of attention and connection. And it was actually good, somewhat to my surprise, because it had been a while. I was reminded what great salvage therapy it is when you really don't know what more to say or do.

When we were done, lying on the couch, where we'd had sex, with the uncooked dinner things sitting out in the kitchen, he looked calm.

"That was really nice," I remarked.

"It was. Been a while."

"Let's not let that happen again."

That glow carried us through dinner. Later, when I took the garbage downstairs, the stars in the black sky caught my eye, and I decided to walk around the block. But the cold bite of the air felt so good, clarifying, after the overheatedness of the house, I kept on walking, all the way down into India Point Park, the lamplit pathways along the water where gay guys cruised in warmer weather, my hands in my pockets. I was reluctant to go back, half wishing some stranger would come along on the deserted path and we'd get into something kind of scary and thrilling, something that amounted to a brief throwing of your life in the garbage. But finally the cold settled in deep under my coat and I turned and headed back, and when I walked inside, I found, to my great relief, Marcus lying there on the couch where I'd left him, half-asleep.

He roused himself just enough to ask, "Did you end up doing your little existential walk in India Point Park?" Before he curled deeper into the couch, leaving me just enough room to scooch in behind him.

SIX

Before I went to New York City for the first time, my freshman year in college, before I ever saw L.A. or San Francisco, ever flew overseas and saw parts of Europe and a few other corners of the world, cosmopolitanism for me was the other schools of Massachusetts—public, private, or parochial—which we'd visit on Speech Team tournament days. These were the times when we'd see faces beyond the roughly one thousand same faces we saw every day at Mendhem High, when we'd infer other lives, other levels of privilege, be they the extreme privilege of the kids from the private schools and the fancy public schools—the boys in frayed corduroy blazers and the girls whose hair fell low and natural in an artfully messy bob instead of standing high and shellacked with mousse—or the kids from scruffier towns with harsher Boston accents, like Malden, Everett, Medford, and Quincy, or the hardworking Black and Hispanic kids from the public exam schools, Boston Latin School and Boston Latin Academy.

These were the times we'd make "outside" friends. For me, it was David Ruth, a junior from Acton-Boxborough High School who had the coolest peroxide-blond haircut and punk-ska wardrobe I'd ever seen, always had the best tapes in his Walkman (Tom Waits, Suzanne Vega, Roxy Music), always was reading some book like *The Basketball*

Diaries or the collected poems of Delmore Schwartz, and consistently won the dramatic interpretation category with his one-man excerpts from plays by Christopher Durang, whom I hadn't even heard of until I met David.

He embodied an extreme level of sophistication for me, some intimation of the life that awaited beyond Mendhem, and I probably annoyed him with my endless cultural name-dropping in a desperate attempt to impress him, although he was actually always nice to me, inhabiting his coolness easily, as though he weren't suspicious that someone was going to outdo him, as Anthony tended to be. I probably didn't realize until I was in college that I'd been completely in love with him, as well as that he was likely gay himself, and by that point he was studying film at the University of Southern California, well out of my reach.

Nat's outside friend was Tommy Markey, a Deadhead from Marshfield who perpetually smelled, as Nat did, of patchouli. On competition Saturdays, they'd sneak off first thing, before the sessions started, get stoned together, and make out, both coming back into the cafeteria or auditorium of whatever school we were at, eyes red, eyelids heavy, cracking each other up. (How Nat managed to compete in that state, and even occasionally win, was beyond my comprehension.)

Tommy became Nat's best friend outside of Mendhem, part traveling companion to Phish shows, part casual boyfriend, which was a cause for enormous jealousy on my part, even if Nat's grimy music preferences, as well as the thought of physical intimacy with her beyond a platonic cuddle, were of no interest to me. It was the thought that she laughed with someone as hard as she did with me, shared secrets and insights as intensely, that needled me.

Jennifer's outside friend was Gisela Muñoz, an extremely brainy, serious Dominican girl from Jamaica Plain who went to Boston Latin and competed in debate. As soon as we got to a competition, she and Jennifer beelined toward each other and were inseparable all day except for when they were competing. Nat, Anthony, and I would look over at the two of them off in a corner, either deep in sober conversation or giggling with an abandon Jennifer never revealed during the school week.

"What are they laughing about?" Nat would ask, and Anthony would drawl, "Probably how they're going to take over Yaaaaaale together next year." And indeed, they did both end up there together.

Anthony's outside friend was, no surprise, a forbiddingly chic, unsmiling Asian girl who went to Cambridge Rindge named Sophia Ando, a severe black asymmetrical blunt cut atop a slash of red lipstick, an oversize, big-shouldered black blazer, a long black skirt, black Doc Martens, and a massive black distressed leather shoulder bag. Without coming right out and saying so, Anthony made it clear that none of us were to approach him when he was sitting with Sophia, whom he clearly saw as a higher life-form than the rest of us. To spy the two of them poring over the latest issue of *Interview* or *The Face*—or, better, the copies of French *Vogue* Sophia brought back from her spring school trip to Paris—was to see two people plotting out the rest of their lives together. Once, when we had a tournament at Rindge, Anthony even secured special permission to not have to come back on the bus to Mendhem with the rest of us plebes, so he could stay the night at Sophia's and spend the next day trawling the thrift shops and record stores with her.

"Of course we stopped in at Algiers for a cappuccino and a clove cigarette," he informed me on Monday while showing off the vintage trench coat he'd bought at Oona's. At the time, I don't think I even really knew what a cappuccino was, except as something mentioned on those General Foods International Coffee commercials, never mind a clove cigarette.

Only Pete Stroman made no outside friends at tournaments. He'd seal himself off inside his Walkman for most of the day, on the bus to and from the destination, sitting by himself, uncomfortable in a jacket and tie, sometimes behind opaque blue John Lennon glasses, coming alive only when rising to the front of a room to perform his speech about the importance of Rush. Then, he'd deliver a passable version of a regular person, moving his hands about and modulating his face, as he'd been carefully instructed by Coach Gold, but he probably won because the speech itself was brilliant, as intricate and dense as a Rush song, full of word patterns that looped and relooped, each time slightly different, until it seemed the speech was not only commenting on Rush but on itself.

I remember hearing it the first time, during an all-team practice session before our first tournament one early October, and thinking that Pete was probably a genius, but in a manner so odd, so inwardly turned, that it might never do him any good. I also remember thinking, then and all the time, that he was the most beautiful person I had ever seen.

Occasionally after a tournament ended, after the competition sessions and the awards ceremony, the hosting school would bring in a dinner buffet—a nuclear bomb of carbs, steaming trays of baked ziti and sheets of cardboard-dry pizza, alongside a cooler of Cokes and Sprites on ice—then clear the cafeteria floor of tables and throw a quick dance party before our buses came for us around eight or nine in the evening. It was a chance to socialize and blow off steam, clear the competitive air, and it was always a bit awkward and surreal, dark except for an amateur set of swirling lights, jackets and backpacks lined up on the tables against the walls as we half-heartedly busted moves to the drum-machine beats and synth stabs of Depeche Mode or Janet Jackson or Simple Minds, whatever the student DJ happened to play.

The chaperones, the parents and teachers, Coach Gold among them, would "monitor" us via open doors from outside, where they traded cigarettes and gossip. On the dance floor, we were among our teammates, but we were also among our competition mates, the outside friends like David Ruth and Gisela Muñoz and Sophia Ando, who, with Anthony, deigned to join the rest of us, barely moving in the most bored manner possible to signal that they were not dancing so much as nodding cursorily to the idea of dancing.

At one such party, I think at Barnstable High School on the Cape, I was elated because I'd once again won the blue ribbon and I was slightly drunk from illicit sips of whiskey from a flask that David Ruth kept slipping to me, an act that felt intimate, as though he were singling me out, which allowed me to project that he liked me back. Eventually, I needed to pee, so I exited the cafeteria and walked down a deserted, dimly lit hallway, hung with the requisite posters: a reminder for School Photos Day, a "Never Forget" tribute for the *Challenger* explosion, a glossy Students Against Drunk Driving broadside—all fuchsia and turquoise, slashes and squiggles abounding.

Before I turned into the boys' lavatory, I spied, at the end of the hall, sitting on the floor against a bank of lockers in the gloom, Pete. I stood for a moment by the lavatory door, unseen and unheard (he had his Walkman on), torn about what to do. Finally, I proceeded down the hall toward him.

"Pete?" I called. He didn't react. I walked closer and doubled my volume.

This time he looked up, clearly saw me, then, oddly, looked away. I was briefly offended, but something compelled me to stay. I squatted down beside him until he clicked off his Walkman, pulled the headphones from his ears.

"What?" he asked.

"Are you okay?"

"Yeah, why?" His tone was curt, annoyed.

"Cause you're out here alone in the dark. You don't wanna do the dance?"

He rolled his eyes. "That music is shit."

"It's too mainstream," I agreed. In fact, as we spoke, I could dimly hear INXS's "What You Need" emanating from the cafeteria. "But," I continued, "you don't want to dance with us for a few minutes before we go? To celebrate your blue ribbon?"

He rolled his eyes again, *pfffft*'d air from his nose. "Not really. It doesn't mean anything."

"Sure, yeah, but you earned it. Your speech was amazing."

He shook his head. "I'm tired of it."

I laughed. "That's Speech Team. Everybody gets tired of their piece. How can you not be? You do it over and over again."

He said nothing to this, just shook his head. I was struck by some new note from him—frustration, depression. Usually, he just came off as aloof.

"So come in?" I asked.

"I'll come in when it's over."

There was no point in further pressing him. I rose. "Okay. I'll come get you if you don't come in."

I turned and walked away, but after a few seconds, he called my name. I turned back, now a good fifteen feet away from him.

"I don't do well at things like this," he said.

"They're stupid! Everyone feels awkward."

"Yeah, but I'm not like you and Anthony and Nat—social butterflies."

I laughed. "Not really. I mean, Jennifer's kinda awkward."

"No, she has her friend." He must have been referring to Gisela. "I don't know what to say, and when I say something, people just kind of go *he-he-he* and then try to get away from me like I'm Charles Manson."

"Well, maybe they think you look more like Jim Morrison, actually."

He ignored that remark. I instantly regretted it, wondering if it came off as a kind of pass.

"It's just fucking exhausting," he said. "I hate these things."

I wanted to walk back toward him, pull him up by the arm, and make him come back in with me. It was disconcerting to see him so bereft. I'd truly always thought that Pete was simply too cool to bother with me, or anyone.

But I did not do that. "I'll come get you if you don't come in," I said.

He shrugged, without looking at me, and put his headphones back on. I just stood there a moment, looking at him through that new lens, before turning around and heading into the lavatory, then back down the hall, into the cafeteria, scanning the room for Nat, in order to tell her what had just happened.

Instead, I nearly bumped into Jennifer, her face flushed and shiny from dancing, her hair slightly awry, her sweater doffed and flung over her shoulders. Just like seeing Pete despondent, it was also unusual to see Jennifer a bit wild and untidy. Still tipsy, I felt a bit like I'd fallen into the kind of dream where everyone you know in real life is suddenly a skewed, vaguely alien version of themselves.

"You look like you're slicing up the dance floor," I said.

She blotted her forehead with the back of her hand. "It is lively, I'll admit it." She pointed behind me. "Are the lavs that way?"

"Yeah. But I should warn you. Pete is sitting at the end of the dark hall, alone."

She blinked. "Really? Why?"

"I don't know. He said he wanted to be alone 'til the dance ended. That he hated things like this."

"Oh, dear." Her lips pursed in concern. "Should I say something to him?"

"I tried but it didn't make any difference. Maybe just pretend you don't see him."

She considered that a moment. "Hmm. That's strange. Well, okay."

I moved past her, but she grabbed my arm. "Can I just ask you something?"

"What?"

"What is the big fucking deal about Sophia?"

I laughed. "What? Did you actually just *curse*?"

"So-*fee*-ah," she repeated. "Every tournament, Anthony glues himself to her like a pathetic puppy. I mean, *what* is the big deal about her? She looks like she's going to a funeral."

It was rare to see her so indignant about something. "You sound jealous," I teased.

"I'm not *jealous*. I just think it would be nice if he would spend some time with his own teammates."

"You spent the whole day with Gisela."

"The *day*. Not now, at the dance. I was just dancing with Nat."

I shrugged. "I guess Sophia is just cooler than all of us." I, too, had felt slighted by Anthony's shunning us all day, but for some reason, I didn't want to give Jennifer the satisfaction of knowing it.

She mimicked my shrug. "I really don't get the mystique." Then she brushed past me, her low dress-up heels clicking on the floor, my laughter tailing her.

Just as I got to the edge of the dance floor, the DJ switched to a ballad, Madonna's "Crazy for You." The moving lights slowed and turned a moody azure. In an awkward shuffle, kids started pairing up. I saw Nat put her arms around Tommy Markey's neck as he fitted his own arms around her waist. Even Anthony and Sophia listlessly embraced each other. I just stood there, suddenly feeling as exposed and out-of-place as Pete had just confessed to me he felt. If only Jennifer hadn't repaired to the lavatory, we could dance together—but as it was, I had no easy port in a storm.

Across the dance floor, David Ruth saw me, saluted comically, then walked around the perimeter, his gelled hair disheveled and sweaty, and came to stand by my side, a red plastic cup in his hand. "It's the *romantic* part," he drawled, saccharine.

"So touching," I drawled back. But, in fact, I *was* touched that he'd come over to stand by me. I felt strangely rescued. He handed me the plastic cup. "I spiked it," he said, and I took a large gulp, grateful for the burn in my throat. I was growing to love alcohol, find joy in its transport, almost as much as Nat loved pot. We both stood there, observing the couples shuffling and rocking in place before us. Jennifer didn't come back until the song was fading out. Then one of the adults flicked on the lights, making everyone wince. A moment later, Pete walked back into the cafeteria, only to sit in a chair by the exit, well away from the crowd, his arms crossed.

Then the rooting about for coats and backpacks, the hugs and goodbyes, the fanning out to more than a dozen idling minibuses in the frigid parking lot. Coach Gold stood outside our minibus as we climbed aboard, head-counting as he always did, smelling distinctly of not just cigarettes but beer, which must have been surreptitiously making the rounds among the chaperones. He was singing as we entered, *After the ball is over, after the break of dawn*, an avuncular paw on each of our shoulders as we boarded. We glanced among ourselves; he was clearly drunk.

Once the minibus pulled out of the parking lot, toward the highway, he stood up in the front and faced us. "I hope this is proving to be an edifying experience for all of you," he declaimed, a bit thickly. "This is the kind of thing that you're going to look back on someday and realize how lucky you were to have had these occasions."

Anthony and I caught eyes, rolled them at each other.

"And I just want you to know, as someone who doesn't have any kids of my own," Gold continued, "how proud I am of all of you. You reflect well on me and you reflect well on Mendhem High."

With that, he sat down in the seat behind the driver, his back to us. Nat and I were sharing a seat, as we always did. I turned to her, whispered, "Maudlin."

But her eyes were unexpectedly glassy. "No," she protested, to my surprise. "He really means it. He's just a big softie."

SEVEN

By the time Nat and I sat at the terminal gate at Logan Airport, the bright and cold Thursday afternoon before Presidents' Day weekend, I was a little bit amazed that it was all actually happening, because it nearly hadn't. I held my coffee with one hand, scrolled my phone with the thumb of my other hand, excited and nervous. I glanced at her, reading her book on massage therapy for animals, for which she was pursuing certification now that she and Aaron had decided to give up farming for a living in order to save for Olivia and Otis's college educations. Her eyebrows were scrunched, her mouth in an inadvertent frown as she read, one leg crossed over the other, the suspended foot bobbing in its sneaker. I felt a rush of tenderness for her, my longest-time friend in the world, wiggled my shoulder against hers.

She glanced my way.

"Hiiiieeee," I said.

She laughed. "Hiiiieeee."

"Are you excited now that it's finally happening?"

"I still feel a little guilty."

"You shouldn't. It's just for a few days."

She was the first to have gotten cold feet, shortly after we booked everything with Anthony's assistant. She texted me: ***Been thinking about it. I just don't feel right about going. We are struggling so much. Otis is struggling in school.***

Mild panic struck me. The truth was, more than I'd admit to anyone, I'd become absolutely obsessed with the trip, with the idea that if we pulled it off and did what we were flirting with doing, then something very pivotal in our lives—okay, I admit it, *my* life—was going to change, some massive boulder in the road was going to give way. And I absolutely could not go without Nat, it just wouldn't be the same. In fact, I *needed* her there if we were going to do this. I nearly texted back but called instead. To my surprise, she picked up instantly.

"But it's all paid for by Anthony, and it's just for a few days over a weekend," I said. "Otis won't even be in school."

She sighed. "It just seems a little weird when you think about it, doesn't it? Are we really going down there to ambush Gold?"

It was clear she was less invested in the idea than I was, which I chalked up to her not having ever been confronted by Gold, as Jennifer, Anthony, and I had. Gold was a benign and neutral memory to her.

"We just want to talk to him," I said. And then, disingenuously: "The plan's not etched in stone, anyway. We can talk about it once we're there and proceed accordingly. And you wouldn't have to come, either."

"Do we even know we're going to find him?"

"Well, we have his address. I guess we just go to his house."

"We don't call ahead?"

"We don't have his number. And I couldn't find him on Facebook."

She sighed again.

"Look, just forget about the Gold part right now and think of this as a cute little reunion, fully paid for, and a break from the cold."

"I guess."

And that had been our last true correspondence, until this moment, sitting here waiting for the flight to board.

I tapped her massage book. "I'm very proud of you."

That elicited a small smile. "Thanks. Let's just hope there's lots of rich people with pets with chronic pain in southern New Hampshire."

A few minutes later came a text from Jennifer: ***I'm at the airport! All*** *by myself, no husband, no kids, no conference prep . . . so discomfiting yet so liberating!*

We're at Logan! I texted back, then snapped a pic of Nat and me, sent it to her.

Jennifer had been the next one to nearly back out, maybe a week after I'd quelled Nat's misgivings.

Hello friends, the email to Nat and me had begun.

I hope the icy depths of winter find you well. This is not a definite reversal, but I wanted to let you know there is a very good chance I won't be able to make our Floridian idyll. This did not come up when you visited, but Raffy has been struggling with depression the past several months and I just don't feel right about leaving him right now, even for a few days. Part of it is that he's growing up to realize what it is to be a brown boy in this country, and he's struggling with that. And it may also have to do with his grandpa, Andres's dad, passing a few weeks ago in Colombia. He's been having a hard time sleeping, nightmares, loss of focus in school, and just a general malaise that is very painful to witness in our little champ.

> *So, again, this is not quite a hard cancel at the moment but just a heads-up that I might be bowing out, in which case I thought you might ask Anthony if he might transfer my plane ticket to one of your significant others, perhaps.*
>
> *I will follow up very soon! I am so sorry to inject uncertainty into our adventure, which in fact I was very much looking forward to.*
>
> *Xoxox Jennifer*

I'm a little embarrassed to admit that my panic over the trip falling apart briefly eclipsed my concern about Raffy. Then I reread the email, processed it. Before replying, I called Nat, of course, who'd also just read it.

"That makes me sad to hear." I paused, recollected our visit to Jennifer's. "Do you remember that Trayvon Martin poster propped up on the wall when we came in?"

"No. There was?"

"Yeah. I wonder if that's what she was alluding to, the part about being a brown boy."

"Maybe," said Nat. I wondered if she'd received the email with relief—here was an out!—rather than dismay. "He was a little sweetheart."

I paused. "Well, what do you want to do if she bails? You wanna bail, too?"

No reply for a few seconds. "Why don't we just give her a few days and see what she says? Even if it doesn't seem very promising."

"Of course. Do you want me to write her back?"

"Yes."

Nat and I just talked, I wrote. *We're heartbroken to hear that about Raffy, who shouldn't have his innocence robbed from him that way—*

At that point, looking at those words on the screen I'd just written, I started crying, startling myself. I just sat there a moment before wiping my eyes with the back of one hand and continuing.

—and of course we understand whatever you want to do, and are sure Anthony would as well, and could easily make changes. So just let us know and we're sending love to Raffy and all of you.

Was that too much? I asked myself. Then decided to let it stand.

Xoxox Tip and Nat

At that point, in the following days, I slid into my own minor depression. The possibility that the trip would not happen felt like an ancient knot inside me fated to stay knotted.

It was a feeling that, for some reason, crescendoed one evening in the office when we were seeing off a colleague: our abrasive but basically good-natured development director, Sharon Leclerc from Cranston, who was going to work for CVS, which was headquartered in the state.

Champagne was going around in clear plastic cups, but no one had thought to buy sparkling water or even Diet Coke as well—admittedly, I was quiet at work about my sobriety—and I found myself taking my plastic cup to the office kitchen to fill it with plain, unfancy tap water. Toasting with that in hand while everyone else giggled over the bubbly, I felt ridiculous, like the world's biggest loser. When the party broke up, I ended up grabbing Thai food with Jono, the other gay guy in the office, and when he ordered a Tsingtao beer with his food, I did as well—perversely. Just to feel on par with him. I wasn't even a beer fan. I wouldn't even touch it, I told myself, but at least there'd be symmetry on the table.

Once it arrived, I could barely concentrate on a word Jono said, so badly I wanted that beer, just sitting there before me, undecanted, unlike Jono's, which twinkled amber in his glass much as the champagne had in its plastic cups. Finally, with what I hoped appeared to be merely a natural reflex rather than the outward expression of a thunderous existential line-crosser, I picked up the bottle and took a sip. I absorbed nothing Jono was saying for perhaps a full minute after that, so obsessed I was with the taste, the texture of the beer in my mouth. It had been so long that I half expected to feel instantly unhinged and start looking about wildly for the person in the room with the cocaine, but in fact that didn't happen. I didn't feel much different than I had a moment before, so, further smiling and nodding at Jono although I was barely processing a word he said, I picked up the bottle and had another sip. Then, once the food came, another, and another, and another, until I'd drunk half the bottle. I marveled at my restraint; Jono had already ordered another beer. And I marveled at my inner state. I felt fine! Unaltered! Why had I thought for so long that I wasn't capable of having a simple beer with dinner? Why had I bought the A.A. line that such an innocent, banal gesture was the first step toward the abyss? A blanket of well-being, of normality and alignment with most of the rest of society, fell over me snugly.

Yet when Jono and I parted ways, only a few blocks from my apartment, terror overtook me at the thought of Marcus smelling beer on my breath, detecting even the faintest shadow of drunkenness. I bought mint gum at the gas station convenience store, zipped up my coat and pulled up the hood, and ended up walking again in India Point Park, the same lamplit pathways by the water, until I felt I was in the clear.

That, I told myself the next day, had been a one-off, something I would not do again until—oh, maybe another year. Or maybe that next dinner with Jono. Maybe it would be something I *only* did with Jono—a kind of ritual, safely contained. With certainty, I knew that I would *not* be coming clean about my half beer in an A.A. meeting, my attendance at which had been dwindling in recent months anyway, nearly to the point of complete dissociation.

But despite this cheap momentary thrill, my low mood persisted. *What was I living for?*, I would find the worst version of myself asking. Several more years of sleepwalking my way through a stupid job, light-years from the kind of writing I'd once hoped I'd make a living at? Several more years of healthy, vaguely artisanal weeknight dinners with Marcus, followed by prestige TV, the requisite annual week in Provincetown, that same anodyne vacation over and over again, the uphill battle not to get too gray, too flabby, too creaky? The trip to Sarasota had sparkled on the horizon like some kind of thrilling threshold, a turning point, Oz rising up from a flat landscape, but now with its prospect evaporating before me, I went through my days in a mild panic of irrelevance. Who, what, would disrupt this terrifying unruffled surface of all the days, years, that lay before me? One night after work, halfway home on my walk, I about-faced and walked all the way to a gay bar downtown, sailed inside, and stood at the bar, joylessly drinking an O'Douls and staring at Katy Perry videos on the screen overhead, until I left and trudged home, unhappier than when I arrived.

And then, to my great surprise—and colossal relief—came the follow-up from Jennifer.

> *Hola, compadres! I'm happy to report we are in a better place. Perhaps I overreacted when I wrote you last, but the fact is, Raffy seems to have returned to some kind of baseline, sleeping better and getting back into the swing in school and with friends. Actually, in the wake of all this, a students of color club has sprung up at his school, started by a lifesaver of a Black teacher and very much cheered on by a handful of parents, including yours truly, and we think his having joined that has provided some degree of . . . solace? Safety? Not quite sure what the word is, but our puppy dog seems happier and that's all I care about. Additionally, Andres is more or less making me go on the trip, all but pushing me out the door. Not that I didn't want to, I was just anxious.*
>
> *Thank you for bearing with me! No need to change any plans with Anthony and I cannot wait to greet you out by that pool in a few weeks!*

Obviously, Nat and I wrote back our hallelujahs. *A lifesaver of a Black teacher*—that line stuck with me. There had been no such lifesaver for Jennifer at Mendhem High. And for the first time, I realized that her lifesaver had maybe been Gisela Muñoz from Boston Latin.

The strangest thing, in all this time, was that we never heard from Anthony. Yes, the trip was fully booked. Yes, we would see him in Florida. And yet it was odd, given we assumed he had our email addresses from his assistant, and certainly in that he and I'd been texting, that he never reached out with a personal note to us in advance of the trip. ***13 days til Sarasota!*** I texted him at one point. No reply for four days, after which he sent a single emoji of an "excited" face.

Then, a few days before the trip, he texted me a link from *The New York Times*, which I clicked. "Anthony Malouf, Pietro Cuccino Creative Director, to Helm Parent Company," read the headline. Apparently, Anthony was now also the creative director for Cuccino Worldwide, overseeing women's ready-to-wear as well as a men's "diffusion" line, whatever that meant, and linens. So apparently that was why he'd been too busy to reach out.

Amazing, congrats! I texted him. ***Will you still be able to make Florida?***

Wouldn't miss it! he texted back almost instantly, to my surprise. ***See you there!***

On the plane, finally up in the air, I announced to Nat, "I think I'm gonna have a few cocktails on this trip with the rest of you."

She put her book down, turned to me. "Oh, really? Is that okay?"

"Well, it's something I've slipped back into here and there, and it's worked out fine. How do you not have a margarita when you're sitting on the Gulf Coast, right?"

"I would be happy to just have mocktails with you. I've got my edibles in my bag; that's all I need."

"Ooh, you brought edibles? Can I do some with you?"

Her eyes narrowed. "Should I be worried about you? I thought you were, like, all A.A. now."

"Well, I was. But I thought about it a lot and talked to a few people about it." This was a total lie; I'd talked to nobody about it, including Marcus, who didn't know yet. "And I decided it's just not sustainable or realistic to say I'm never going to pick up a drink for the rest of my life. Alcohol wasn't really my problem anyway. Coke was. You know that."

"I know, but . . ." She trailed off, pondering. "I'll admit, I'd have a hard time, too, never having a beer again. Or a margie."

Good, I thought. She'd come around. "So we'll have some margies together? All salt-rimmed and stuff, very Jimmy Buffett?"

She shrugged. "It's not like any of us are gonna be driving. It doesn't look like we need to leave this resort."

"So true. It's a self-contained paradise. From the room to the pool to the beach."

"But believe me," she said. "I thoroughly intend to do an edible at least an hour before we do you-know-what."

"What?"

"If we see you-know-who, I mean."

Oh. She'd meant Gold. "Well," I said, careful to downplay my desperation about the whole thing, "it's not entirely set in stone that we're going to see him. We'd need to talk it out first, right?"

"The thought makes me vaguely nauseous."

"Why? You're the only one he never said something horrible to."

She just looked at me and rolled her eyes.

"What?"

But we were interrupted by the flight attendant, coming around with drinks. Nat asked for a sparkling water, then so did I.

"What?" she teased, as we toasted with our plastic cups. "No cocktail?"

I laughed. "I'm holding out for the good stuff."

My favorite moment—my *first* favorite moment—flying to warm climes in the middle of a miserable New England winter is feeling that blast of warm air coming through the crack between the plane and the jet bridge as you disembark. It's always a bit shocking, as though you can't believe other people in other places have been enjoying this weather, drifting out of their homes and onto their lanais in bare feet and shorts, while you've been mummifying yourself every morning before leaving the house, tramping through icy, dirty slush to get to the car, where you sit, desperate, waiting for the heat to kick in and the engine to turn over, as the radio tells you to expect another week of subfreezing temperatures and roads marred with terrifying black ice.

And so we tasted that warm blast, and then we were completely bathing in that warm air as we waited for a car at the airport.

Nat hugged herself. "This feels so good," she said.

"I know."

The view from the car was an unbroken expanse of blue sky, palm trees, and dull, square buildings of off-white or sand.

"Everything looks like it was built maybe ten years ago," Nat said.

Momentarily, we were on a bridge sailing over an expanse of shimmering turquoise water, an island looming ahead. It was Longboat Key, with manicured lawns and pristine, large newish homes, all of them gleamingly white, and in a moment, we were passing through a private gate and pulling up under a portico to a building that could only be described as corporate contemporary chic, which also aptly described the lobby we entered, with vaulted ceilings, walls of glass looking out onto the expanse of pool, every cherry wood or white plaster surface so immaculate, so unlived-in, it looked like they had been installed literally moments before we arrived.

We were halfway to the desk when we heard, from the island of massive, vaguely mid-century couches nearby, "You two!"

We turned. It was Jennifer, in shorts, sandals, and yellow capsleeve T-shirt, waving to us with her phone in her hand. We hastened toward her, smiles and hugs all around.

"This place is so *luxe*," I said. We three perched back down on the sprawling white sofa, nearly the size of a small yacht.

"Would you expect any less from Anthony?" asked Jennifer.

"Where is he?" asked Nat.

Just at that moment, a young, dark-haired woman in what appeared to be the resort staff uniform—a short-sleeve khaki shirt and shorts, conferring a kind of safari look—strode our way. "Are you the guests of Anthony Malouf?"

We all nodded.

"He said he should be here by five. There's a light lunch and drinks waiting for you outside by the pool," she said, "and then Mr. Malouf requests your company for drinks and dinner in his cabana out on the beach at six o'clock so you can all catch the sunset together."

The three of us looked at one another, burst out laughing. "This feels very Agatha Christie!" declared Jennifer.

I cracked up. "Evil under the sun!"

Laid out for us on an umbrella'd table by the pool was a salad festooned with pecans and strawberries, crab finger sandwiches, glass pitchers of lemon water, tiny wedges of key lime pie. We ooh'd and ahh'd all around before sitting down and setting to it.

"We're so glad you were able to make it," Nat said to Jennifer. "And so glad to hear Raffy's doing better."

Jennifer's brow furrowed slightly. "Well, just when we thought he was in the clear, he had another nightmare last night, which of course sent me away this morning under a cloud of guilt."

Nat and I frowned, shook our heads. *He'll be okay with Andres*, I nearly said—then, thinking better of it, remained silent. And thus a few moments of silence ensued while we nibbled.

"But!" Jennifer finally continued, as though she sensed that she alone could speak next, "he has proudly insisted on wearing hoodies to school every day as an act of solidarity with Trayvon. Which makes me very proud of him."

"Otis did that, too, for a while, with his friends, in solidarity," Nat added, and Jennifer murmured, "I love that," but then some of the same silence befell us momentarily.

I almost said something about the Zimmerman trial, which was coming up later in the year, but I truly didn't know if pushing forward with the topic was called for or perverse, so I didn't. Instead, reaching for the blandest possible segue, I gestured out toward the Gulf of Mexico, impossibly blue against the white sand. "I still can't totally believe we're here."

It felt like the right pivot, because both Nat and Jennifer instantly overexclaimed, "I know!" which led to a usefully diverting conversation about the last time all of us had been in warm climes in winter, followed by an only marginally sincere conversation about whether such trips were worth it at all, given that one had to return to the same miserable weather from whence one had come after a few days.

As we chatted, I wondered if either of them would bring up Gold. He was on my mind—the fact that we were basically in the same town as him felt both thrilling and forbidding—and yet steadfastly I refused to be the one who invoked him. In fact, sitting out in the golden warmth, which loosened muscles in my neck and shoulders I hadn't even known were locked up, suffusing my whole body in a kind of delicious narcotic relaxation, I briefly wondered if we really needed to follow up on the Gold thing at all. Then, just as quickly, I abandoned that thought. I absolutely would not let the good weather lull me away from the real reason we'd—I'd—come.

As lunch plates were cleared, Nat asked if we'd mind if she went up to her room to unpack bags that had been brought up for us by the staff while we ate. I heartily seconded that; I was excited to see my digs. It turned out that our rooms, on the sixth floor, were contiguous, so we had a funny rom-com sort of moment when we all said ta-ta before disappearing behind our separate doors.

I sailed straight through the large, similarly corporate-upscale room—every surface azure or sand, vaguely abstract beach tableau hung over the king-size bed—to the massive sliding doors that led straight out onto a spacious balcony overlooking the Gulf. The whole sensation was indulgent and luxurious in the cheesiest, best possible Julia Roberts–discovers-fine-living-in–*Pretty Woman* sort of way, and without so much as a second thought, I beelined to the bar, opened a small bottle of tequila, poured a glass, took it out onto the balcony, sank into a chaise, and drank it right down, followed by another from the bottle, as I stared out at the sea and felt that exquisite, half-forgotten tequila warmth steal over me like a dear old friend. At one point, my phone buzzed and it was Marcus, texting, ***Got there safely?*** And I intended to answer it in a moment but instead dozed off in the chaise to the sound of gulls cawing.

In my dream, Marcus was hammering up something in the house, despite my protestations that he was too loud. But then I awoke with a start, to realize that the hammering was actually a banging coming from the other side of the frosted-glass divider between my balcony and the one next door.

"Tippy!" It was Nat's voice.

"Huh?" I called.

"It's six o'clock."

"It is?" I reached down for my phone, in the process upending the empty tequila glass. Indeed, it was.

"I knocked on your door a few times but you didn't answer."

"I fell asleep out here, it was so nice."

She laughed. "Nice. Should I go down and tell them you need a few minutes?"

I sat up in the chaise. "No, no, just give me five minutes to freshen up and I'll go down with you. Meet you in the lobby."

In a moment, the two of us were walking, arm in arm, down a

wooden walkway toward an enormous blue-and-white-striped canvas-tent cabana, its backside to us. It was the only such one on the beach.

"Do you think Anthony had that specially set up for us?" Nat asked.

"Wouldn't surprise me."

Rounding it, entering on the open side that faced the sea, we found, in facing beach chairs, Jennifer and Anthony, chattering away, each with a mesmerizing pale yellow drink in hand. The inevitable whoops, exclamations, and embraces followed; Jennifer and Anthony had clearly already had a moment to reconnect, but it was Nat and Anthony's first time seeing each other, to my knowledge, since high school.

"You look the same!" Anthony exclaimed, standing back from her. "You still look seventeen." Which was, in fact, true.

"You look—better!" replied Nat, which was also true. As I'd noted over Thanksgiving, once-pudgy Anthony was now almost frighteningly lean and lithe, his toned legs and arms exposed in some sort of unconstructed white linen sleeveless tunic and short-shorts ensemble, those hammered metal bracelets he'd worn in the *Hello Mister* photos intact, leather sandals tossed aside so that he greeted us in bare feet.

"Sit, sit," Anthony instructed us, pouring drinks for Nat and me from an enormous glass pitcher on a white table laden with guacamole, fruit, and ceviche, all of it set out in matching white bowls and platters.

We settled in, the four of us facing one another in beach chairs, as the sun slowly descended toward the line where blue sky met bluer water. I sipped; the taste—sweet, tart, and bitter, a divine combination—sparkling on my tongue. "This is delicious," I said. "What is it?"

"Limoncello, prosecco, and mint," said Anthony. "My favorite spring-summer drink when I'm working in Italy." He didn't seem to notice that I was now drinking, whereas I'd sat there with Diet Cokes over Thanksgiving, and I was grateful for the nonrecognition, glad I'd not told him I was in recovery. He reclined back in his chaise rather regally, like a pasha, beholding us, one leg slung over the other. "How was everyone's flight?" he asked. "Are the accommodations adequate?"

He clearly was looking for a barrage of affirmation, which of course he got, Nat and Jennifer rhapsodizing about the spaciousness of the rooms, the dazzling views off the balconies, the impeccable service. My drink kicking in, feeling again that irresistible wave of warmth and well-being that had settled over me at lunch and then on my balcony with the tequila, I beheld Anthony with amusement and affection. He really hadn't changed that much, I decided; he still wanted to impress, to make it clear his tastes had far surpassed his upbringing.

He then continued to impress me with his ability to sustain at least a veneer of interest and curiosity in Jennifer and her stories about her life, her kids, her town, all of which I imagined must have seemed a bit dull to him. But then again, he'd always been impressed by Jennifer's intellect, so it didn't surprise me that he wanted to know all about her professor life.

"It's so *unnerving*," she was saying. "I'll be up there, *deep* into a lecture about, I don't know, W.E.B. Du Bois. And they're all sitting behind laptops and I have no idea *whatsoever* if they're taking notes or if they're on Facebook or whatever, which they totally could be, because the whole campus is wired." She was getting drunk, and it was funny and charming to see her become louder and more emphatic than usual. "I mean, the late eighties, even the nineties, what's the worst you could do during a lecture? Doodle in your notebook or even read a magazine surreptitiously? You're still somewhat engaged. But for all I know, I'm competing with kids watching, you know, *Gaga* videos with the sound down, or with one earbud in."

Which of course led into Nat and Jennifer's detailed laments about losing their own kids to screens and the various deals they had to cut with them to get them off said screens for a few minutes at dinner, et cetera, and weren't we glad we weren't glued to screens when *we* were growing up, except TV screens, of course, but that was different because—because—well, it was just different!

Anthony poured another round of drinks, then another. At one point, we all rose, drinks in hand, a bit woozy, and exited the tent to stand barefoot in a line on the sand, to ooh and ahh as the sun fell into the sea. Anthony, well lubricated, put an arm around both Nat and Jennifer. Soon the four of us were enlaced, years having fallen away in the matter of an hour.

In the fading light, staff—in those safari-like khaki uniforms—marched out with a massive tray of lobster tacos, set them down, then built a firepit right outside the cabana, which lit up our faces as we dive-bombed the tacos.

"Is messy and casual okay with you guys tonight?" Anthony asked, all fake fretting. "We'll do a proper dinner out by the pool tomorrow night."

Nat hooted. "Are you kidding? This is *amazing*." I glanced at her, contentedly nipping at her fingertips as she ate. It made me happy to see her in this setting, being attended to, every pleasure provided, awash in prettiness and niceties.

"I am in *heaven*," echoed Jennifer.

It's hard to pinpoint exactly how conversations flicker between the present and the past—exactly what thought or remark triggers a lurch forward or backward—but that's more or less what happened as we continued to eat and drink, the four of us talking about the Obamas or the precipitous and slightly Orwellian rise of Whole Foods one minute, then talking about some old piece of Mendhem the next, something stupid like the fact that the rock-garden fountain in the foyer of the Happy Panda was still intact, as Anthony and I had noted over Thanksgiving.

But our portal to the real stuff, the as-yet-unspoken stuff, was in fact Gisela Muñoz. Because, in the course of yet another discussion about food, Jennifer mentioned that her friend Gisela was always raving on Facebook about the CSA she had joined, and how she simply thought *everyone* should join a CSA.

"Wait," I said. "Is that Gisela from Speech Team? Gisela from Boston Latin?"

"Yes!" exclaimed Jennifer, as though she'd herself forgotten. "Half the time I forget that's when we first met, not in college."

"I remember her," Nat said. "What's she doing now?"

"She's vice president of a bank. In Hartford."

"That sounds thrilling," drawled Anthony, now soundly drunk.

Jennifer laughed. "We can't all be as glamorous as *you*, darling." She still had some sort of a crush on Anthony, that much was easy to see. Something about him brought her to life, made her giddy, in a way that Nat and I hadn't seen when we visited her.

"I guess that's why she's always going on and on about her CSA vegetables," Anthony persisted. "It's probably the most exciting thing in her life."

Jennifer shrieked again, delighted. "You're still such a bitch!"

That was that. It was now officially "Whatever happened to . . . ?" time, and of course that brought us around, after a few other long-forgotten subjects, to Pete Stroman.

"That breaks my heart," said Jennifer. "I wonder if he got worse after high school, or if it was always that bad. You know?"

"That's so true," mused Nat. "Because Aaron—my partner, Aaron—had very bad depression in his teens and twenties, but he said it got better in his thirties. And now he's fine, more or less. I wonder if it works in the opposite direction for some people."

We all pondered that quietly a moment. Then Anthony finally said, "He could've been a model. Easily. I wonder if he knew that. He was not only beautiful but tall enough."

"I agree," I said. "But do you think that would've made him happier?"

"No. I'm just saying that he had an amazing face. More than people even realized then."

"I guess in his mind that didn't make much of a difference," said Jennifer.

Anthony looked up at her. "Can I ask you something? Frankly?"

She half smiled, game, sipped her drink. "What?"

"Were we racist toward you? In any way we didn't realize?"

The question seemed to catch her by surprise, and she inhaled sharply. Her subsequent pause, I have to admit, was mildly excruciating. Were there things she remembered us saying, Gold-style, that we did not?

"No," she finally said, after what appeared to be genuine consideration. "Not that I recall. You were good friends. We had fun. Of course, you all gave me the razz for being so fucking prim and proper."

"*Fucking!*" Anthony echoed her. "Did Jennifer Douglas just say *fucking*!"

She whooped, delighted. "She does now!" Then, more subdued: "But that's really how I was. That's how my respectability-worshipping mamma raised me and I didn't know anything else. And I think—" She paused a minute. "I think I realized pretty quickly after we moved to Mendhem that it was better to be the opposite of a white person's stereotype than to embody it."

We were all silent for a moment, processing this. "You mean, like, a racial stereotype?" Nat finally asked.

Jennifer nodded, sipped her drink. "Exactly. I'll tell you the one line I got over and over again—not from you guys—that drove me crazy. *I just want you to know, I don't think of you as Black.* Kids told me that all the time. As though it was some kind of compliment. Was I supposed to be, like, 'Gee—thanks! God forbid you think of me as what I actually am!'"

"That's fucked up," I said. And felt like the world's biggest hypocrite as I said it, because that's exactly what I'd privately thought of Jennifer.

"I got it so much," she went on, seemingly warming to the topic, which at least suggested to me that she felt comfortable—or drunk—enough to talk about it with us. "Once I asked this boy—I can't even remember his name—'What *do* you think of as Black?' And he answered: '*Sanford and Son*.'"

She cracked up, and we groaned dutifully. "So at least he didn't think of me as living in a junkyard. I mean, that's good, right?"

We were all still laughing when Jennifer interjected: "Oh, but wait! Tip and Nat, I remember something else." She regarded us both with a Cheshire cat smile.

My stomach dropped. "Uh-oh," I said. "What?"

"I know you called the other Black girls the Dreamgirls. The ones in chorus."

She said it in a kind of singsong, as though to take the sting out of it. I felt the blood rush to my face, then glanced at Nat, to find her in the same state of mortification. She and I glanced at each other, then back at Jennifer, who seemed to regard the two of us with amusement. I glanced at Anthony, whose gaze toggled back and forth as though he were at a tennis match; I'm sure he was loving the drama and happy to not be implicated.

"We did," Nat admitted flatly.

And I echoed her. "That was shitty. We had snarky little nicknames for everyone and I guess we didn't really think about—"

"But think about what going to Mendhem High must have been like for them," Jennifer cut in. "And they didn't even live in a nice house out in the fancy part of town, like I did. They lived in the *apartments*."

"Yeah," I said. I was past my shame by this point and just wanted to be honest. "I didn't really think about that stuff back then. For them or for you."

"I didn't really either," said Nat. "But I genuinely did *like* them. I was in chorus with them! Janis, Liz, and—who was the other one?"

"Angie," Jennifer said quickly, passing her glass to Anthony and signaling for him to refill it for her. "An*gel*ica. And yes, they were sweet-hearts. And I for one was glad they were there, even if we weren't close." She took her glass back from Anthony, sipped. "And look, guys—do I think what you called them was really that bad? No. I even thought it was slightly funny, because it was kind of true. I mean, they were *always* singing."

"But you remembered it," I said.

She nodded. "I did. Maybe because it was *friends of mine* who said it."

"Where—?" began Nat.

"In the hallway. The two of you passed the girls and, Tip, you turned to Nat and sang, *We're your Dreeeemgirls—*" Jennifer made the stylized sweeping gesture, Supremes-like, with her right hand. "And, Nat, you cracked up. And neither of you knew I was behind you."

It bothered me intensely that she remembered this so vividly. Had she seen Nat and me in an entirely new light after that—trusted us less?

"Jennifer, I'm really sorry," was all I could say. "Sorry I said it and sorry you heard it."

"I am too," said Nat.

Jennifer, more than anyone, seemed to want to break the brief silence that ensued. "I am not holding anyone up to 2012 standards for something that was truly not that terrible a thing to say in 1987—or six—or whenever it was," she declared, raising her drink. "If anything, I wish I could go back and smack *myself* for the things I put up with back then. But I just didn't know any better. And look—I survived! We all did!" She raised her glass higher, in a toast of sorts, and we followed.

And then she pointed her glass first at me, then Anthony. "And it couldn't have been easy for the two of you—and that's something I'll admit never crossed *my* mind back then. Unworldly girl that I was."

"Listen," added Natalie, pointing to me. "I was his best friend and I wasn't sure myself."

"Well," I said flatly. "You're right. It wasn't easy. I hope kids don't have to go through it quite that bad today. Gay kids, I mean. Or gay-seeming. Whatever."

I looked to Anthony, wondering if he'd back me on this, but instead he rose, pulled cigarettes from his shorts pocket, and went to stand outside, by the firepit. "I just removed myself mentally," he said matter-of-factly before lighting one. "I was out of there before I was out of there."

"You shouldn't smoke, Anthony!" Jennifer called after him sharply.

But Nat rose, joined him. "I'll share that with you." He handed it to her, and something about watching the two of them side by side, sharing it, broke my heart, but in a good way.

"Did anyone ever give you shit for anything?" Anthony asked Nat, then exhaled.

"I mean," she began. "I don't think anyone knew that the 'Farb' in 'Farb-Miola' was Jewish. I think most of them thought that it was one name, like 'Farbmiola.'"

We all laughed. "Farbmiola!" Anthony exclaimed, in a silly *abbondanza!* accent.

"And we went to Unitarian church! No, I was just called a hippie chick and a stoner, which was fine with me."

"Speaking of which, did you bring pot?" Anthony asked.

She smiled and pulled a tiny metal case out of her shorts, extracted a joint from it.

I gasped. "You brought that on the *plane*? How?"

Nat merely smiled slyly. "I have my little tricks."

"You are my *savior*!" Anthony exclaimed. Soon, they were passing both the joint and the cigarette back and forth.

"You two burnouts!" I called. "Go back to the smoking area."

We all laughed. We'd actually had a smoking area, a patch of asphalt outside where students sixteen and older could smoke. The idea of it now seemed bonkers—a memory from the Stone Age.

Nat held the joint toward Jennifer and me. "You guys want?"

Jennifer shook her head, raised a palm in demurral. "I'm not good with pot. You'll literally have to drag me off the beach."

Her refusal was the out I needed as well. "I'm good," I called.

Anthony exhaled, stretched his arms over his head, turned to the sea, then back to us. "Well, *I* was called a hairy terrorist in high school," he announced. "By none other than our speech coach."

In the dark, Nat, Jennifer, and I glanced at one another. He didn't know I'd already mentioned this to them, and I imagine they, like I, had been waiting to see if he'd bring it up.

"You're actually gonna tell the whole story this time?" I asked. I remembered my shock when he'd started to cry, retreated to the bathroom, as he'd begun the tale at Happy Panda.

"Am I chic enough for ISIS?" he asked, striking a mod pose with his cigarette, sucking in his cheeks like Paris Hilton in front of a camera. "Edgy enough?" He was drunk now, silly drunk, like he'd been that night he came to my house many years ago.

"Tell. Us. What. Happened!" demanded Jennifer, each word punctuated by a clap of her hands.

He sighed dramatically, as though winding up, flicked his cigarette into the firepit, then turned to us. "I'm rehearsing with him one day," he began, "I think it was fall of senior year, because I remember I was very anxiously waiting to hear from NYU—and he interrupts me and says, out of nowhere, 'What kind of name is Malouf? Pale*stin*ian?' Just like that. With that tone."

"Oh, no," interjected Jennifer.

"Oh, yes. So I said, 'It's my dad's name. It's Lebanese.' And he says—and I kid you not—he says, 'Ah, that's what I thought, a hairy terrorist name.' And he's kind of, like, smirking while he says it. So I just go, '*What?*' and he goes, 'Oh, you don't know that Lebanon has basically become a'—I forget the word he used, something like a staging ground—'for terrorists who are trying to destroy Israel? What, you don't know what's going on in your own home country? And then he goes—I totally remember this—'what kind of Arab are you?'"

"Are you fucking kidding me?" Hearing the story in its entirety now, I actually *was* fairly shocked. And also somewhat relieved to hear that Gold had said to Anthony something just about as fucked up as what he'd said to me, and with that same breeziness.

"Not in the least," said Anthony. "He says this to me with this smirk on his face that I will never forget."

"I remember that smirk," said Nat.

"And what did you say to him?" asked Jennifer.

"I think I said, 'Well, my father was born here and nobody in my family has even been there since my grandmother went back for a month in, like, the sixties, before I was born, so except for going to Lebanese church with my grandmother sometimes, and the food, and a few Arabic words my grandmother uses, I don't even really know anything about it.'"

He paused, crossed his arms over his chest. "But mostly I just remember this overwhelming sense of shame and, like, *dirtiness*, and wanting him to know I had no association with the place. Which was true. But I remember feeling *very* hairy and *very* swarthy for months after that—more than I ever had before."

"Ha!" laughed Jennifer. "Swarthy!"

"It definitely started me on a journey," continued Anthony. "But when I looked back on it over the years, I was like, who the fuck was he to single me out that way?"

"Oh, he *loved* to single you out." It was Jennifer again, in a sharp tone, to whom we all turned. "Really make you feel the thing about yourself you were most trying to just fly under the radar with."

"He did that to you, too, right?" I dared to ask her, trying to draw out more this time.

"Did he ever."

"What did he say to you?" It was Anthony. I was glad he'd asked; maybe Jennifer, fresh off hearing his own recounting, would elaborate.

She opened her mouth, holding us in suspense a moment, then exhaled and shook her head, as though newly flabbergasted by whatever he'd said. "It was just bananas" is all she ended up saying. "Bananas and *so* wrong. *So* much wronger than 'Dreamgirls' or anything anyone else ever said to me, because it seemed so—pointed. Like he was really trying to bring me low."

I desperately wished she'd just come out and say what it was, but clearly she didn't want to.

"More than anything," she continued, "I wish I'd told my mother. She'd have reamed him. *Reamed* him in the way that only an angry West Indian mother can."

I noted this with interest; I hadn't known her mother was West Indian. In fact, I'd known nothing about her family except that they'd moved to the Boston area from California because her father, who'd been some sort of engineer, had been transferred.

"Why didn't you tell your mom?" I asked.

She shook her head again, frowning, seemingly disappointed in herself. "I was too ashamed. I didn't want to see the look on her face when I told her what he said."

"What did he say?" insisted Anthony.

To which she merely raised a palm, to signal she didn't want to go there, before continuing: "And actually I *didn't* want her going in and reaming him. And she would have. Him and the principal, too. And that was the last thing I needed at the time, when I was so close to getting out of there. Because after he said that, I remember thinking to myself, 'It's okay—I am getting out of this town in a few months and *never* looking back.'"

She'd said nearly the same words the first time she'd touched on the Gold moment, I recalled. A bruised silence ensued.

"He definitely had a mild case of foot-in-mouth syndrome," Nat finally said.

To which Jennifer laughed harshly. "Mild? More like raging."

"Yeah," said Anthony. "I don't think it was just a lack of a filter."

"Well—" Nat began, chastised, then looked to me.

"There *was* something perverse to it," I said. I was siding with Anthony and Jennifer over her in some subtle way, I knew, but I also found it just slightly annoying that Nat, not having been zapped by Gold like the three of us had been, seemed keen to minimize him.

"Well, okay," Nat finally averred.

Yet more silence, the firepit crackling outside the tent, moon rays sparkling on a still sea, only the very gentle lapping of water on the shore before us. Some of the evening's previous lightness and bonhomie had been lost, I sensed. But, I decided, if not now to push the agenda, when?

"So we're paying him a visit tomorrow?" I asked. "I have his address."

More silence ensued. It was hard to read everyone's faces in the half-dark.

"Are you sure it's his address?" Jennifer ventured.

"Almost certain. Sixty-seven-fifty-three Bellwood Drive, last purchased in 2003 by Gary Gold for 187,000 dollars. That was a year after he retired from Mendhem."

"How are we going to get there?" Nat asked.

"I rented a little car at the airport," Anthony said. "I figured we might want to venture off the compound."

"I suppose we could just drive by," Jennifer finally said. "See where it leads."

"But exactly what are we going to say when we see him?" asked Nat. "I mean, like I said to Tip a while back, did he do anything *that* wrong? It was the eighties. He just said some stupid things."

"Well," began Jennifer, who then paused, thinking. "I guess I would ask, 'Do you remember what you said to me that day?' And then if he didn't, which I doubt he does, I would repeat it back to him. And I would simply say, 'I just want you to know that stuck with me the rest of my life.'"

"Me too," I added. "That's what I'd say. Nothing too vicious."

"Me too, basically," said Anthony. "And I would say something on Pete's behalf as well. Mention what Pete said in his goodbye note."

Nat exhaled smoke, frowning in the gloom. "But we got stuff from him, too, right? I mean, he was a good coach."

"He was," I said. "He helped me lose my Boston accent. For that, I'll forever be grateful to him."

Jennifer, with the others, laughed. "Absolutely," she said. "And we should tell him that. But I don't think there's anything spiteful or vengeful about calmly telling him that his words had consequences. That's more like restorative justice than revenge."

Anthony tossed his second cigarette into the firepit. "What's that?"

"It's a whole school of thought," Jennifer said. "In criminal justice, it's when—okay, say a young man, a teenage boy, commits a crime of some sort, some kind of nondeadly assault. So instead of the traditional court system locking him up for *x* many years and ruining his life, he would go before a counsel of his community and his peers, and his victims, if they wanted to, would have the chance to explain to him the damage he's inflicted, and he would have a chance to respond, and then the community would come up with some kind of reparative action for him, like—" She paused. "Oh, I don't know, *x* number of hours working in the kitchen of a home for abused women. That sort of thing."

"I *love* that," said Anthony. "It's so much more humane."

"So we could think of this as a very low-key form of restorative justice for Gold," concluded Jennifer.

"We're not even going to make him go work in a kitchen," I added.

But Nat, staring into the firepit with her arms crossed over her chest, was silent. Finally, Anthony put his arm around her.

"You don't have to come if you don't want," he said. "You can just stay here and chill by the pool and we'll report back to you."

She lay her head on his shoulder, dreamy for a moment. "No," she said at length. "I want to see him. I'm not averse to what you're talking about. Just letting him know. I think it's fair. We're definitely not going to viciously attack him, right?"

"No!" insisted Jennifer. "I have no desire to do that."

Nat came back inside the cabana, sat. Since high school, I'd admired her ability to continue carrying on a coherent conversation after getting stoned. It seemed to confer a soothing buzz on her without scrambling her brain. I always descended into mental chaos, finding every stupid thing hilarious while simultaneously not being able to follow the logic of a sitcom.

"I'm game then," she said, picking up the remains of the taco on her plate.

Jennifer, Anthony, and I glanced at one another. "I guess we're doing this," Anthony said. "Drive over after breakfast?"

"What's the game plan?" I asked.

Anthony came back into the tent, refreshed his drink. "I guess we go up to the door and—ring the bell."

"Oh my God," said Nat, freshly dismayed. She dropped her head into her palm.

"And then," I continued, "assuming he comes to the door—assuming he's not out *golfing*—do we just give him a minute to . . . process us?"

"Well," said Jennifer—who, ever since she'd explained restorative justice to us, had assumed a somewhat alpha vibe on the matter—"I think we should say something kind of neutral, such as, we were all planning to take this little reunion trip down here, and then one of us kind of *stumbled* on the fact that he—Gold—lived here."

"How did we just *stumble* on it?" Nat asked.

I raised my index finger. "I know. We'll say that, um, my mother ran into, uh, Mrs. Dufresne downtown—"

"Mrs. Dufresne!" exclaimed Jennifer. "Honors English senior year!"

"Right," I continued. "And they got to talking and Mrs. Dufresne mentioned that Gold had retired several years ago and moved to Sarasota, and my mother told me, and I told all of you."

Jennifer laughed. "That's a bit tortuous, but I guess it'll do. And then I suppose he'll either be delighted to see us and invite us in, in which case we can come around to the Reckoning"—she emphasized the words, with a bit of mock drama—"in good time, or he'll put us off for one reason or another, in which case we'll have to get right to the point."

Anthony topped up his drink. "That sounds good," he said. Then he raised an index finger. "Hey. You don't think he'd ever, like, call the police on us, do you? Or go to the press? Because that would not be a good look for me—especially with this new position."

We all paused on that a moment. "I have a hard time seeing it go that way," I finally said. "Especially if we're nice about the whole thing, like we said we would be."

"Agreed," said Jennifer. "Believe me, I have no intention of doing anything that's going to summon the police. In *Florida*."

Anthony sipped. "Yeah, I guess you're both right."

Then there was a long stretch of silence except for the faraway buzz of a motorboat way out on the water.

Nat rose. "If we're doing this tomorrow," she said, "I'm going up to get a good night's sleep. And I should call Aaron and the kids before it gets too late." She turned to Anthony first, kissed and hugged him.

"Thank you for such a magical first night. This is really lovely of you to do for us."

"I'm just loving having you all here," he answered, as though the resort were his own.

Away went Nat, the soft thud of her footsteps in the sand receding.

"She doesn't seem enthusiastic," Anthony said, several seconds later, when she was likely well out of earshot.

I felt protective toward her, as always. "I think maybe because she never had a moment with Gold like we did," I said. "But we made it clear we're not going to attack him."

"How's Nat doing, Tip?" It was Jennifer asking me.

"Huh? What do you mean?"

"Is she happy? She's got a sadness around her I don't remember from high school. Like, maybe a little bit—" She paused. "Lost?"

I was torn between knowing exactly what Jennifer meant and feeling it was a little mean of her, from the perch of her tidily packaged career and family, to point it out. Was there even a touch of smug superiority to it, unleashed by the alcohol?

"She's had her struggles, like all of us, but she's okay," I said, trying to keep the defensiveness out of my voice. "She's got two great kids who I adore and her current boyfriend is a really nice guy. And she does what she loves, farming, even if it's not lucrative. I certainly wouldn't say she's *lost*." I couldn't keep some remonstrative sting out of the word. For the first time since we'd reunited, I felt a bit of the anger at her that I'd felt after the Yale weekend blow-off.

"Okay," Jennifer answered—too brightly, I thought, as though she were agreeing to indulge my sanguine portrait of Nat. She had to know that I, too, had not fared as splendidly as either her or Anthony, and suddenly I imagined a line dividing her and Anthony from Nat and me, glittering achievers on one side, dinged-up schlubs on the other.

Jennifer, after a moment, rose. "I'd better call home, too, before the kids go to bed." She kissed me, then Anthony, goodnight on our cheeks. "This really *was* a lovely first night," she said to Anthony. She cupped his chin between her thumb and index finger. "And you know you're just as drop-dead as you were in high school."

"Oh my *God*," Anthony groaned. "Predator!"

"Dramatic exit!" I cried as she sailed out of the cabana.

"Drunken exit!" she called back, her laughter fading as she walked back up the beach.

"She still wants to bone you," I said. "After all these years."

"I'm glad somebody does."

"Please. I'm sure you get plenty in New York. Or *Milan*."

He said nothing, just knocked back the rest of his drink. Then: "I suppose you have to go up and call the hubby, too."

"I do. In a minute."

Then, wobblingly, he rose and, to my great surprise, pulled off his white linen tunic thing, then pulled down his shorts, to reveal his expensively toned and hairy but manicured body in a white Speedo. "So come swim with me first."

I hooted. "What? I didn't wear a bathing suit like you."

"So swim in your underwear. There are towels here. Or swim naked. It's dark; no one can see."

So I rose—woozy with drink, as well, I realized, as I pulled off my shirt, then shorts, right down to my boxer briefs.

He appraised me, head to toe. "You look okay," he said.

"Wow, thanks. So emphatic."

He smacked me lightly on the butt. "Come on!" Then he ran down to the water and into it for a few broad strides before he arced forward and dove in headlong, a lean shadow cutting into the shimmering surface of the sea.

"Ah!" he exclaimed when he surfaced. "Come in, it's *sooo* warm."

So I ran and dove until I, too, surfaced alongside him. "Oh my God!" I exclaimed. "It *is* so warm. That's heaven."

"It's warmer than Tulum," he said, floating on his back.

I didn't know where Tulum was, but I didn't ask, floating on my back alongside him, marveling at the vast emptiness around us, the silence save the tiny splashes of the water on the shore and the faint, faint sound of the cool jazz piped in around the pool up at the resort. Above us were bold stars I never noticed in Providence, a gaudy cut-out moon.

"It's really nice you've done this for us, Anthony," I said.

"I'm happier than I've been in a while," he answered. Then I felt his fingers grasp my outstretched hand, and I grasped it back, and in a moment we were standing in the water, chest-deep, kissing. I felt twenty-one again.

EIGHT

The teachers of Mendhem High were a pasty, unglamorous lot, the men former Mendhem sports heroes, a gaggle of Gallaghers, Callahans, and O'Briens who'd ventured not farther away than Fitchburg or Salem State before coming home to teach math or social studies. One or two of them were of a leftward bent, incorporating *A People's History of the United States* into their senior AP classes, but overall, their passion resided in coaching the teams on which they'd once been stars. The women were marginally more sophisticated, true lovers of Hawthorne or O'Neill or French lit when they were sixties coeds at Wheaton or Simmons or Emmanuel, then went on to get their teaching certification at Lowell State—women who went to see theater or the symphony in Boston or even New York on holiday breaks, who stuck to a lean budget the whole academic year in order to spend two weeks per summer in the European capitals, who frequently sent their own children to private or parochial schools, in a sort of implicit rebuke of the worthiness of the very system that employed them.

They were all from Mendhem or the immediate area, all spoke through their nose, all wore a tweed blazer over a cable-knit sweater and a plaid wool skirt, all married tax lawyers or accountants or, in a few tittered-over instances, lived quietly with a female "roommate."

They all shoveled their own compacts out of the snow on the mornings they lacked the good fortune for school to be called off that day. They all believed in the value of intellectual pursuit and the life of the mind, even if they didn't exactly burn and glow with passion.

Gold, as I've suggested before, was a square peg in a round hole in that school, and not only because he was—to our knowledge—the only Jewish teacher. He was among the few who hadn't lived his whole life in town or the immediate area, having grown up, if I remember correctly, in New Jersey, then having come to Boston for college—Brandeis or Tufts, I think. He lived not in town but on the nearby coast, in Newburyport, a town that has since been impeccably restored and gentrified but in the eighties was still a slightly exotic hybrid of shabby and artsy, fraying sea captains' mansions and an abundance of taverns, diners, and dusty curiosity shops, alcoholics and heroin addicts roaming about freely. To our knowledge, he did not have kids or even a wife or steady girlfriend, though on a few Speech Team bus trips, he brought along a mousy young woman with lank hair and large Hillary Rodham–style glasses who appeared half his age, but in retrospect was more likely a thirty to his forty.

But it was the figure he cut, more than anything else, at once dorky and attractive, that set him apart. Not quite fully short but certainly not tall; that goofy crown of tight dark curls that grayed a bit with each passing year; the oversize square-frame glasses, the pilly sweaters and tweed jackets, the plaid shirts with the pearly buttons, the knit, blunt-ended ties, the corduroy pants that flapped around his ankles, the suede earth shoes that were probably the ugliest footwear I'd ever seen. I think he fancied himself professorial or bohemian, but in fact he was just goofy, *nebbishy* as Nat would say, his hands slightly flapping at his sides as he walked—waddled, even?—down the hall, in tandem with his flapping pant-ends. I guess Wallace Shawn comes to mind, although there was the matter of Gold's actual face, which was—despite all the surrounding dorkiness—undeniably handsome, square-jawed and dark-eyed. But then there was his voice—that faint *Joysey* accent, somewhat wheedling and grating.

Gold was just odd. I don't know how else to describe him. I remember distinctly his telling us that only three things in life could bring him to rapture: Maria Callas, the band Mott the Hoople, and a good Reuben. *Bring him to rapture* were exactly the words that he used. Why he felt compelled to tell us this, I don't know. Like I said, he was odd.

I was thinking about all this the following morning, showering and then fixing the kind of coffee you fix in hotel rooms, those individually wrapped pods you slip into a small plastic coffeemaker. I was moderately hungover. After the moment with Anthony in the water, which filled me with a kind of giddy victory—or perhaps vindication—we'd toweled off, mostly silently, come back up to the resort. I went up to my room and, too afraid Marcus would hear a drunken slur in my voice if I called, texted him goodnight, claiming that I was on the brink of falling asleep and would call him in the morning. Maybe, too, I was afraid he'd hear adulterous guilt in my voice; sure, we had our don't-ask-don't-tell policy, especially when we were in different cities, and Anthony and I in fact hadn't done much more than make out in the water, then the cabana, for a few minutes before we stumbled together back up to the hotel and parted ways for the night. But was horsing around of a graver order of, say, *emotional* infidelity if it felt like picking up on unfinished business from the past? If, while engaged in it, you'd allowed yourself to fantasize about what might have been—what could maybe still be?

I'd woken to Marcus's terse text reply—***Thanks for finally checking in. Goodnight. Hope you're having fun.***—and when I did sit down with my coffee and call him, it went to voicemail.

Anthony, Nat, and Jennifer had already been out at breakfast by the pool for a good half hour, I learned upon arriving down there, and

Anthony, I further learned, had worked out in the resort gym even prior to that.

"I just make myself do it," he said matter-of-factly, reaching for the fruit salad, "regardless of my indulgences the night before." He'd returned to his baseline cool—no wink or grin or conspiratorial glance my way commemorating our nightcap swim.

"That's impressively disciplined of you," I said, sitting down next to Nat and putting my arm around her. It was another picture-perfect Gulf Coast day, but I found that, amid my cotton-headedness, the sun felt more like an assault than a balm. I was glad I'd brought down my sunglasses. Jennifer wore them, too, I noticed, and I gestured between mine and hers to note the commonality.

"I'm right there with you," she remarked drily. "I was never a heavy drinker, but ever since I turned forty, I pay the price if I have more than two."

"That's why I'm a grass girl," said Nat. She seemed the chipperest of the four of us, looking cute in a striped T-shirt and jean shorts rolled just above the knee.

"That's why you were scarfing down those lobster tacos last night," I said. "Miss Munchie."

"It's true, they were *so good*."

They sipped coffee while I partook of the fare they'd already attacked, family-style plates of scrambled eggs and lox, bagels and croissants, fruit salad, crispy bacon.

Nat addressed Jennifer: "Did you call home last night?"

"I did. I tucked the kids in over the phone and all seemed well. And Andres texted me this morning that Raffy slept well through the night. Which was a relief on my conscience. And you?"

Nat nodded. "Otis told me all about his earth science presentation. Igneous, sedimentary, and metamorphic. Remember that?"

Anthony groaned. "Not fondly."

Jennifer laughed. "They *really* did not know how to make science interesting in our day, did they?"

"Remember having to memorize how to diagram all the molecules?" I asked. "I hated that more than algebra."

When two of the khaki-clad servers came around to clear the table, Anthony clapped his hands together. "Are we ready for the Solid Gold hour?"

Nat's mouth opened in surprise. "You wanna go right now?"

"Why not? We're all showered and ready, right?"

Jennifer considered, then shrugged. "We may as well just rip off the Band-Aid."

But Nat just sat there a moment, that half-surprised look still on her face.

I put my hand on her back. "You really don't have to come," I said. "Just stay here and relax. How long could it take anyway? We'll probably be back for lunch and we'll tell you all about it."

But she slammed her palm lightly, resolutely on the table. "No. I'm coming. Let's go."

We all leaned in toward her. "You're absolutely sure?" asked Anthony.

"Absolutely."

A few minutes later, as Nat, Jennifer, and I waited under the porte cochere, Anthony pulled up in a black Escalade SUV. The three of us erupted in laughter.

"Anthony!" Jennifer cried, climbing into the front seat while Nat and I climbed into the back, instantly intoxicated by the scent of newness. "You are *insane*! A Toyota Camry would've sufficed."

"Don't insult me," said Anthony flatly, pulling away from the resort.

Shortly, we were on the Ringling Bridge connecting Longboat Key to the Sarasota mainland—an endless, bland strip of blue sky, water on either side, and palm trees. Jennifer touched up her makeup in the mirror behind her sun visor, while Nat and I held hands in the back—Nat turned slightly away from me, staring out the window.

I could feel her hand shaking now in mine, so I squeezed it. "Listen," I told her. "We are unequivocally not going to be mean."

By this point, we were on the mainland, Anthony turning our small yacht of a vehicle off a shopping strip into what seemed a network of residential streets, an infinite landscape of fairly modest white- or sand-colored single-level ranch homes, landscaping tidy if not lush.

Jennifer pointed at the GPS mounted to the dashboard. "We are now a mere nine hundred feet away from destiny."

Anthony slowed to a crawl. "This should be it up here on the left," he said. "Sixty-seven fifty-nine, fifty-seven, fifty-five, and here we go."

We were crawling up on the opposite side of the street upon a butter-yellow ranch house, fairly indistinguishable from the rest, a well-tended lawn. First I saw the mailbox.

"Gold!" I exclaimed, reading the name stenciled on the box.

And then we saw him. Gold, 1987 with the addition of twenty-five years, sitting on the front steps with the newspaper in his hands, a red coffee mug by his side. That same tight crown of curls now entirely snowy white, peeking out from under a Red Sox cap. The body still slim but smaller-looking, slightly hunched, in a polo shirt, shorts, and flip-flops.

"Oh my God, it's him," Anthony said, hushed.

But Gold had barely had a moment to look up from his newspaper at us before Nat cried out, "Keep driving!"

We all twisted around toward her. "What?" Anthony asked.

Now she was crying, her hands to her face. "Keep driving, please!"

"Anthony, drive on," said Jennifer sternly.

"But—"

"Just drive *on*, Anthony."

"Okay!"

Which he did, down the street, then a left, then a right, all of us silent while Nat cried and I rubbed her back, until we were back on the main commercial road and he pulled into the parking lot of a Denny's.

Jennifer, Anthony, and I glanced at one another warily while Nat continued to cry, then to take deep gulping breaths, her face in her hands. A vague idea I'd had last night, a germ of an idea I'd forgotten this morning, seemed to become clear to me now—and perhaps, based on the looks I exchanged with Anthony and Jennifer, to them as well.

I continued to rub Nat's back. "What is it, honey?" I finally ventured.

She raised her head, sighed, wiped her face with her palms. She even smiled, ruefully and sardonically. "Guess what?" she said, taking my hand. "I haven't told you guys everything."

"I got that feeling," Anthony said.

"We had a thing," she said. "A romantic sexual thing."

It was what I had nearly expected to hear, and yet it was still shocking, and somewhat sickening. Wild rage toward Gold coursed through me. I was right—he *had* been a creep that way. I'd always sensed it.

"When?" I asked.

"It started senior year," she said. "*My* senior year. When you'd all moved on. The year Speech Team was just me and a few freshmen and sophomores."

Again, Anthony, Jennifer, and I glanced at one another, wondering how to proceed. It was surreal to think that the man she was talking about was now a quarter mile away, rather old, sitting out on his modest stoop in the sun.

"He'd do things, like he'd put his hand on my head and it would stay there, and then I'd feel the caress."

"I *told* you I remembered things like that," I said.

"Or he'd interrupt me when I was practicing and tell me I was beautiful. 'You look beautiful in that pool of sunlight right there' is what he said exactly."

"Oh, *no*!" exclaimed Jennifer. Which almost made me wince, because I think I sensed where Nat was going.

"And then one night when we were coming back from a tournament, when the kids were falling asleep in the back of the bus and I was sitting right behind him up front, he turned around and asked me quietly if I wanted to drive out to his place at the beach the next day. A Sunday. It was spring and he said it would be so beautiful out there."

"Did you report him?" Jennifer demanded. "Did you tell your mom?"

But Nat said what I thought she'd say: "No. I went. I wanted to." And she started crying again—softly this time, not convulsively. I rubbed her back. "I was actually totally in love with him by that point. Or infatuated, I guess."

"Oh my goodness," said Jennifer quietly. "Nat, I'm sorry. I didn't mean to—"

"No, of course not!" Nat interjected. "I mean, I get it. I know what he did was wrong. I figured that out a long time ago. But I *did* end up going to his place all summer. I had a job at that ice cream place in Newbury and I'd drive there after work and tell my mom I was staying at a friend's. And then I went to college in the fall and wrote him probably a letter a week, no replies, and then one day he wrote back and said that he was already in a relationship—*already*, he wrote—and would I mind not writing him anymore? He didn't allude at all to what had happened between us, and he wrote it in this sort of formal tone, like he was politely but firmly asking me to stop stalking him."

"Of course he did," Jennifer cut in sharply. "He was making it sound like the advances had only ever come from you. Covering his ass, so you could never use the letter as evidence."

Nat shrugged weakly. "Yeah, probably. But then he writes, *You know how special I think you are and what an incredible woman you're going to grow up to be.* And, quote, *It was an honor being your coach.* That's exactly what he wrote. And that was the last I ever heard from him. And I never reached out to him again after that. I wasn't going to be some *Fatal Attraction* girl."

"That's just what he wanted," Anthony said. "For you to go away completely."

Again, Nat shrugged. "And I never told anyone except for Jack—that was my first relationship after college, Olivia's father. Which I regretted, because then Jack constantly told me that being with Gold had fucked up my ability to make any future relationship work, because the power dynamic had been so unbalanced."

"Ouch!" cried Jennifer. "That's mean. And that's certainly not true."

Nat looked at her wistfully. "I think there might be some truth there."

I tightened my grip on her hand. "I don't think that's true either," I said.

"But he made me laugh so much and he made the *best* pancakes," exclaimed Nat, laughing.

"Wait," interjected Anthony. "Who are we talking about now? Jack?"

"No. Gold."

"And we know what pancakes do to you," I added. "They're your kryptonite."

Nat laughed at this, allowingly. "It's true. I will *always* remember sitting out on his deck with him, wearing his flannel bathrobe, eating his perfect pancakes, and looking out at the marsh while he played the Byrds."

This had such a Proustian finality to it, so clearly was a moment in time her memory had polished to a sheen, that for several seconds none of us said anything, unsure how to proceed.

"Well," Anthony said finally, "I'm not judging you. Him, yes. You, no. I had something with a forty-eight-year-old guy when I was a freshman at NYU."

Oh really, you did? I thought. *Curiouser and curiouser!*

"I thought it was all equal," he continued, "and very grown-up of me and just fine because it was totally hot and thrilling for me, but of course after about six months, he dumped me. Pretty much told me what Gold told you. And it's only been the past few years that I've realized how wrong and fucked up of him it was to play with a kid like that in the first place."

Jennifer inadvertently *tsk*'d, as though to acknowledge a distinction between the two stories, I surmised. But instead, her hand still on Nat's knee, she said, "Well, my dear, that's it. We're not going back. Who would like to go see the Ringling Museum?"

But Nat put a hand atop Jennifer's and cried, "No! I want to go back. I'm ready. I just needed to get that out of my system."

Again, a round of wary glances among Anthony, Jennifer, and me. "Honey, are you sure?" I asked. "We don't want you to get all upset again."

She dabbed away the last remnants of tears around her eyes. "I won't," she said. "But at least now you know that my relationship with him wasn't—neutral, like you all thought. I've never forgotten him either."

Anthony, Jennifer, and I glanced at one another. "Are you going to bring it up?" I asked. "What you just told us?"

Jennifer answered before Nat could: "She has the right if she wants to."

Anthony, pondering this, shook his head, blew out air. "Karma's a bitch," he said. "I wonder if Wifey's home."

But Nat just shook her head. "I don't know yet. I'll decide in the moment. But I'm resolved to see him."

"If his wife *is* there, just his fear that you may say something," said Jennifer, addressing Nat, "may be justice enough." Then she lightly bit her lower lip. "Now *I'm* suddenly the one with cold feet," she said. "Just seeing him sitting there like that. An old man in his little cap."

"He's not that old," I said coldly, earning a startled glance from Jennifer. Suddenly, the thought of not following through induced panic in me. I was only minutes away from redressing a mortification lodged within me for twenty-five years. I would *not* be denied this, I decided. Even if I had to approach him alone while the other three stayed in the car. I would not get that close to courage, to justice, to closing the aching gap of years, and just walk away.

Anthony sighed, paused. "Look," he said, "we decided we were coming in a spirit of . . . friendliness. Even gratitude. For the joys of Speech Team. So let's just start on that note."

We were all quiet for a moment, distracted as we watched a very elderly couple emerge from their car and walk with infinite slowness and fragility, arm in arm as though they were propping each other up, in baby steps toward the Denny's entrance. Their legs, exposed in shorts, were stick-like, blue veins prominent beneath papery white skin, their knees and ankles knobby.

"Toddling their way toward their Grand Slam Breakfast," drawled Anthony.

Jennifer slapped him lightly on the arm. "That's us in a few years."

A moment after they'd disappeared inside, Nat, her voice flat with resolve, said, "Let's go see Gold."

In the back seat, she and I continued holding hands as Anthony steered back into the network of ranch homes, then crawled back up to Gold's house. There he was, still on his front steps, staring into space with the newspaper cast off by his side. Had a tremor of what was to come touched him? Had he been sitting there ever since, the words of long-ago years coursing through his more tender old man's conscience, the horror of forgotten cruelties resurfacing? Was he wondering how to respond—with grace? With anger? Disingenuous forgetfulness? By darting back inside, locking the door behind him, and plugging fingers in his ears against the doorbell?

I saw him squint beneath the brim of his cap once we stopped.

Anthony silenced the engine, pulled the key from the ignition. "You guys ready?" he asked.

Nat's hand was again trembling in mine, but she raised her chin and said, "Let's go."

We took the liberty of walking together diagonally across his neatly trimmed front lawn, forgoing the narrowly paved walkway, until we stood about six feet from him. Through the screen door, I saw the silhouette of a woman pass through the kitchen and out a back door. But mostly I could not take my eyes off Gold. I'd thought I might be overcome with anger upon finally seeing him.

But oddly, I wasn't. Instead, I was thrilled—almost moved to tears. He lived! Again, as with the night before in the cabana tent, that sense of decades collapsing away in a moment, that your own mind and heart hadn't gathered weight and slowed, that you could almost taste your youth again, that sweet, impulsive stupidity, the lightness of thinking you knew everything while not yet realizing you hardly knew anything at all.

Since my father had died three years before, I'd often wondered what it would be like to walk into my mother's house and, without shock or ceremony, merely find him there again, in a V-neck lambswool sweater, scanning the *Boston Globe* through his readers, or with his beloved Manhattan and a plate of crackers and cheese in front of the Patriots game. We'd had nothing in common, seldom said anything meaningful to each other, did not even share the simple pleasure of watching a football game together, because I'd hated contact sports my entire life. And yet I longed for the laconic assurance of his presence again, our own companionable disinterest in each other, the certainty that he would care for and protect me, even if he did so unceremoniously, never putting words to his actions. Staring at Gold, I felt an approximation of what I imagined that father-reunion moment would be like; his past missteps, even my own, didn't matter, because here he was again, alive, and more conversation was possible.

Gold stared at the four of us blankly, then smiled courteously. "Hello, there," he said. It was the same voice, that faint *Joysey* twang underneath the middlebrow teacher's cultivation. "What can I do for you?"

"Mr. Gold," began Anthony, his voice pitched higher than usual. "We're your former students from Mendhem High in Massachusetts. We were all on Speech Team. Anthony Malouf," he said, pointing at himself, then each of us in turn, "Natalie Farb-Miola, Jennifer Douglas, and Tip—Thomas—Murray. Remember, from the eighties?"

"We were all having a reunion in Sarasota," Jennifer broke in, "and thought we'd visit, because we got your address from Mrs. Dufresne."

His brows were still knitted, and we were waiting for that moment of recognition to burst onto his face. But instead he just nodded slightly, as though he were politely registering what we had to say.

"All right, then," he finally said with that same vacant affability. "Well, all right. That's terrific."

"So you remember us?" It was Nat, whose shoulders still trembled slightly under my arm. There was a faint, froggy waver in her voice, and a note of desperation.

"All right, then," he said again—a bit more emphatically, like someone politely trying to wrap up a proceeding. "Wonderful. Very good." And then, as though to signal that we should leave, he picked up his newspaper and made some show out of shaking it out, in order to resume reading.

The four of us glanced at one another, none of us bold enough to say, in front of him, what was becoming increasingly clear. He then gripped the railing of his front steps, as though he were bracing himself to rise. And it was then, seeing him in that moment of physical frailty and mental vacancy, that my tenderness turned, on a dime, to a taste for cruelty.

"Do you remember what you taught?" I asked him, with a certain hard bluntness.

"Tip!" shushed Jennifer.

"Do I remember what I taught?" parroted Gold, sounding offended.

"Yes," I said. "Do you remember the names of the other English teachers?"

"Of course I do!" But that was followed by nothing but a perturbed look.

Anthony turned to us, mouth curled down. "I think our mission has been botched," he said quietly. I glanced at Nat, whose eyes were glassy with unfallen tears.

And then a woman's voice called from inside the house: "Gary?" She was at the screen door presently, a birdlike woman, small, tanned, ash-blond hair brushed back unfussily, probably about sixty, in a short-sleeve coral blouse and tan shorts. It was Janet, the woman from the photo we'd found, nearly a decade later.

She stepped out onto the top step, caressed Gold's shoulder lightly with her right hand, as though to soothe him. "Can we help you?" she asked. She had the faintest southern drawl.

Anthony, politely, reiterated who we were. At which point the wariness in her face melted and she smiled.

"Oh, how lovely!" she exclaimed. "That's very sweet of you to come visit." Then she knelt down by Gold's side, put an arm around him as one would a child. "Sweetheart, these are your old students. From Mendhem."

He smiled now, sparked with more recognition, but it seemed to be of her, not us. "Isn't that wonderful?" he asked. "That's just top-rate."

"Yes, it's very nice," she said. "They came to tell you what a wonderful teacher you were." She looked up at us. "Isn't that right?"

"Of course!" said Anthony. "And what a wonderful Speech Team coach."

Janet's hand rose to her mouth. "Oh, my goodness. Did you hear that, Gary? They were on your Speech Team. Oh, that's marvelous."

Gold nodded along with her. "Absolutely marvelous," he said.

At this point, angling herself slightly behind him so that he couldn't see her face, she looked at the four of us—pointedly, regretfully, the frown and the shake of the head. *I'm so sorry,* she mouthed at us, then lightly tapped her own temple.

Now the four of us looked at one another, at a complete loss. I could barely understand the rage I was feeling. If we'd arrived to find out he'd flat-out died, I'd have been less furious, felt less foolish for my efforts. My heart was pounding, my palms clammy.

Jennifer spoke: "Well, alright then, Mr. Gold, it was wonderful to see you after all these years, and we wish you the very best." She stepped forward and offered her hand. Suspiciously, he took it, shook it lightly. Then we all did the same.

"It's so nice to meet you," Jennifer said to Janet.

"And I'm Janet," she said. "Thank you so much for coming." Then, to Gold, "Gary, let me walk our friends over to their car."

Once the five of us had got there, Janet, her back to Gold, said in a low voice, "Kids, I'm so sorry. He has early-onset Alzheimer's. It started about eighteen months ago. And he's okay with me and our daily life, but everything else—" She shook her head. "He doesn't recognize his own sister and nieces anymore. They were just here last week."

Jennifer and Anthony murmured their apologies, but Nat and I were silent.

"It is so sweet," she continued, "that the four of you came to see him. I can't tell you how tickled that would've made him if it had happened only a few years ago."

"We're so sorry," said Jennifer. "If we had known, we wouldn't have come, honestly."

Janet put a hand atop her arm. "No, it's wonderful that you came!" She paused, an idea coming to her. "In fact, would you mind waiting just a moment while I get my phone and then I can take a picture of the four of you with Gary? His sister and nieces would love to see that."

The four of us looked at one another again. I was about to decline, to savor the coldness of it, when Anthony said, "Of course not."

We stood by the car while she hurried back inside, Gold occasionally glancing our way uneasily as he pretended to refocus on his paper.

"Well, this is sad," Jennifer said. "And hardly the outcome I'd have guessed."

"This is a fucking sham," I said.

They all looked at me. "Tip!" cried Jennifer. "The man has Alzheimer's."

"How do we even know that for sure?"

The three of them regarded me, puzzled. "Just take a deep breath," Anthony instructed me.

In a moment, Janet reemerged on the front steps, phone in hand, waved us over. We trudged across the lawn again.

"Gary," announced Janet, "I'm just going to get a picture of you with your former students so we can send it to Susan and the kids, okay?"

Gold fairly slapped down his paper, frowning, and shook his head, in a manner I found so funny, as though he were a cranky sitcom grandpa, that I released a short, sharp laugh. Jennifer shot me a dismayed look.

Then Janet to us: "Why don't you kids gather around Gary and sort of scrunch down and put an arm around him?"

Which we did, awkwardly, Jennifer's hand on his right shoulder, Nat and Anthony just behind us, my hand on his left shoulder. After twenty-five years of hearing his words in my ears, here I was, touching him, the container if not the substance of the man. I was torn between rage and loss, not sure if I wanted to shove him or lay my head alongside my hand on his shoulder.

"Alright, then," Gold grumbled. "Let's leave well enough alone."

"Gary, smile!" chided Janet, half squatting with her camera six feet in front of us. "Wonderful. Why don't one of you give me your number and I'll text it to you?"

Anthony did so.

"There we go," Janet said. "I love how easy everything is these days." Then she turned back to Gold, sat by him and put an arm around him. "Sweetheart," she instructed, "let's say goodbye to your old kids. Students, I mean."

"Goodbye, Mr. Gold!" called Jennifer, Nat, and Anthony. Yet by this point I was trembling.

He gave us that same forbearing nod, raised a palm to us. "Alright then," he said again. "Very good. Off you go."

Janet walked us to the car again. "I can't tell you all how kind it was you came by," she said.

"When did you both meet?" It was Nat, to whom Janet, then the rest of us, turned. I thought she looked a bit defiant. "Were you and Mr. Gold together when he was teaching?"

"No, dear. We met at a conference in North Carolina when we were both still teaching—I was a junior-high school teacher in Virginia—and after about a year of seeing each other, we made a plan we'd retire down here, because we were both planning to retire at the end of the same school year, in 2002. The school year of 9/11."

We all nodded, and then she smiled, with a sob breaking through. "And I am just so sorry you missed his recognizing you by about only a year. It's been—it's been the hardest thing, as you can imagine. The past eighteen months or so. I'm sure I can't go on caring for him alone like this forever. I've been talking about that with his sister, about what to do." She was dabbing her eyes with the back of her index finger now.

"I am so very sorry," said Jennifer. "It must be extremely hard on you."

She cry-laughed again. "I certainly didn't intend on losing him this early!"

Then I suddenly heard myself talking, barreling through the politeness: "We had actually meant to discuss something with him."

Anthony, Jennifer, and Nat turned to me, shocked. "Tip!" from all three of them—Anthony in a warning bark, Jennifer in a small scolding hiss, Nat in a note of alarm.

Janet now regarded me, a new, faintly colder glint—what I hoped was apprehension—in her eyes. "Oh, really? What's that?"

I met her gaze squarely. "We were just curious if he remembered certain things about Speech Team."

Janet frowned, shook her head. "Anything that he remembers comes out in a jumble that makes no sense."

It was a mercy cue, but I wouldn't be cowed. "I don't suppose he ever told you some of the things he said to us. When we were too young and isolated to defend ourselves."

"Tip!" hissed Jennifer again, sharper and louder. "Enough!"

"No, it's *not* enough," I snapped back; Jennifer blinked, almost winced, in shock. Then I plowed ahead on a rush of vengeful adrenaline I'd not seen coming that morning. It was the same feeling I'd had, in fact, when I walked out of the fishbowl after he'd said what he said so many years ago—my heart pounding, my palms moist, everything in front of me blurry and vertiginous.

"He actually said really awful things to all of us when we were alone with him," I continued. "Really inappropriate things that he'd probably be fired for today. About our ethnicity and our race and our sexuality." I stopped briefly, glanced at Nat.

"*No*," she mouthed at me, looking terrified. It was just enough to stop me short from taking the enormous liberty of divulging her secret as well.

"So we wanted to ask him," I continued, "if he remembered, and why he said what he said to a bunch of teenagers, and if he knew that every single one of us has never forgotten what he said. And one of us even killed himself recently and he even included what Mr. Gold said to him in his final note. His suicide note. Mr. Gold had apparently said something about his being autistic, probably autistic, and Pete—that was his name, Pete Stroman—never forgot it."

The color had drained from Janet's face. She just stood there for several seconds, her mouth half-open, absorbing my words. Then she crossed her arms over her chest and her face hardened, a warning glint in her eyes—an entirely new Janet.

"And that is the reason you four showed up at our house today? To ambush him?"

"We certainly weren't planning an ambush," Jennifer said. "We thought we might just talk about it with him—if he were open to it."

"Well," rose Janet's voice, raspier now, as her eyes glassed with tears. "You can certainly see now he's in no state to have that conversation with you. I'm very sorry."

Three words were on the tip of my tongue. I held them there, aware of their power, before I unleashed them, with all the fury of my beat-up, pent-up sixteen-year-old self, only words to fight back with: "Karma's a bitch."

Janet's eyes widened in horror. "Tip!" cried Anthony, Jennifer, and Nat in chorus. Then, just from Jennifer, in a deadly low register: "Tip—*enough*."

Janet, crying freely now, pointed back at Gold, who watched the whole thing vacantly from the steps. The next-door neighbor had stepped out, I noticed, was watching the proceedings keenly from their own front steps.

"You don't know the first thing about that man's life or why he was the way he was," Janet said, her voice shaking. "The first thing about what life was like for *him*, with the parents he had and the situation they were in. But you were just going to come here in his retirement and *torture* him."

"We certainly weren't going to torture him," said Anthony.

But Janet took no heed. "Well, I hope you all know who you actually ended up upsetting today. Because"—and she pointed back again—"*he* doesn't even know who you are."

Now the neighbor raised a hand. "Janet," she called. "Is everything okay?"

Janet, shaken, ignored her. "Please go," she said to us instead. And when, in the first moment, the four of just stood there, frozen, she said, louder and more forcefully, "Please just get off the grass and *go*."

Then she stalked back up the walkway, arms crossed. "Mrs.—" called out Jennifer, who then stopped, realizing she didn't know Janet's surname. Then: "We're so sorry."

Janet didn't reply, just waved off the neighbor, as though to signal that whatever had transpired had come to an end, then sat down beside Gold (who continued to stare at us blankly), put her arm around him and then her head on his shoulder, her eyes closed, as though she intended not to open them until we'd driven off.

"Come on," said Anthony to us, extracting the car key from his pocket. "Let's go." And we all filed back into the car, Nat and I in the back again.

"Where to?" Anthony asked.

"Let's just go back to the hotel," Jennifer answered curtly, after an excruciating pause.

We drove on in brooding silence broken only by the robotic voice of the woman narrating the GPS instructions. I felt what I likely could have predicted I'd feel even before I'd opened my mouth: not better, not catharsis, but worse, hateful and hated—flooded with regret over the entire trip, a feeling that I'd just sledgehammered whatever old bond we'd reestablished the night before.

Then Nat, turning to me in the back seat, broke the silence, her voice quiet but indignant: "I can't believe you said what you said to her. After the way we saw him."

Before I could even reply, Anthony joined in: "I can't either, Tip. Wasn't it clear that once we knew what was going on, we were supposed to drop it? You ended up dumping it on her, not him."

"It's why we went!" I protested. "It's why we're here in the first place."

"But you knew you weren't going to get contrition out of him." It was Jennifer now, staring straight ahead in the passenger seat, her voice heavy with what sounded like contempt. "Or some kind of meaningful recognition. So why bring it up?"

"Why *not* bring it up?" I wanted to double down on my chastisers, a familiar feeling from childhood, that petulant refusal to admit wrong.

"All you did was tell Janet something about him she probably already knew," said Anthony.

"And I'm glad I did!"

"Are you?" Jennifer shot back. "Do you really feel better?"

So they'd decided they'd come down on me tag-team style, Jennifer and Anthony. That didn't surprise me. They suddenly seemed like bookends of smug success. It was Nat's more sullen rebuke that stung me the most.

"I do feel better," I said—a lie, because I would not let Jennifer have the upper hand. Then, because I felt so lousy I could only dig a deeper hole for myself: "I wouldn't expect either of you"—by which I clearly meant the two of them, up front—"to understand what it feels like to be completely stuck in place and going nowhere."

Jennifer finally turned around, looked at me with withering disdain. "Oh, *poor* Tip!" she crowed. "Poor Tip Murray with all his disadvantages and barriers."

"You weren't thrown in a trunk and dumped out on the edge of town in the middle of winter—were you, Jennifer?" I was nearly yelling now. "You might've been different and that might have been uncomfortable, but you weren't tortured for it. Were you? Be honest. Oh, and don't think I don't remember that weekend at Yale when you blew me off, either."

Now her jaw dropped. "*What?*"

"*What?*" I mimicked. "You don't remember blowing me off because you were too embarrassed by me in front of your cool new friends? Well, I do."

Before she could answer, Anthony, in what sounded like an attempt at a conciliatory register, broke in: "Tip, *I* was tortured, too, okay? I got stuffed and locked in my own locker once and I had to scream and bang until a janitor came along."

"You did not!" I'd never heard such stories from him.

"Yes, I *was*."

"Then why didn't you *tell* me?" It now seemed like the cruelest betrayal, that he'd have let me suffer in isolation, let me think that I was the only proto-faggot in that school who took the hits for the rest of us.

"Because I was embarrassed, okay? I just wanted to get through it and get out of there—like all of us. And we all have. So now I think we should put Operation Gold behind us and just try to enjoy the rest of this trip."

"I honestly don't know if I can do that at this point," said Jennifer, who'd turned back around.

I looked at Nat. She regarded me regretfully, lips pursed, then turned away, staring out the window, her chin cupped in her hand. That quiet gesture was the last blow for me; I slunk down in my seat, my arms crossed, staring sullenly out my window, suddenly feeling like a complete child.

By that point we were back on the long, dull main road of Longboat Key, the same stretch of palm trees and white homes, but in reverse. We fell into a silence that lasted after we parked in the lot under the resort. Once the elevator brought us back up into the lobby, we dispersed. There was no talk; it just sort of happened. Jennifer and Nat stayed on the elevator, presumably en route to their rooms; Anthony strode to a lobby couch, sat, and pulled out his phone in a businesslike manner, presumably to look at work messages.

At a total loss, I wandered out past the pool, down the boardwalk, then onto the beach, where I took off my sneakers and sat, my arms around my knees, looking out at the sun glittering on the water. Shame and regret bore down on me, unbearably. I'd spoiled everything, taking the situation into my own hands because it had felt good in the moment. How on earth did I ever think I deserved the success of an Anthony or a Jennifer? Whatever they'd been through, they were adults, had learned to subordinate their anger to their needs and goals, to keep their eyes on the prize. Even Nat, whom Gold had perhaps trifled with the most, had had the grace to not take it out on Janet. What a fool I'd been the night before for considering myself an adult among adults.

I stood up, walked back up to the bar beside the pool, and asked the bartender, a handsome young man in that same khaki safari uniform, for a shot of tequila. I stood there and knocked it back, relieved by the instant fire in my throat and—finally, because I was alone—the lack of need to sip carefully, pace myself, project the impression of indifference to the drink. I ordered another, warmth coursing through my mind and body, diffusing the shame, then ordered another. When I demanded my fourth and the bartender asked if I wanted to slow down, I laughed and brayed back, "No!" He paused, then poured. I drank it, then another in quick succession, turned, and wove my way through a terrace of tables, chairs, and potted palms, toward the ocean.

"Hey!" called the bartender, but I didn't bother looking back. The water looked amazing, dazzling and irresistible with sun on its surface, and as long as our plan had failed and everyone now hated me, I was at least going to swim.

NINE

The banging was coming from somewhere, muffled and murky, as though I were leagues under the sea and it was originating above the water level, reverberating around my ears below. And the next sensation was of an unpleasant hardness beneath me, and then my eyes opened and, with a sick rush of pain and dizziness behind my eyes, I realized that I was facedown on the concrete floor of my balcony, the sun much lower over the water than I remembered it.

I had no idea how I'd arrived there, could only remember standing at the bar, knocking back tequilas. Oh yes, then a very dim memory of walking toward the ocean and deciding to swim. But that's where my recollection stopped.

On the balcony floor, my phone lay beside me. I picked it up. There was a text from Marcus: ***Call me back please so we can finish talking. I'm worried about you.***

Finish talking? I propped myself up, my head pounding and everything around me spinning, to find that, indeed, Marcus and I had talked at 12:47 p.m. for all of forty-six seconds. I had no recollection of that. And then came that sinking feeling, mortification, as I realized I'd done it again. Blacked out.

Then the knocking again, which I now realized was someone

knocking on my room door. I lay back down again on the concrete floor, curled up fetally, hoping it was merely the cleaning lady, that she'd go away. But then came: "Tip? Are you in there?"

And then almost simultaneously a buzz and a new text on my phone, from Nat: ***I'm knocking on your hotel door. Where are you?***

"Nat, hang on a sec!" I called, but weakly.

"Oh my God, thank God," she called back. "Are you okay?"

"Hang *on.*" I hadn't meant it to sound so nasty, but I knew it did.

I managed to sit up, put my head in my hands, massaged my forehead. The room was still spinning and I felt nauseous. Still clutching my scalp with one hand, I got up, walked back inside, and opened the door to find Nat, her face all balled up with worry.

"Come in," I said, then turned and collapsed facedown on the bed, both to stop the spinning and to not have to face her. But I felt her sit down beside me on the bed, then I felt her hand stroking my back.

"How much did you drink?" she asked.

"I don't remember," I said into the pillow.

I then felt her lie down fully beside me. "I thought you said that going back to drinking wasn't a problem."

"It wasn't. For a few days."

A pause. Then: "Do you remember what you did?"

My horror winched tighter, chased by more nausea. "I had a few tequila shots."

"Then you tried to run into the water in your clothes and the guy at the bar ran after you. And then Anthony saw the fuss and came down and they both had to drag you back up. But you resisted and pushed over a huge potted palm by the pool."

"No."

"Yeah, actually. And Anthony said you kept asking the bartender where you could get coke."

"Are you serious?" I found this detail particularly humiliating—in its utter predictability. Put enough alcohol in me and I'd start asking any random stranger where the coke was.

"That's what Anthony said. And they had to get you in the elevator together, and then Anthony said that you walked in the room and passed out on the bed."

Passed out on the bed? Then how had I ended up facedown on the balcony? I would not look up at Nat. It was too much. "I wish I'd drowned instead of what you just described to me," I said, into the pillow.

I felt her hand on the back of my neck. "Tip, stop. Look, you can just go back to A.A. when you get back to Providence. I mean—you will, won't you?"

"I haven't gone in months."

She laughed. "Really? Big surprise."

Eventually I turned on my side, away from her, but reached around to pull her arm over my chest and squeeze her hand. I kept my eyes closed to fend off the spins. "I'm sorry about you and Gold," I said. "Why'd you never tell me? Even when all this Gold stuff was coming up recently. Sometimes it felt like you were keeping something from us."

She was silent, leaving me to wonder if I shouldn't have asked. Then she said: "I was ashamed. And today, I was *so* scared you were going to say something to Janet."

"I wasn't going to."

"Oh, Tip." She laughed again. "You *so* were about to say something. I could see it there on the tip of your tongue."

She was right, of course, so I said nothing. Then from her: "I actually feel worse after having seen him. Not better. Seeing him like that, I mean."

"Me too."

"This trip fell apart fast."

"Yep." I dared to ask: "Have you talked to Anthony and Jennifer?"

"Just Anthony after he told me what happened with you. He said, 'Let's all decompress and figure out what to do later.' It didn't sound like he was jumping on the next plane home or anything."

"But he probably will," I said.

"Well," she said, "maybe it's best we all just go home?"

I didn't reply. The logistics of getting home seemed overwhelming; as it was, I could barely move my head. I made myself take deep breaths, trying to stave off that hysterical sense of catastrophe that engulfed me after coming out of every blackout, that borderline suicidal feeling that I'd never feel normal again, that there was no point in even trying to set the ship aright yet another time. I realized that over the past many months of not drinking, I'd taken for granted the blessed absence of that pitch-black feeling—especially after I stopped going to meetings, the whole point of which were to hammer into one's head, daily, that one was in a better place without drinking, because apparently the human head seemed unequipped to remember such a thing on its own from day to day.

Then there was a buzz, and a rustling as Nat extracted her phone. "It's a text from Jennifer," she announced. "Can she come by the room?"

I wanted to say no, to avoid her seeing me in this condition. But then I remembered that this was precisely the effect of these relapses, how they made me push away people, including Marcus, until I felt I was respectable enough to be countenanced by them again, and this time I determined, fuck it, let them see, it's better than hiding.

"Sure," I said, "but you better tell her I'm hungover."

"I think Anthony already told her everything."

Another wave of shame overcame me: Jennifer, my overachieving high-school friend, the scholar and professor and wife and mother, the keeper of a beautiful home. And me, the early fortysomething alcoholic, the childless inhabitant of an upstairs unit in an irrelevant city, the anonymous scrivener of inconsequential content, the vessel of unexamined entitlement and emblem of resentful mediocrity, as she'd more than pointed out to me in the car coming from Gold's.

I forced myself to get up out of bed, go scrub my face, and tame my hair despite the migraine, dizziness, and nausea.

She knocked as I was exiting the bathroom, and I let her in. She took one look at me—I saw her nose wrinkle minutely as she smelled the liquor coming off me; I'd not remembered to brush my teeth—and smiled forlornly, shook her head. "Tip," she intoned, in a tone so full of kind pity that it nearly devastated me.

I rolled my eyes, to acknowledge my own abjectness. "Sorry you have to see me like this," I said, stepping aside. "Come in." I walked to the bed, where Nat had sat herself up against the headboard. I did the same, fingers clamping my scalp again, and Jennifer perched at the foot of the bed, posture erect and perfect as ever.

She and Nat exchanged hellos in that commiserating tone women use when they mean to nod to recent unfortunate events.

"How are you doing?" Jennifer asked Nat.

"Trying to get past that shitshow. What about you?"

Jennifer laughed lightly. "*Very* much the same."

But there was something perfunctory and purposeful in her manner, and then she said, not entirely to my surprise, "So—I'm actually going back on an 8 p.m. flight tonight. Raffy's still having a very hard time sleeping." Her voice broke slightly as she said it. She then smiled, apologetically, as though the moment had not happened at all.

"Oh!" Nat half exclaimed. "We were just wondering how the trip was going to end."

"Yes, well, I think we've realized that reunions can have diminishing returns and that there's a reason why we turn the page and find a better fit for our lives."

This came out of Jennifer's mouth so fast, so spontaneously, and with such an abruptly hard edge, that Nat and I both laughed, in a kind of spasm, to cover our shock, and our hurt.

And then Jennifer, almost as though she'd shocked herself, laughed sharply. Then, for several excruciating seconds, nobody said anything. As what she'd said sank in, it occurred to me that I could not think of a recent occasion in which someone had said "fuck you" to me in such couched terms. And yet—I knew too well—it was of my own making. I'd ruined everything.

"Of course," I finally said. But this time I tried to match the nasty edge that had been in her words, and to pair that with a pointed look her way. "We all have to do what we have to do."

"Of course," Nat echoed me, but more tenderly. "It's just sad it all ended this way, after such a great night last night."

More unbearable silence followed. Jennifer glanced downward, fiddling with the hem of her shorts. I knew she'd caught the hurt in my own tone, and I was glad.

Then she looked up. "I hope you know that when I said that about reunions, I meant with Gold. It was wonderful seeing you guys again."

But to me, her tone had spoken for itself. I said nothing.

"I'll be glad to see my own kids again, too," Nat said. "It's tough being away, isn't it?"

Jennifer nodded and smiled cursorily at this, then rose. I thought, to my great dread, she'd be coming around the side of the bed for those obligatory valedictory hugs, but in fact she did not. "Get back safe and be well," she merely said, and exited, closing the door softly behind her.

Nat and I turned to each other. "Wow," she said. "That was abrupt."

"I wish I hadn't gotten back in touch with her in the first place," I said.

"But she *wanted* to come here. Didn't she? Remember when she was like, 'Let's have an adventure?'"

"I guess she's had enough adventure."

No sooner had I said it than a wave of nausea overcame me. I rushed to the bathroom, slammed the door behind me, crouched over the toilet, and retched.

"Are you okay?" Nat called.

"Yeah," I managed to reply. I reached for toilet paper, wiped my mouth, flushed, slowly rose, splashed more water on my face, brushed my teeth. I did, in fact, feel better for having puked. I exited the bathroom and sat back down on the bed, at a respectful distance from Nat, who was still up against the headboard.

But then she looked up from her phone. "Oh shit, I forgot! Please call or text Marcus and let him know you're alright."

My eyes narrowed. "Why—" I began.

"Yes, he texted me, worried. I told him I'd go check on you."

Yet another sick wave of shame. This was always one of the mortifying things awaiting you after a blackout—the realization that Loved One A, not having heard from you, had reached out to Loved One B to see if you were okay. The realization that you'd disrupted and slowed others' business with worry over you.

I picked up my phone. *I'm okay*, I texted him. *I'm with Nat. I'll call you in a bit.*

In reply, a few seconds later, a terse: *OK*

And then, only seconds after that, a text from Anthony, on our group thread: *Where is everyone? We need to discuss something.*

I relayed this to Nat, who raised a curious eyebrow, then texted him back: *Nat and I are in my room. Jennifer just said she's going back tonight.*

Then from Anthony: *I'll come to your room, Tip. Jennifer, please join us—you may not want to leave yet.*

"New drama," I reported to Nat. "Anthony's imploring Jennifer not to leave for some reason. He's coming to our room now."

"Aren't you glad you puked already?"

I chuckled with her, sourly.

In a moment, Anthony knocked, and I rose to let him in, squaring to look him in the face.

There he stood, phone in hand, his face a wide-eyed parody of excitement. "Did you find the coke?" he asked.

I was actually relieved he'd started on a flip note; all my life, I'd preferred to be mocked than spoken to in true anger. "Listen," I said, closing the door behind him. "I'm sorry. I'll apologize to the bartender and I'll take care of the damage with the plant. The palm, or whatever."

He put a weary hand on my shoulder. "I already took care of it. But you could definitely apologize to the bartender for backhanding him in the face."

"I didn't do that," I said.

He laughed. "Oh yes, you did. Very Joan Crawford of you. Thankfully not too hard." He sat in the chair opposite the bed. "Hi, Nat."

"Hi, Anthony. What did you do all day?"

"I just holed up in my room and worked. What about you?"

"Same. I studied and I went for a little walk on the beach at one point."

Anthony nodded, then asked, "So, guess who I just got a call from?"

Nat and I glanced at each other. "Who?" asked Nat.

"Janet."

Nat's eyes widened. "Seriously?"

"Yep. She had my number from texting us the picture, remember?"

"Oh, that's right."

"Listen," I said. "I'll apologize to her, too. I went too far."

"Actually," continued Anthony, "she asked us to come back tonight. She says there's something she wants us to see."

"What?" I asked.

"That's what I asked her. And she said she couldn't really explain it over the phone, that she had to show us. But she was almost begging us to come back. She said she felt so awful about today."

"What did you tell her?" Nat asked.

"That I was open to it but I had to ask the three of you."

Nat and I looked at each other again. "She wants us to come back *tonight*?" Nat asked. "It can't wait until tomorrow?"

"That's what she asked."

"You can't go tonight," Nat said to me.

I sighed. "Yes, I can. I can suck it up."

Now Anthony frowned at me. "When did the problem drinking start? You didn't drink the night we went to Happy Panda."

"*You* sure did," I snapped back. "I had to drag you home."

"Well, now we're even."

I just rolled my eyes and shook my head. "Look, I said I can go tonight. I guess if she"—Janet, I meant—"wants us to come back that badly, I owe it to her, after what I did."

Anthony and I both looked at Nat. "I guess so?" she said. "I mean, the worst is over. I've seen him and now I know what to expect." She paused, then laughed sharply. "He doesn't even know who we are!"

After which Anthony pulled out his phone. "I'm calling Jennifer," he announced, dialing. In a moment, he greeted her, related the same news, concluding with: "I feel like we kind of owe it to her." Pause, then: "Can't you postpone the trip back until tomorrow?" Pause, then: "I'll pay for it." Slight wince and aggrieved eye-roll. "I'm sorry, I didn't mean—" Pause, then, "Well, exactly, and now I feel bad about it, and that's why I think we should go hear her out." Pause again. "Yes, I know." Pause. "I've had the same feelings today." Pause. "Well, yes, I know, I don't have *kids*, thank you for reminding me, but I do have a life and I do have *feelings*." Pause, then in a more conciliatory tone: "I know." Pause, with a glance my way, which made me queasy. "I *know*." Pause. "Okay. Thank you."

He put the phone down. "She said that if she can switch the flight to tomorrow for not much money, she'll come."

"Really?" I asked. "I'm surprised. She seemed pretty through with us a moment ago."

"She did," Nat added.

"Well," Anthony continued, "that's what she said. And that she'd just come to your room, Tip, ready to go."

Nat touched my hand, gestured toward the balcony. "Why don't you go call Marcus?"

I reached for my phone, grimacing. "I suppose I should." Just before I pulled the balcony's glass door behind me, I heard Anthony say to Nat, sotto voce, "*That's* why I'm glad I'm single."

To my slight surprise, Marcus picked up amid the second ring.

"Hey, it's me," I said.

An unhappy grunt of recognition, then: "You're okay?"

"Yeah. I'm in the hotel room with Anthony and Nat. On the balcony, I mean. They can't hear me."

"But they both know you got wasted."

Ouch. I'd known it was coming. "They do."

"Do you remember what you said to me?"

"I don't." I braced myself.

"You said you weren't ever coming home."

This truly startled me. "I did?"

"Yep. You said you liked the view from your balcony so much that you weren't ever coming home."

To be told the things one said and did in a blackout—it's like getting a glimpse of the Hyde inside your Jekyll, to know the things your id is capable of if sufficiently unleashed. Or maybe it's not your id. Maybe it's just your dumb, drunken self.

"I'm sorry," I merely said. "I was obviously talking bullshit."

"Yeah, well."

"That's not what I want."

"Well, I need a break from you. I'm going to Julia's tonight for a while." Julia was his work bestie, a fellow nurse. "She has a guest room."

"You don't have to do that." I felt that mad, desperate hangover panic start rising up again in my chest.

"No," he said emphatically. "I really do. You are not in this relationship anymore. And it started even before you relapsed, but I have to say I'm not surprised that you did, because you've obviously stopped caring about it. I've totally noticed that you stopped going to meetings, but I made myself stop policing you, because it's not my job."

"Of course it's not!"

"No, it's not." He sounded like he was trying to convince himself. "I'm sorry, Thomas, I love you, I really do. And I'm not saying this is the definitive end, but I need a time-out. I'm just exhausted from caring about you and getting so little back."

"Oh, shit." I sat on the edge of the chaise, squeezing back tears. "Don't say that. I do care about you."

"Yeah, but I think you've never really gotten the help you need, the *real* help, 'cause you're stuck back there."

"Back where?"

"Back there in your past and all the abuse at school. I mean, this whole trip."

"This trip is just a little reunion with friends!"

"The only friend you were really in touch with, that you really cared about, is Natalie."

"Well, yeah, but, you know, people get back in touch!"

"Did you find your old teacher yet?" Sarcasm edged his voice.

"We did. Today."

"How'd it go?" His voice had softened a notch.

"He has Alzheimer's. He didn't know who any of us were."

After a pause, Marcus burst out laughing. "I'm sorry," he managed. "That is just the richest, most ironic thing I've heard in a long while."

"I know." I laughed along with him, slightly, despite my aching head. "It's like a de Maupassant story."

"*The Necklace*," he said, not missing a beat, impressing me.

"Exactly." To have laughed with him, even briefly, sparked in me memories of good times with him, times when I'd felt lucky to have someone with whom to snicker and marvel at the world, a coconspirator. "Marcus, come on, don't move out."

"I am, for now. I really need some love and support myself. And can I just say one more thing?"

My heart was sinking again. "What?"

"I really hope you go back to your meetings when you get back, because they're a good stabilizer from day to day. I can see it even if you can't. But I don't think just talking about what you're grateful for and making lists of your character flaws—"

"Defects. In A.A., they're called character defects."

"Fine—defects—is enough. I even wonder if it's counterproductive in some way. I think you need some real therapeutic help from a trauma specialist, which we can totally find for you."

"A *trauma* specialist?" The word sounded utterly ridiculous. "I wasn't in Cambodia."

But he ignored my crack. "You have your whole forties ahead of you. You don't really wanna carry around that baggage from when you were fourteen, fifteen, for another decade, do you? You're a man, now, Tip. You're not that beat-up kid anymore."

It was the word *man* that set me off, my tears. "I don't feel like a man, though, Marcus."

"I know you don't. But you deserve to."

He let me finish blubbering for half a minute. Then he said: "Just try to take care of yourself for the rest of the trip. Just stick close by Natalie, okay?"

"I will."

"Okay, I'll talk to you later then. And you should know that they are tearing the downstairs hallway apart, redoing the stairs."

"Okay. Bye, Marcus. I love you."

"Yeah, I love you too, Tip."

I sat there a moment, smearing tears away from my face. I'd have to return to an empty house. The unbearable silence that would hang over the framed prints, the dishes, the pillows, the dust as it floated in front of the windows in the shafts of sunlight.

I rose. I hardly cared at this point that Nat and Anthony would see my puffy face. They already knew what a mess I was.

But when I turned and stepped back in the room, I found there, chatting with Nat and Anthony, Jennifer, a little purse in her lap.

"You're coming?" I asked her.

"I postponed the flight until tomorrow morning."

I said nothing, slid the balcony door closed behind me, and sat back down on the bed.

"Are you okay?" she asked me.

"I feel like shit but I'll be fine. Thanks for asking. So—" and I turned to address Nat and Anthony as well. "We're gonna go find out what this is all about?"

Anthony rose, followed by Nat, pulled the car key from his pocket and dangled it theatrically before us. "Let's go," he said.

As we walked down the long hallway toward the elevators, Jennifer grabbed my wrist, held me back just before Anthony and Nat turned the corner.

"I'm sorry I did that," she said. "That weekend at Yale. I *do* remember."

I felt myself blush scarlet. "I'm humiliated that I even brought it up. I didn't want you to know I remembered."

She looked at me keenly, her fingers still loose around my wrist. "I was in a transitional state," she said.

"Yeah. I know that now."

"I also didn't fully appreciate at the time how badly you wanted to stay friends."

"I did." It was the one final admission of need, I told myself, she was ever going to get from me again.

TEN

I leaned away from Nat in the back seat of the car, fearful I still stank of tequila, as we retraced our route of late morning amid darkness, water glistening on either side of the Ringling Causeway that connected Longboat Key to the Sarasota mainland. We were mainly quiet.

"What . . . could . . . this . . . be?" Jennifer intoned finally, in a kind of ironic, rhetorical announcer's voice.

"Anthony, did she give you any hint?" Nat asked.

He shook his head. "She had to show us something, she said."

"I hope he's not sundowning," I said.

Jennifer, in the passenger seat, twisted her head back toward me. "Oh, yes, I've heard of that."

"What's that?" Anthony asked.

"It's when," I explained, "people with Alzheimer's get very restless and agitated in the evening."

Anthony laughed. "Maybe he'll start yelling at us. Telling us to stand up straight and make eye contact."

Now Jennifer laughed. "*Artic* and project!" she cried. It's what Gold would blurt out at us when we were practicing, *articulate* shortened to *artic*.

I pointed my second and third fingers at my own eyes, then toward the others, then back, in a flicking gesture. "Focal points!" I barked.

The others laughed, and then we were pulling off the main drag back into that anonymous cul-de-sac, Anthony stopping the car in front of that same pale yellow ranch, its front door open, revealing a rectangle of light from within. "I can just see the seashells now," he said.

"Say what?" asked Jennifer.

He pulled the key from the ignition. "I just know their house is gonna have seashells everywhere, like, conches, and be done in corals and periwinkles."

"You're such a snob, Anthony." It was Nat—an unusual bit of genuine distaste in her voice.

"And how do I know this?" he continued. "Because that's exactly how my own mother decorated the little place I bought her and my father in Pompano Beach. Despite my protests."

We weren't halfway up the front walk before Janet appeared, opening the screen door for us. I was struck again by her slightness. How could she manage caring for Gold alone?

"Hi there!" she called, oddly ebullient, then waited until we were all on the front steps. "I'm so glad you all came back. I felt terrible about today."

"Janet, I'm sorry," I instantly said. "I was rude."

She put a hand on my arm. "No, no. I'm glad you told me what you did, because it gave me a chance to tell you what *I* did. And I'm glad I had your number from texting you the picture. Because if I hadn't, I don't know how I would have reached you, because I didn't catch where you were staying."

"At the Resort at Longboat Key Club," supplied Anthony.

Janet's hand flew to her collarbone. "Oh, my!" she exclaimed. "Very fancy." She said it with just a note of teasing, toward Anthony it seemed, which endeared me to her. And then: "Well, all of you, come in."

And so we did, one by one, following her down the entranceway, around the corner, into the living room. Anthony was more or less right—the house was an assemblage of, if not periwinkles and corals, than beiges and taupes and, if not seashells, then black-and-white "art" photographs of Gulf Coast beaches in faux-rustic bleached-wood frames.

And there, almost swallowed up completely in a gigantic suede recliner, in front of a TV show about wildlife—lions and hyenas viciously fighting—was Gold. To my surprise, he was wearing a red sweatshirt imprinted with the profile of a tall-hatted pilgrim, *Mendhem H.S.* emblazoned beneath it. It was the sweatshirt of our high-school sports teams.

"Mr. Gold!" Jennifer exclaimed. "You're wearing the Mendhem Pilgrims sweatshirt!"

He only stared up at us blankly, but Janet said, "Yes, indeed, he's kept it all these years and I dug it out for tonight to get him in the spirit."

The spirit? The four of us glanced at one another, uneasy and curious.

"Isn't that right, Gary?" Janet was now talking somewhat louder and more slowly, that voice people use with children, pets, and old people. "It's your students from the debate team who came back to see you tonight."

None of us, politely, told her it was actually the Speech Team, of which debate was merely a category.

She pivoted toward us, clapping her hands together. "Who wants what? Wine? Beer? Coke? Fizzy water?"

Merely the thought of wine or beer nauseated me. "Fizzy water, please," I said, and the others echoed me.

"Sit, sit," insisted Janet, gesturing toward the boxy beige couch at an angle from Gold. It was long enough for the four of us, so we all sat together, side by side. "I'll be right back, and I'll bring some snacks, too."

Then she was gone and it was just the four of us and Gold, his eyes on the TV but darting over to us every few seconds, as though he were annoyed we were distracting him from the program, wondering when we would leave. I glanced by my side at Nat, who stared into her lap, as though she couldn't bear to look at Gold, then I put an encouraging arm around her. On the TV, a pack of hyenas tore a lion cub apart.

Jennifer perched forward on the couch. "Mr. Gold," she intoned, louder and clearer than usual. "Are you sure you don't remember us from the Speech Team?" Then, to my mild shock, and then amusement, she mimed, while still seated, standing up ramrod straight, opening before her a stiff folder, lowering her head solemnly, then raising it with eyes wide, lips apart.

"Listen my children, and you will hear/Of the midnight ride of Paul Revere," she declaimed.

"You never actually read that, did you?" Anthony interrupted.

She turned toward us, rolled her eyes. "It was the first thing that came to my head," she said, then turned back to Gold.

But he merely stared at her confoundedly, as though she were out of her mind, then scowled and said, "Gimme a break, young lady."

I laughed. I couldn't help it. So did Anthony and Nat—and then Jennifer, who sank back into the couch. "Oh, well, I tried," she said.

"I heard you."

We all looked up. It was Janet, coming back in with a tray of beverages and various crackers and dips, which she placed before us on the coffee table before lowering the volume on the TV to a murmur.

"Oh, come on," Gold protested.

"It's just for a little while, Gary." Then, to Jennifer: "I used to try to do memory triggers like that with him, too. And they seemed to work, for a while. But not so much anymore. And he can be snappish, as you just saw." She pivoted toward Gold. "Isn't that right, my dear heart?"

"Yes, my dear heart," Gold replied dutifully.

The four of us, pained, shared minute glances.

Janet sat back in her own recliner, face-to-face with Gold's, alongside it a reading lamp and a stack of books and magazines on an end table. I imagined this was their nightly setup, Gold staring at the TV, engrossed in images he could no longer decode, while Janet sat across, reading, the occasional watchful eye on him, the man who now knew her only in the abstract, as a comforting familiar presence, if not in the entirety of the catalog of their shared decade. Whatever memories they'd made between meeting at that teachers conference and this moment, whatever markers and milestones, were hers alone now—an odd asymmetry.

"Please," Janet implored us now. "Help yourselves."

To my surprise, I found that amid my dimming drunkenness, an edge of appetite emerged—it was also basically dinnertime by now—so I spread pimento cheese on a Triscuit and nibbled it between sips of seltzer. The others followed, politely.

"So are any of you in the Boston area still?" Janet asked, herself rising to kneel before the coffee table to fix herself a napkin of bites.

One by one, we told her where we lived. She seemed, not surprisingly, most dazzled by Anthony's answer.

"I love New York City so much! Gary and I had a few wonderful weekends there." She twisted around to address him. "Didn't we, honey?"

"Didn't we what?" he asked, his eyes fixed on TV. The scene was more tender now, baby lions suckling their mother.

"Didn't we have a nice time in New York City when we went?"

But this time he didn't answer at all, prompting her to turn back to us and shrug, as though she were used to this kind of brush-off.

"Well, we did," she continued—to Anthony more than the rest of us, as though she wanted to impress upon him her urbane bona fides. "We saw the wonderful revival of *Fiddler*, which actually was what *I* saw on my first trip to New York as a little girl—the original one, I mean. And I think that was the same trip, in the winter, where we saw all those beautiful—um—those saffron-colored flags that were set up all through Central Park. Did any of you see that?"

"Of course," said Anthony. "Christo and Jeanne-Claude's *Gates.* That was the art thing of the year. I think 2006, right?"

"Five," Janet corrected firmly. "I remember because I became an aunt for the second time that winter. But wasn't that magnificent, all that vivid color through the park in winter?"

"It truly was," said Anthony, without condescension, which relieved me, because Janet was endearing, talking about art and culture, her eyes bright, as though she were remembering things that had once thrilled her, things she had once shared with Gold, before their life together had become what I imagined was a monotony, even a prison of sorts, of care and feeding. I could imagine them together, before his mind went, the two of them talking about books and plays and politics, Gold likely fairly didactically, as had been his way with us, Janet often deferential but still with enough spirit to sometimes contradict him, assert her own point or taste, perhaps even bring him around. It reminded me that, for at least some people, the decision to become teachers had to have started with some love of art and culture and history, some pleasure from having learned those things themselves and a desire to pass them on, even if the job became the stuff of repetition, tedium, and a patient vigil toward retirement as the years passed. In their one free decade together, I imagined, they had rediscovered these joys, freed from the numbing weight of lesson plans, grading, and parent-teacher conferences.

She then turned to the three of us—me, Jennifer, and Nat—as though she were coming out of a slight reverie and remembering her manners. "And I love New England, too," she said, possibly forgetting that Jennifer's New Jersey was not quite technically of the region. "I had some very nice times there with Gary before we sold our places and moved down here together."

"Where did Mr. Gold live again?" asked Jennifer.

"Newburyport."

It was not Janet who had answered, but Nat. I glanced at her, startled by the quick note of authority in her voice.

"That's right," said Janet, nodding toward Nat, seemingly nothing more than mildly impressed that she had remembered such a bit of trivia. "Such a pretty town. We would walk along the river and Gary would tell me every time that it was the same river that Thoreau and his brother had traveled on. He loved that period and he loved living in the same area as those writers—Thoreau, Emerson, Louisa May Alcott."

"It's true," I said. "He did love that Civil War period. He got me to read Whitman for Speech Team."

Still kneeling on the carpet, Janet straightened herself up, rose. "Well, related to just that, this is what I want you kids to see." She plucked something from her end table, held it up for us—a DVD in a clear plastic case. "I don't think I would have ever thought of this again if the four of you hadn't come by today." She popped the DVD from the case, walked on her knees to the DVD player in its console under the TV.

"So, until about a year ago," she continued, dropping the DVD in its deck, which slid back inside the player, "Gary and I were in a golf club. An amateur golf club for retired folks in Sarasota, nothing very competitive. I'm not really a golf maniac, but I went along for Gary's sake, because he really loved it." She glanced at him, perhaps a touch guiltily, for speaking of him in his presence. "I don't think he had a lot of luck with sports and teams growing up, so here was his chance to finally have some of that later in life." Then directly to Gold: "Didn't we have fun at the golf club with our friends, Gary?"

He regarded her blankly, sitting back in his chair. "Oh, yeah." He nodded, his voice a facsimile of fellow feeling. "A lot of fun."

Janet turned back to us. "So there's a fellow on the golf club named Murray Adler who fancies himself a kind of—um, amateur reporter, like a documentary maker. And he'd bring his little video camera with him to the course and make these little videos that he called 'Portraits of the SSGC,' the Sarasota Seniors Golf Club. And then at our New Year's Eve party, he'd show them and then he'd give everyone a copy as a gift, with a small bottle of champagne." She stopped, blushed. "It must sound very silly and amateur."

"No," I said. "It sounds very nice." I was dead-set on undoing my rudeness of the morning.

"Yes," echoed Jennifer politely. "What a lovely thing to do."

"And after you all left this morning," continued Janet, "I remembered that on Gary's, he talked about—" She paused to gesture at the four of us, her face bright. "The Debate Team!"

We looked at one another. "He did?" Anthony asked.

"Yes! And I was so tickled when I remembered this, I got out the DVD and watched it, and after I did, I decided I just had to see if you'd all come back and watch it with me." She paused, then—for some reason—turned specifically to me. "So? You will?"

I glanced from her to Gold, whose own eyes darted between Janet and the four of us, as though he were desperately trying to square our quartet of unfamiliar presences alongside Janet's familiar one.

I then looked at the others. "Of course," I said. "Right?"

"Yes, of course," Nat murmured, followed by Anthony and Jennifer, who sat forward on the couch, followed in turn by the three of us.

Janet beamed in relief. "Okay, wonderful, then." She clicked the remote at the DVD, and suddenly we were looking at the Gold of a few years back, in his golf gear and that same Red Sox cap, sitting, legs crossed and with a beer in his hand, in one of those bucket-like collapsible beach chairs, the golf course in the background—dotted with players and their carts—staring into the camera, the screen's lower third reading: "Gary Gold, October 2007."

And then a disembodied voice, a thicker Jersey accent than Gold's—clearly Murray, behind the camera—said: "Okay, wonderful, so today in our 'Portraits of the SSGC' series, we have the inimitable Gary Gold, late of—where in Boston are you from, Gary?"

"Newburyport, Massachusetts, just north of Boston," said Gold, a note of weary indulgence and forbearance in his voice.

"Newburyport, Mass, right. Gary Gold, otherwise affectionately known within SSGC as King of the Cabbage."

Gold laughed. "You had to lead with that, didn't you, Adler?"

Janet froze the DVD. "That's golf slang," she told us. "The cabbage is, um, the thick vegetation. Gary was always hitting the ball into the cabbage, hence he got that nickname."

The four of us nodded respectfully and she resumed the DVD.

Murray again: "And for how long have you and your lovely consort Janet Milken graced our fair community?"

Janet glanced at us, blushed, and laughed. "Murray's quite the character," she said, as Gold on the DVD answered beneath her: "We just passed the four-year mark and we're delighted to be here."

"And we're delighted to have you. And what is it you like about the Sarasota area?"

Gold cocked his head thoughtfully. "What is it we like," he repeated. "So much. Where to start. We like the weather! Well, I should say, *I* like the weather. Janet's from Virginia, where the weather's not quite so bad as in New England. I like not having to dig out my car from four feet of snow!"

"Yes," said Murray. "The easy life."

"Yes, the easy life. And well earned. And we like the folks down here. I had my doubts about moving south at first, then we get down here and we find it's full of a bunch of schmucks from Jersey like you, Adler. So it all turned out okay."

On the tape, Gold and Murray laughed together. "Takes a schmuck to know a schmuck!" Murray exclaimed. In the TV room, Janet and the four of us laughed a bit, too. Gold's sarcasm, benign with the faintest edge of hostility, was slowly drifting back to me now, across twenty-five years.

"Okay, terrific, then," continued Murray. "And what do you like about SSGC?"

"Ah, gee," Gold exhaled, as though he were faintly put off by the banality of the questions. I wondered if the beer in his hand was indeed his first. "Like about SSGC. Hmm, well. You know, I like the camaraderie. I like the chance to come out here and work on something that's low-stakes and kind of mindless. I don't care if I'm a duffer. I don't care if my handicap isn't going to win any awards. I'm just happy that when I leave, I leave, I can go home and have my dinner, and I don't have to stay up grading a bunch of God-awful illiterate papers all night."

The four of us hooted inadvertently, Janet glancing at us, seemingly sharing our delight.

"Oh, my!" Jennifer exclaimed.

"Mr. Gold!" cried Anthony. "Shady!"

But Gold continued looking at the screen, perhaps—or perhaps not—recognizing himself. "Ah, come on," he protested mildly, as though he understood the context, which made the four of us laugh a bit more.

Janet restarted the DVD, which she'd briefly paused.

"That's right," said Murray, "you were a teacher. High-school teacher, correct?" Gold nodded. "I was getting to that. How many years?"

"Thirty-six years, Adler."

"Holy moly. In—where again?"

"Mendhem High School, Mendhem, Massachusetts."

"And what kind of school was that?"

"By Massachusetts standards? Pretty mediocre, if you want the truth. I wish I'd ended up in a more Jewish community, like Brookline. Or even at a private school. But, you know, the past is the past. Who cares now?"

"Well, he's right about that," I interjected. "It was pretty mediocre."

Janet froze the DVD again. "That wasn't his first beer that day," she told us, then turned. "Was it, my love?"

"Ah, my love," he replied, oblivious.

She turned back to us. "But wait," she said. "It gets better."

The four of us glanced at one another. It was clear—we were thoroughly hooked now.

Back on went the DVD. "So," fumbled Murray, "what are you saying? You didn't like teaching?"

Gold considered, cocked his head, raised his beer to the camera. "I like retirement. How's that for an answer?"

"We all like retirement," said Murray. "But I wanna hear about your teaching. Thirty-six years."

"Yep," said Gold. "Thirty-six years. Thirty-six years of hearing 'Merry Christmas, Mr. Gold,' all day on December twenty-second. Lemme see, what else. Thirty-six years of a town obsessed with the football team, a town that couldn't raise the money to build a proper theater in the school, even though the money was certainly there. So they had to use the cafeteria for plays. Thirty-six years of blank-eyed, incurious, cud-chewing—"

Janet froze the DVD. "I think he means gum-chewing there," she said, but by this point, the four of us were transfixed, occasionally glancing over at Gold, our eyes wide with shock and, frankly, growing admiration. "I don't think he ever thought this would be seen by anyone from Mendhem, obviously, so he really just let loose."

"Clearly!" laughed Jennifer.

Janet restarted the DVD.

"—unintellectual, uninspired drones," concluded Gold. "Parent conferences where all they cared about was that I keep their grades above a C+ so they could stay on their teams. I don't think I can remember a parent asking me once if their kid seemed intellectually curious."

"You didn't like your job!" Murray exclaimed. "For thirty-six years."

Gold raised his beer again, shrugged. "Listen, we do what we have to do. I had great summers. I saw much of the world." He gestured airily with his beer, then sipped. "And listen, of course there were some exceptions. There always are. I loved my Speech kids, okay?"

Janet turned to us. "This is it," she said.

"What's that?" Murray asked.

"My Speech kids. In the eighties, I ran the— I was the coach for the Speech Team, when the kids would compete against different schools in the area. In debate, original speeches, reading literature and poetry, stuff like that."

"And this was a source of joy?" asked Murray. I couldn't tell if he sounded relieved or incredulous.

"This was a source of joy," Gold conceded.

"Why?"

"Why." Gold, on the tape, blew air out of his mouth, briefly stymied. "'Cause these kids were the misfits, okay? They didn't fit in this incurious"—that *word* again! It must have been playing in his head for thirty-six years!—"provincial community. There was the smart Black girl—"

Jennifer's hands flew to her lips. "Oh my God!" she exclaimed.

"—pretty much the only one in the whole school, the poor kid. A couple of—" He paused. "Gay kids, basically, I'm pretty sure. A cute little hippie girl. These are the kids I remember from the golden years."

"Eh?" It was Murray.

"When we really picked up speed and brought home a lot of trophies. It was all downhill going into the nineties."

"Ah." Murray again. "So these kids were your rainmakers."

"Made me proud. I'm telling you, just the square pegs. But they all actually loved words. Language, literature, oratory. How to put it all together. And that's what I did with them after school, tried to make these kids more polished. And we had a hell of a good time on the bus on Saturdays and I was damn proud of them coming back with their medals."

A tear raced down my cheek. I couldn't help it, and perhaps it was partly that I was still somewhat drunk. But we were all wet-eyed, it turned out, including Janet, lightly, who paused the DVD yet again.

"I just had to let the four of you hear that before you left," she said. "Can you see now?"

"Of course," I said, picking up a napkin from the coffee table. There was quite a stack there, I noticed. Had she foreseen all this? Anthony, Jennifer, and Nat were reaching for them, too.

Across the TV room, Gold tried to sit up in his chair, looking agitated. "What the hell," he managed.

Janet sidled over to him, took his hand. "It's okay, Gary," she said. "They just heard something nice you said about them on the DVD and they got emotional, that's all."

He gestured toward us. "What the hell?"

"We're sorry, Mr. Gold," Anthony said, wiping his nose. It was odd to see him crying, his face so unattractively uncomposed. It was odd to see all of us crying, honestly. The whole moment might have been the oddest in my life up to that point.

"It's just," continued Anthony, "that's sweet what you said on the tape."

"Alright!" said Gold, that same tone of false comprehension.

Janet let us compose ourselves somewhat, watching us as we did.

"Is there more?" Nat finally asked.

"Not really about the four of you. Murray starts asking him about his favorite authors, his favorite books, stuff like that."

The four of us just sat there, completely at a loss for what to do next.

"Listen," continued Janet, "I was thinking. Why don't the four of you tell Gary what you wanted to tell him in the first place? Do you think you can do it in a sort of, um, low-key register so he doesn't get riled up?"

The four of us looked at one another, none of us able to say what we were thinking.

But she seemed to intuit it. "Even if he doesn't really understand you, I think you'll feel better for saying it," she said.

I sat there, fully torn about the usefulness of this idea—it felt somewhat ridiculous to me, in fact—when Jennifer surprised me by starting right in.

"Mr. Gold," she began, clasping her hands and leaning toward him from the couch almost as though she were declaiming for Speech Team. "You were right. I *was* almost the only Black girl in that school." Her voice was patient, low, and kind. "And you knew that." She gestured toward the TV, where Gold's image now sat frozen, a nanosecond after he'd said *coming back with their medals*, a comically pained look caught on his face amid the digital freeze.

"So can you understand," Jennifer continued, "how humiliating it was for me when—I'm trying to do honor to one of the most important speeches ever given by a Black woman in America, trying to do this honor in Massachusetts in the 1980s of all places. And you told me to do it in—and I quote you here directly—a *slave* voice. A *mammy* voice, you said. Because you thought that would sound more authentic and win me first place. You told me to go rent *Gone with the Wind* and to—and I will never forget this as long as I live—'put some chitlin in it and talk like Mammy.'"

I nearly gasped. So *that* had been the indignity she'd withheld from us all this time. She certainly wasn't holding back now. Her voice was shaking.

"Oh, Gary," said Janet softly, her hand still in his, as though she were determined to shepherd him through this.

"Yes," continued Jennifer. "You said it didn't sound right that I was doing it in a, and I quote because I remember this exactly, *contemporary white voice*. And that I would not properly transport the audience to the time and place when she, Sojourner Truth, gave the speech. And I was alone with you in that glass room and shaking, but I made myself summon all my composure and explain to you that, actually, nobody *knew* what Sojourner Truth had sounded like, because recording hadn't even been invented yet, but that she had been a *northern* slave, a New Yorker, before she gained her freedom, and had actually spoken *Dutch* the first years of her life, so if she had any sort of accent, it was probably a Dutch one—not something out of *Gone with the Wind*."

"*Gone with the Wind*," Gold suddenly repeated. "Classic film."

It was the first time in our presence he'd put together two phrases lucidly, and it briefly stopped Jennifer cold, sparking her to a short, surprised laugh, before she continued.

"Yes, indeed," she said, her tone sardonic. "Classic film. But Mr. Gold, I just want you to know, it was so awful for me, because—"

Suddenly, her voice broke, as it had in my hotel room, and, to my great shock and dismay, she sobbed. "Because I didn't think you saw me that way. I thought you saw me the way you said right there." She gestured at the TV. "Intellectually curious." I watched her, transfixed. She'd made herself stop crying, but her hands, still clasped together, were trembling.

"I just wanted something more from that school," she continued. "And you gave it to me. And then you spoiled it that day. No, wait. You nearly spoiled it. But I didn't let you, Mr. Gold."

She was pointing a finger at him now. I wondered if this was how she was in class, in front of her students, when she became really impassioned about something, to the point where she seemed to be indicting them for insufficient interest. It was such a break from her steadfast unruffled surface, even if she'd become somewhat less tightly wound than in high school.

"I didn't tell anyone about that, even my mother, who'd have let you have it *good*. But I stood my ground." At once, her eyes re-welled and she broke into a smile. "I did the speech the right way. And I still won, Mr. Gold. I won first prize."

She paused, briefly spent—but only briefly.

"And can I say one more thing? You were the first of many men—many white men, let me be clear—in a long career now, that I've had this quicksand relationship with. Respect one minute. You see me. And I know it, and I see you, and we have this moment, this bond, which is so beautiful, because it's usually over something we both love so much—literature. Letters. The American archive. And then you turn around and devastate me with some casual remark."

Her tears welled over again and she brought her napkin to her face.

"And half the time, you don't even know you do it. And it is so painful, Mr. Gold. But I will say this, Mr. Gold." She shook a finger toward him again. "You still gave me that moment. You said, 'Go ahead, Jennifer. Do it. Do Sojourner Truth.' And I know that somewhere in there, you really saw me, because you just said it, right there." She pointed at the TV again. "So I can forgive you, Mr. Gold. Because you messed up, but overall—you saw me."

Gold stared at her blankly.

"You saw me," she said again, now sounding truly spent.

Jennifer sank back down into the couch a bit. For a moment, nobody said anything. Then Gold looked up at the ceiling, exasperated, muttered, "What the hell—"

"Shhh, Gary." Janet stroked his arm, continuing to hold his hand with the other. "Just let them finish."

Anthony, Nat, and I looked at one another—each of us wanting the other two to proceed. To my mild surprise, Nat leaned against Anthony and said, "You go."

"Really?"

"Yeah, you go, Anthony," I said.

Anthony turned to Gold, raised his palms aloft somewhat stagily. As with Jennifer, it was such an echo of how we might have started a Speech Team presentation, I nearly laughed.

"Mr. Gold, do you remember what you said to me?" Anthony paused—it must have been a rhetorical pause, because surely he knew that Gold could not possibly remember. "You told me my last name—Malouf—sounded like the name of a quote-unquote hairy terrorist. And that the Lebanese were trying to destroy Israel. Or something like that. I mainly remember you telling me I had a terrorist name. Alone in a room with you, practicing."

I dared to glance at Janet. This time, she evinced no dismay as she had at Jennifer's revelation. I sensed that, by this point, she'd steeled herself for the very worst.

"But I've thought about this the past few months," continued Anthony, more brightly. "And the funny thing is that, in a strange way, I have to thank you. Because honestly, up until that moment, I barely thought of myself as an—uh, as an Arab. I mean, my parents were both Catholic. I didn't think of it as any different from being half-Italian, from my mother. I had one grandmother who made meatballs and another who rolled grape leaves. Big deal."

Gold shrugged. "Big deal," he said, mimicking Anthony's tone, that same kind of cadence he'd used with Jennifer, meant to assure us he was following the thread.

"But then for the first time," continued Anthony, "I left that day thinking of myself as part of some dirty, bad group. Things I'd see on the news about terrorists that I never associated myself with. And

I went home and asked my dad, 'Dad, are Lebanese people terrorists?' And he said, 'Lebanon was a beautiful country that was destroyed by the Muslims and the Jews.'"

Gold perked up, to my surprise, and laughed. "The Jews, huh?" he asked.

"That's what my father said. And so, to make a long story short, when I wasn't reading fashion magazines, I started reading about Lebanon, about the Middle East, and actually learning about this place I was from. And then I started learning that before the war, Beirut was actually this *incredibly* glamorous city."

"That's very true," Janet interjected at this point.

"Full of artists, writers, jetsetters—*not* terrorists. The Paris of the Middle East, they called it," Anthony continued. "And a few years after the war there ended and things were coming back, the late nineties, I went there for the first time and had the most amazing time—met the most amazing, cultured, creative people. And I've probably been half a dozen times since then and made some of my best friends there. I was so in love with the tiles in the old floors that I put them in my last collection."

He even put that in an article, I almost said.

"So, Mr. Gold, the point being, all of this I have you to thank for, because it started with you calling me a hairy terrorist."

Gold regarded him frankly, a kind of challenging look on his face. "Well, alright, then," he finally said, nodding his head firmly.

Janet stroked his knee with one hand, tapped her temple at us, as she'd done that morning.

"That's okay," Anthony said. "I actually feel better." Then he turned back to Gold: "And, I would just like to add, Mr. Gold, I would also like to thank you, because the presentational skills you taught me have helped me in my career. People always tell me that I'm able to explain my ideas well, even about a new season collection, and I can only assume that's because of Speech Team."

"Alright, then," Gold said again. He seemed to be settling on this as his standard rejoinder, a fallback cadence.

"That's lovely to hear," said Janet. "Also, you should know, his feelings about the Middle East evolved. Especially after he read Jimmy Carter's book. I don't think he would have said to you the past few years what he said—so long ago."

Anthony, receding self-consciously back into the couch after his aria, smiled weakly. "That's nice to hear."

Then all eyes turned to Nat and me. She nudged me. "Why don't you say what you have to say?" I read between her lines—she didn't yet know what she wanted to say, or if she wanted to say anything at all.

I put my arm around her. "Okay." Then I turned to Gold. "Mr. Gold," I began. Then—what? I'd told this story so many times the past few months that now, oddly, it felt meretricious telling it once more, even to its source. "I know you probably don't remember, but one afternoon, you took me aside alone, just like with Jennifer and Anthony, and you told me I should stop running around the school being a mincing homosexual."

Janet put her head in her hand, shook it. "Gary," she moaned, half-laughing. And then, for a moment, we all laughed. The revelations were becoming a kind of *Saturday Night Live* sketch of "Most Offensive Teacher Ever," each new divulgence a beat in a parlor game of rising stakes.

Even Gold, taking his cue from us, laughed in a short, sharp bark. "Homosexual?" he mimicked me.

"Yes. A mincing homosexual, a mincing, flaming queen, or something like that."

"His views on that evolved as well," Janet cut in. "He thought Obama should support gay marriage."

"That's good to hear," I said. Then back to Gold: "But Mr. Gold—can you imagine how confusing this was for me? You were the one who told me to read Walt Whitman. 'Song of Myself.' And it was *so gay*."

We all laughed again.

"And," I continued, gesturing at Jennifer, "it's like Jennifer said. I thought you got me. I thought I was safe with you. And then you turned around and said that. And I walked out of there that day thinking, *Oh, okay, if it's not okay with Mr. Gold, then it really isn't okay.*"

Here, I'll admit, I did choke up again.

"I'm thinking, *I have to change this, I have to get over this.* And it wasn't until, like, halfway through college, that I could say to myself, *No, Tip, it* is *okay, a lot of people are like this, and they are perfectly fine, and you have to accept this.* Even though that's more easily said than done."

He shrugged agreeably at me, as though conceding my point.

"But I guess, like Jennifer said, I have to thank you, too. Because on some level, you saw us and you let us read the stuff we needed to read. Or you even went so far as to suggest it. Because I guess based on what you said later"—I gestured at the TV—"you must have thought at some later date that what you said was wrong, right?" I looked at Janet. "Did he ever say anything about it to you?"

"Not specifically about what you just said," she said. "But when we first started dating, I told him I didn't like his jokes. About gay people. He said he didn't have anything against gay people, but I told him I didn't like them, anyway, and I told him to stop. And then his tune changed, and whenever he brought it up, it was all about how"—she gestured at me and Anthony—"your community should have rights. And I said to him, 'I'm glad you came around, Gary. I like this version of you much better.'"

She seemed to have no further discomfort about talking of him in his presence, I noted as she spoke.

"It sounds like you made a better version of him all around," Jennifer noted.

She smiled, accepting the compliment. "That's what a relationship is, right? Two people helping each other make a better version of themselves. Or I guess that's what it should be."

Then she sighed that sigh of a chapter closed. Inevitably, all eyes turned on Nat. My hand had been in hers for most of my own storytelling, and now I squeezed it, looked at her carefully. "You wanna say something?"

Nat looked down at our hands together, then up at Janet. "I actually just want to say something on behalf of Pete Stroman. That was our team member who committed suicide recently."

"I am so sorry to hear that," Janet said. "Had y'all stayed in touch with him?"

"No," said Nat. "We weren't close to him on the team because he was hard to get close to, and I think it's clear to us all now that he was on the spectrum. The things we didn't have words for back then, but we knew he was different."

"Of course," said Janet. "We all know now."

"And it was the little note he left on Facebook that actually brought us all back together"—she gestured at the four of us—"and ended us up here. So it only seems fitting. Apparently Mr. Gold at one point said something to him about him being robotic, or nonhuman, and apparently it stuck with him all his life because he actually mentioned it in his final note."

Janet nodded. "I see." She shook her head, exasperated. "Well, once, on our second or third date, Gary asked me why I hadn't had my nose fixed when I was young."

We all cried, "No!" Then shared her exasperated laughter.

"And that wasn't the only doozy," she added.

Anthony began: "Why didn't you—?"

Janet raised her palms aloft. "I almost did. I didn't pick up his calls for two weeks. And then finally one day I did and I said, 'You need help. No man says that to a lady he is ostensibly vying for. What is wrong with you?'"

I felt fondly for her when she said that. I could hear in her both the southern girl and the teacher, each its own version of not putting up with any BS.

"And," she continued, "to his credit, that's when he went to see someone. And came back around and said he'd learned a few things about his father, cause and effect and all that. Some of what I mentioned to you earlier today. Which has to do with what happened in Europe before they came over, and I don't want to use any specific words right now that he might pick up on." She looked at the four of us keenly. "But y'all can understand what I'm alluding to, right?"

It was obvious. We all nodded gravely, murmured. I'd never considered such a thing about Gold in a million years—never remotely thought about his childhood, his parents. What high-school student pictures their teachers as children? As fully rounded humans?

Janet put her hand back in Gold's. "But the fact he went to see someone—that showed me he cared enough to make the effort. And I'm really glad he did, because as you kids can see—I mean, as you remember, apparently—he has good sides as well. Very good and sensitive sides, good instincts underneath the *total* lack of a filter." She laughed abruptly. "And he had really mellowed in recent years and become *much* more thoughtful and solicitous of my feelings."

She stopped talking and started crying, her hand to her eyes.

"Oh, I'm sorry!" exclaimed Jennifer.

"No, no, no, no," insisted Janet, laughing and crying. "I'm sorry, but of course, that's the hardest thing, just when you think you're going into another chapter with someone, a sweeter chapter—"

"Of course," I said.

"But please!" She briskly dabbed her eyes, looked up at Nat. "I feel badly, dear, because I interrupted you. Please go on."

Nat was looking at Janet, frankly, her own eyes glassy. "That's it," she said. "I was spared. He never said—" She paused, then laughed. "—wildly inappropriate things to me. He knew my mom was Jewish—

in fact, they even knew a few people in common—so I guess he saw me as, you know, part of the same tribe, or maybe he was just on his best behavior with me."

Janet smiled. "Well, my dear, I'm glad *someone* here was spared the wrath of Gold."

We all laughed. I squeezed Nat's hand, leaned into her, but she betrayed no reaction save a quick squeeze back.

Janet turned to Gold. "Gary!" she declaimed. "Have you heard everything your old kids wanted to say to you?"

The four of us glanced at one another. Janet was, it seemed, becoming increasingly cavalier with him, the awkward line between talking-to-Gary-Janet and talking-to-us-Janet having faded somewhere in the prior hour.

Gold looked at her as though she were slightly mad, or at least a slight nuisance. "What?" he barked.

She was smiling. "Did you hear everything your former debate students wanted to tell you?"

He frowned. It was, I thought, that moment in a film or a novel where he'd reveal that he'd been, on some gut level, comprehending us all along, where we would all leave feeling some peace, some closure.

"Oh yeah," he said to Janet. "Good stuff."

"Good stuff?" she asked back.

"Good stuff," he repeated.

She turned to us. "And there's your answer," she said. "But do you four feel better?"

We looked at one another, at a loss. "I can't believe we actually just did that," said Jennifer.

"Me neither," I said. "I've never done something like that before."

"I will say this," said Janet. "Sometimes I like the fact that I can now say whatever I want to him. I take advantage of it quite frequently!"

We laughed.

"Not that I'm mean," she clarified. "But maybe just more blunt than I used to be."

"Of course," I said.

Awkwardness always sets in for a moment when business is finished, and now it did. We were sitting up straighter, taking final sips, wondering how to start a graceful extraction of ourselves. Janet seemed to allow us this moment, saying nothing, looking down into her lap.

Gold pointed at the TV. "Where's the show?" he asked.

We laughed.

"He knows the encounter session is over," said Jennifer.

Janet reached for the remote. "I'll put it back on for you, my love." And she did. "Just say goodbye to the kids," she instructed him, actually gently guiding his chin and turning his gaze toward us, as we rose.

"Alrighty," he said. "Good stuff."

"Goodbye, Mr. Gold," said Jennifer. She started toward him, stopped, then continued, bent down to kiss him on the cheek. He grimaced slightly.

"Goodbye, Mr. Gold," said Anthony, who reached down to squeeze his indifferent hand.

"Goodbye, Mr. Gold," I said, doing the same.

"Goodbye, Gary," said Nat, who followed Jennifer's lead with a kiss, which earned another bewildered grimace from him.

Of course, Jennifer, Anthony, and I glanced at Janet, to see her reaction to Nat's rather shocking final address, but she'd turned, her back to us, to retrieve a napkin that had fallen to the floor, and when she turned our way again, we weren't even really sure she'd absorbed the goodbyes. She squeezed Gold's hand briefly.

"Gary, I'll see our friends out and be right back."

But he clutched her hand and frowned. "Don't go," he said.

"I will be right back." More firmly this time. She laid his hand in his own lap. "Just watch your nice show." She was already around the corner when she said it, the four of us following her.

On the front steps, we all hugged her. "Are you glad you came back?" she asked us.

The four of us looked at one another, nodded. "That was very thoughtful that you called us back," Jennifer said.

She looked searchingly at Jennifer. "Do you really forgive him?"

"I do," said Jennifer, with a kindness, I reckoned, intended more for Janet than Gold.

Then she looked at Anthony and me. "Of course," I said.

"Of course," echoed Anthony.

Instinctively, I put a hand on Nat's back, to acknowledge the lacuna.

"And good luck with him," added Jennifer.

"Thank you," said Janet. "And good luck to all of you. How long are you here for?"

"Until Sunday," I said.

"Are you going to the Ringling Museum?"

"Absolutely," said Anthony, if only to please her.

"I was a docent there until recently, so I will call in the morning and ask them to comp you. It's Anthony—"

"Malouf," he said.

"Anthony Malouf plus three."

"That's very kind of you, Janet."

She waved us off from the front steps as we pulled away in the car.

At which point there were exactly four seconds of somber, very pregnant silence. Before Anthony screamed: "Goodbye, *Gary*!"

We erupted. "I. Almost. Fell. Over. And. Died," proclaimed Jennifer.

Then me: "I. Did. Too."

"That was *my* moment!" cried Nat. "That was as much as I was gonna get!"

"You. Are. A. *DRAMA*. Queen!" cried Anthony. "That was out of a *LIFETIME* movie!"

We were screaming, tears running down our faces. It was the only way we could unload the overwhelming strangeness of what had just happened, this being back in the now, this all of us having the same information, being on the same page, not having to navigate the twisted hilarity of Gold's oblivion or the sweet delicacy of Janet's feelings. Anthony couldn't even drive, he was laughing so hard. He pulled back into the same Denny's parking lot we'd sat in that morning and he collapsed over the wheel as we just screamed and cried and kept repeating "Goodbye . . . *Gary*," over and over, laughing harder with each repetition, each of us trying to outdo the others' mock gravitas, Nat screaming in my lap.

It was the kind of insane, shriekingly unhinged, your-brain-isn't-fully-formed moment you have in high school, all the time, but that you have with decreasing frequency over the many years to come, until when you do, you think you'll need a full day to recover, because you're not used to pulling from such an animal place in yourself, your adolescence, all mad feeling and no self-regulation.

Finally, in glacial increments, we calmed down—heaving, exhausted, our faces drenched with tears. Then Anthony said that after all *that*, we really deserved to find someplace better to have dinner than Denny's, and so we all pulled out our phones and set about to the task.

As we did, Janet's words came back to me. *Have you heard everything your old kids wanted to say to you?*

Old kids. God. She'd nailed us. Me, at least.

ELEVEN

Did we have catharsis? Did we have the restorative justice of which Jennifer had spoken? Were we *healed*? Or, per the *TV Guide* blurbs of our childhood promising "a very special two-part episode" of a sitcom staple, or an afterschool show taking on a "tough" issue like drunk driving or peer pressure, did *the kids learn a valuable lesson*? About, say, how everyone's got a little bit of good in them? How you never really know someone until you really *take the time* to get to know them? And how everyone, no matter how much they've hurt you, deserves a second chance?

That's basically what we discussed—once we were over our screaming fit and had homed in on a slick Peruvian restaurant on Sarasota's Main Street, the recipient of a deluge of local media accolades—when we were sitting outside, Anthony with an Old Fashioned, Nat and Jennifer joining me in elaborate mocktails, out of solidarity, I sensed, because I'm sure they both probably wanted a very stiff drink after the trip to Gold's. Then there was the ordering of an array of ceviches served in an array of faintly gauche, color-tinted jumbo martini glasses, all our ooh'ing and ahh'ing over it, followed by an endless succession of those so-called small plates that cost more than normal or even large plates anywhere else. It was ridiculous, but I think it was also the interval we needed, the mind cleanser rather than the palate cleanser, before we turned back to the visit.

"He just *wasn't there*," Anthony said. "It's like we were talking to a—like a baby or a pet or something."

"Oh, Anthony!" It was Nat, aggrieved. "Don't talk that way about him. I hated seeing him like that."

Jennifer pointed her fork at Nat. "I was wondering if it was hard for you," she said. "Harder for you than us, if you don't mind me saying."

Nat mused on that. "It was surreal. I knew he didn't know who I was. Who we were. But his expressions were still so familiar to me. His tone. A lot kept coming back to me."

"The tone was totally still there," I agreed. "Kind of sarcastic, bored—but funny."

"I loved the video," Jennifer admitted. "Hilarious."

"He was *such* a bitch about Mendhem," Anthony said. "So spot-on. I wish the whole town could see it."

We laughed. "A special screening!" I said. "Can you imagine?"

"He had some serious Jew alienation," said Nat. "The Christmas remark."

"Speaking of Jewish issues," I added. "Talk about things you don't know growing up. I wonder what exactly happened to his family."

"I wasn't going to ask," said Anthony.

"Me neither," said Nat. "I didn't want to know."

"He never mentioned it to you?" I asked. "Back when you were—hanging out?"

She shook her head gravely. "Not that I can remember. But I think I would've remembered that."

Jennifer nodded, her mouth full, before swallowing and speaking. "It colored my feelings about him, I'll admit," she said. "New information." She paused, plucking more fish pieces from a martini glass onto her tiny plate. Then: "You know, quite frankly, I think it was easier talking to him as he was. Rather than if he were understanding. I felt very liberated to say exactly what I wanted to say—even some things I didn't expect to say." She paused. "And I knew I wasn't going to get any pushback."

"I love what you told him," I said.

"I love what *you* told him. And you, too, Anthony."

I turned to Nat. "So, did you—consider saying something?"

She paused, sighed. "I did. I'd thought I might do it on the way over. I was totally shaking just thinking about it. But then, with Janet, I just could not. I mean, she obviously was not the woman he was talking about when he wrote me and basically asked me to back off. I don't think he met her for about another decade. But still—"

"I get it," I finished for her.

"Exactly. I just couldn't let her know that the man she'd been in love with the past ten years had been—"

She trailed off. The wrongness of it all was re-impressed upon me again, in the blank space where she did not complete the sentence.

Jennifer reached across the table and rubbed her hand briefly. "So instead you talked about Pete," she said. "Gave him his due. That was lovely."

"Could you see him on this trip with us?" Anthony asked. I glanced at him. He'd softened over the past couple days, I thought, let himself come down to our level and simply be among us, interwoven, not at a haughty remove, not even the benevolent pasha of the first night in the beach tent. I liked this version of him: comfortable in his material comfort, no longer brandishing it about as though he couldn't afford to have anyone forget about it for five minutes.

"That would be extra weird," I said.

"And it's already *been* super weird," said Jennifer. Then she glanced up at the three of us. "But, let me be clear, not weird in a way I regret, actually. Now that it's all said and done."

So I asked that question: "Well? Did we get our restorative justice?"

She pursed her lips, considered. "That requires the offender to have really heard you," she said. "Really absorbed. So—no, I guess. But I still don't regret it. Because—" She paused again, gestured lightly with her fork and furrowed her brow. "Because *something* feels different."

We leaned in slightly.

"I feel like—I had cut Mendhem out of my life. Everything that happened there. It's like, the day I went to college, I cut it away"—she glanced at me, like a reflex, as she said it—"like it had never happened, like I'd gotten through it and I'd never have to live in a place like that again, where there was no version of me anywhere to be seen. Now my real life could begin, I thought. And it did."

"And you did amazingly," said Nat. I thought I detected the faintest, unintended trace of jealousy in her voice. I remembered her wide eyes as we drove into Jennifer's posh town, pulled up to her impeccable jewel box of a historic home, lush hedges neat as a pin.

Jennifer shrugged off the compliment. "But, the truth was, Mendhem was the first—well, *most* of the first—eighteen years of my life. You can't just erase that. Real things happened there, people I met, who made me who I became, for better or worse. And I guess in the past few months, being back in touch with the three of you, and the trip, and seeing Gold—I feel like the me of today is connected back to the me of that time in a way that feels—not *entirely* comfortable, but still—coherent? Harmonized, I guess, to use a somewhat academic word."

She'd been looking away slightly as she spoke, across the street, but now she turned back. "Does that make any sense?"

Anthony nodded quietly and put an arm around her, which—to my surprise and perhaps a pinch of jealousy—she snuggled right into, as though she'd been waiting for his arms all along.

"I know what you mean," I said. "I feel that way, too. I don't feel so bad about those days, now, actually."

She fixed on me. "It was a long time coming, right? It's so strange to not really know you need something until it happens."

Then we all looked at Nat. She'd become the odd man out, somehow, the special case, with her story she could not fully tell.

Her eyes welled. "I just want this relationship to work out," she said. "I really love this guy and I can't drag the kids away again." She veiled her face in her hand, cried. I leaned over, wrapped an arm around her shoulders. "I'm so tired of starting from scratch."

Jennifer grabbed her hand again, squeezed it hard. "Look! You figured something out."

"I guess so," she snuffled.

"Who knows if you hadn't come down here?"

"I guess so."

After that, after Nat dabbed her eyes with her napkin and gave us all a sheepish look, we simply ate for several minutes, not saying much. It was a relief. A sense of equipoise overcame me, an almost narcotic feeling of being perfectly okay in that moment, completely who I was, with people who completely knew who I was, whose lives I knew, too. It was such a sharp feeling that I realized I'd not felt it for longer than I could remember.

Not since many, many months ago with Marcus, it occurred to me.

A little jazz trio set up on the sidewalk across the street from the restaurant, opened with a trumpet-led "Hello, Dolly."

Anthony put his head in his hand, shook it. "Just when everything was so nice."

Jennifer regarded him. "How can you stand being such a snob?"

"Were you craving a Dixieland version of 'Hello, Dolly' right now?"

"Well, no, but—"

"Okay, then."

Anthony got drunk enough at dinner that Jennifer had to drive the yacht-size rental car back to the resort, Anthony singing along to Paula Abdul's "Opposites Attract" on the radio in the passenger seat beside her, Nat and I in the back as usual.

"Let's go on the beach!" Anthony cried out in the lobby, loudly, once we'd emerged there from the parking lot below. And so we followed him, indulging and somewhat chaperoning him—a reversal of my own beach messiness hours ago—until we were walking down the boardwalk single file, slipping off our shoes before heading out onto the sand and sitting, four in a row, on towels we snatched from the pool on the way down. In the dark, only a very faint line existed between the water and the sky. I wondered what Marcus was doing at that moment. Curled up with Julia at her apartment, the two of them with dinner plates in their hands, wineglasses on the coffee table, watching *Game of Thrones*, or—worse—discussing what to do about me?

Jennifer was leaving first thing in the morning. That's what hung in the air, or at least I thought. The original happy plan, four of us over four days, had been dashed, and as this reality settled over me, so too did an emptiness, tinged with a grudge, a dim echo of the Yale-weekend feeling. I'd never liked it when plans changed; I took it too personally.

"What's the latest on Raffy?" I asked her.

She was in profile, staring at the sea, but turned to us now. "Last text from Andres was that he fell off to sleep just fine." Then: "Sometimes I feel guilty that all my worry goes into my boy and not my girl. But Chloe always seems so . . . fine. A very tidy package."

"That's what *you* were like in high school," Nat said.

I glanced at Nat, a bit startled by the force in her voice.

"I felt tremendous pressure to maintain that surface," Jennifer answered flatly, looking straight out at the sea.

Anthony leaned into her, lying on one elbow, now fully indulging her adolescent crush, it seemed to me. "Do you still?"

She regarded him, smiled, brushed some of his bangs off his forehead. "Yes, but I don't always succeed. As you saw today, my dear."

He laughed. "I certainly did."

"And I try to remind myself," Jennifer continued, "that I don't always *have* to be that tidy package. That it's okay to show feelings—including anger and sadness and all that. It's human. But y'all can understand why that can be dangerous for us, right?"

She was looking at the three of us in the dark, as though to signal she wasn't being merely rhetorical—that she *really* wanted us to understand what she meant. Not dangerous for *me*. Dangerous for *us*. I thought I knew what she was getting at—what she wanted to hear from us. But—what if I was wrong? Overinterpreting and being presumptuous?

"I do," I said anyway. I didn't want to disappoint her.

"I feel the opposite," Nat said. We all turned to her, confused, before she clarified: "Olivia is my angst-ridden one and I call Otis my mellow fellow." *Oh*, I realized. She'd steered the conversation away from what Jennifer was digging at, perhaps not deliberately but obliviously, and I didn't quite know how to steer it back.

So, with a final glance toward Jennifer to suggest I noted the departure, I asked Nat: "Do you still talk to Jack and Julian?" The two men who'd not wanted to help her raise the babies they knocked her up with. She'd wanted kids, anyway, she'd told me at the time—both times—so why not have them and just muddle through from there?

"Jack, yes, a few times a year. Julian, no. We've just trailed off. But of course I do see him every time I look at Otis."

"Right."

More silence, then Anthony asked: "What is having kids like?"

"Who are you asking?" It was Jennifer. "Nat or me?"

"Both of you."

Jennifer and Nat glanced at each other. Then Nat said: "For me—it's loving someone like you never knew you could love someone. Like, with such depth and fullness that it hurts. And the love coexisting with this constant fear that something's going to happen to them or they're going to be hurt."

"That is so spot-on," Jennifer said. "And—" She paused, shook her head slowly. "Let's face it, it's also saying goodbye to your life—that you knew—and the autonomous person that you once were, roaming freely in the world. Accepting that you won't really know that person again for about twenty years. I remember my first flight, plane flight, about eighteen months after Chloe was born. I left her with Andres and went to an overnight conference and freaked out on the flight because she wasn't tethered to me—mentally or physically." She paused. "Then I had a drink and rejoiced."

Nat laughed. "I remember that feeling."

Anthony regarded them both closely in the dark. "I wouldn't want that."

Jennifer laughed. "I don't think it's something you fully want until it's in front of you. Then you don't have a choice, and you just cope."

"I'd be up for it." It was me speaking, surprising myself. "I'd welcome someone grounding me like that, getting me out of myself."

"Tip!" It was Nat, sharply. "You *have* that person. His name is Marcus and he's a great guy."

"I know. I'm not sure I have him anymore though."

"You still have time," she said. "I'll help you."

Then Jennifer: "Tip, can I strongly suggest something? Get a dog with him. It'll work wonders. When we got Dudley, a lot of our family tension just magically evaporated because we were all obsessed with him."

"I second that," said Anthony. "Alexis keeps *me* grounded." He was referring to that blindingly white dog I'd seen in the photo spread, lounging with him in his blindingly white apartment overlooking the Manhattan Bridge. He'd already shown us several selfies of the two of them on his phone. "And she never talks back."

Jennifer regarded him. "I can't believe you named your dog Alexis. That is the gayest thing I've ever heard."

We cracked up. "Of *course* I named her Alexis," Anthony conceded. "What else could it be?"

When we settled down, Jennifer turned to Nat. "We're taking the kids to Martha's Vineyard for the first time this summer," she said. "Would you want to meet up with your kids in Boston for the afternoon?"

Nat's face lit up with delighted surprise in the dark. "I'd love that!"

"Maybe do a whale watch? Raffy's obsessed with whales."

"Yes!"

"Great." Jennifer turned to Anthony and me. "And you two can come join us if you're nearby."

She then sighed, rose to her knees. "But now, speaking of the progeny, I'm afraid I better go up and call them. And pull my stuff together for the flight tomorrow morning. Anthony, I'm so sorry I'm bailing early. Tell me how much and I'll send you a check for the two hotel nights if you can't get refunded."

Anthony frowned. "Stop."

Nat rose with her. "I'd better go up and call home, too."

And thus began the round of hugs meant to send off Jennifer.

"I'm so glad we're back in touch, Tip Murray," she said as we embraced. "We'll stay this way?"

"We will," I said. I didn't even care if she meant it, or how deeply she meant it. Mostly, I was just grateful that she gave me what I needed to hear.

She pulled back, looked me in the eyes. "Will you please take care of yourself?"

So I gave her what she clearly needed to hear: "I will."

She and Nat trudged up the sand, back onto the boardwalk, leaving Anthony and me side by side, alone, on the beach. He got quiet. I imagined he wanted to bring a drink back down to the beach but felt he couldn't in my presence. My own desire for one, in fact, now that my hangover of earlier had all but evaporated, was strong—a craving tugging at my consciousness that, exhaustingly, I had to keep batting away.

"Do you mind if I have a cigarette?" he asked me at length.

"No. In fact, I'll share it with you."

So he pulled his pack from his pocket, lit and drew on one, passed it to me. I inhaled lightly, not having had a cigarette in a very long time, still felt woozy, but—I'll admit—pleasantly so. We eased down on our towels, propped up only by our opposite elbows, passed the cigarette back and forth.

"It's so funny, isn't it?" he asked.

"What?"

"They are *mothers* now." He sounded half-incredulous. "These other human beings literally *came out* of their own bodies. How fucking weird and, like, *Alien* is that?"

"I hope I never find out."

This made him laugh. "But you know why I'm jealous of them?" he then asked.

"You just said you don't want kids."

"I don't. But I'm jealous because they had this thing that literally separated their youth from their adulthood. You know? Like, a bright line."

"I know," I said. And I did—I knew exactly what he meant. "And they also know that some part of them will go on."

"Right." He handed me back the cigarette, but then actually, briefly, caressed the stubble on my face. It felt friendly to me, rather than seductive. "Do you feel like you have something that makes you an actual grown-up?"

"Not so much," I said. "A job, a relationship, a mortgage, a few trips here and there. It all feels a bit flimsy, really. Like playacting."

He exhaled smoke up at the sky. "That's exactly how I feel," he said. "You know the one thing that makes me feel like an adult? Taking care of my mother. Marie."

I laughed ruefully. "Yeah," I said. "I know what you mean. And then what happens when they—"

He cut me off: "Right?" Then pondered more. "But there has to be some aspect of life with—" He faltered. "Oh God, I'm sorry, Tip, I'm flaking."

"Marcus?" I supplied.

His face lit up. "Yes! I'm sorry."

"So, what?"

"—life with Marcus that—"

"Yeah, I know what you mean," I said. "And I'll tell you. It's when I get up in the middle of the night, to go to the bathroom or something. And I see him there. Then I feel this deep . . . gratitude, I guess. That I found someone to go through all this with. And I suppose that's underneath all the other feelings, the banality and the restlessness and the not feeling worthy of him."

He regarded me curiously, as though he were actually seeing me, sizing me up. It was disconcerting.

"I hope you don't mind that I told you that," I said.

He shook his head, stuck what little was left of the cigarette into the sand. "Not at all." Then he sidled over to me, nuzzled up against me as though he wanted to spoon. I indulged him. It was nice, actually, with the beach breeze and, once again, the dim, blandly luxe sound of chill-out music far away, from the pool area.

"But you don't want any of that," I said. It was a challenge—I admit it. "You said so in *Hello Mister* magazine. It would throw off your decor or something."

He laughed softly. "So, you read that," he said, quietly triumphant.

"I was seriously not going to give you that satisfaction. But, yes, I saw it at the pharmacy and I bought it."

"You know it's all a performance, Tippy."

"It's everything you ever wanted, Anthony." I put some camp irony in my voice when I said it, a little *Dynasty* frisson, so he wouldn't take it too much the wrong way.

"Yeah, I know," he admitted. "But people can change."

Could they? I didn't answer.

Then he said it again: "They can change, right?"

TWELVE

Before I went to bed, I wandered out to my balcony—site of my drunken naps—and just stood there, leaning over the railing, staring down into the pool, all rippling white and blue with its underwater lights. At length, a figure in one of the resort's plush white bathrobes stole out from the lobby beneath me, walked barefoot right up to the pool's edge and stood there, clutching the robe, as though undecided. A swim cap obscured their hair. Then, abruptly, they shrugged off the robe to reveal their full nakedness, crouched, and dove soundlessly into the pool, swimming underwater for several seconds. A brown body cutting through the lighted blue and white. Was it—?

They broke the surface, shook out their head, then let out the shortest, sharpest yelp of joy, as though they were incredulously, giddily pleased with themselves.

It was Jennifer. I stood there—mesmerized, shocked, delighted. *I see you, girl!* I nearly cried. But I muzzled myself, stood back slightly from the edge of the balcony so as to not catch her eye, and watched as she proceeded to frog-swim several more laps, mainly underwater, perhaps to make no noise. Finally, in the middle of the pool, she surfaced, threw back her head, laughed curtly again, then frog-swam to the edge where she'd left her robe. She clambered inelegantly out of the pool and into the robe, then, leaving a trail of wet footprints behind her on the poolside floor, pitter-pattered back into the lobby, out of my view.

I just stood there a few moments until I finally broke out laughing, my hands over my mouth. "Miss Naked Professor!" I said aloud, doffing my own clothes as I headed into the bathroom.

When I woke the next morning, nine-ish, I remembered first that I had watched Jennifer swim naked in the pool, and only then that she was already gone. It stabbed me briefly with a little panic and grief, a feeling that a micro-family was falling apart, and then that feeling only intensified when Anthony, eyes glued to his phone, hustled over to where Nat and I had just met to have breakfast out by the pool, even before I'd told Nat about the delicious spied-upon Jennifer moment of the night before.

Anthony looked at us and sat down—but only after a moment's pause, as though he were calculating whether he even had the time.

"Kids," he began, pouring himself coffee from the carafe. "I have some bad news. I have to get back to New York today and then hop in the car straight to Connecticut. I already booked a flight at noon."

"Oh, no!" cried Nat.

Such were my own feelings. Save the first night in the tent, we'd yet not really relaxed, just had a vacation, because we'd been consumed with all the drama around Gold. And all the more so, how could he curl up next to me on the beach the night before, albeit platonically, then quit me in the morning? I felt like a jilted lover.

"Why?" Nat asked.

It was a complicated story, something about how Pietro Cuccino had decided to buy a small amount of fabric from a revived old factory in Connecticut that wanted to compete with the storied Italian mills as a weaver of luxury wools, so Pietro Cuccino had put in an order with them, but it appeared their computer system had misread the order and a bunch of wool was coming out a slightly different kind of plaid, with the wrong color blue threaded through it, and Anthony's bosses in Milan were demanding he go to the factory immediately and assess the mistake. I only absorbed half the story because I was stewing in my feelings of abandonment, truncation.

He stopped abruptly, sipped, then pointed at Nat and me. "You two, *stay* and enjoy yourselves. A charming little vacation for two." He reached in his pocket and put the key to the rental car on the table. "Explore glamorous Sarasota! I'll call my own car to the airport."

"Are you sure?" asked Nat.

"Absolutely." He gulped the last of his coffee and stood.

"You're not even going to have breakfast?" I asked.

He raised his palms skyward, shrugged. "This sucks. But!" He paused. "We did it! We gave Gold a piece of our minds!"

His voice was rich with irony, and Nat and I both laughed.

"Can I bring you both to New York soon and put you up in the Cuccino guest apartments?"

So you can ditch us again? I wanted to ask. But I didn't. Nat looked at me, then at Anthony. "That would be so fun," she said.

"It totally would," I echoed dutifully.

He came around the table, arms outstretched. Nat and I both stood, hugged him. Then he stood back apace, regarded the both of us, put a palm to each of our cheeks. "I love you guys," he said. "We're gonna be okay."

Then he was hustling across the pool terrace, head hunched back down toward his phone. Then he stopped, wheeled back around. "Nat!" he called, and we both looked up.

"You did right by Pete," he called.

She shrugged and laughed. "Okay!" she called back.

He blew us a kiss with both hands and hustled back into the lobby, toward the elevator, to pack and leave.

Nat and I turned to each other. "People come and go so quickly here," I said. Acutely, I felt our shared smallness; neither of us, clearly, had lives pressing enough to be calling us back prematurely.

She socked my arm lightly. "It's you and me, buddy. What are we gonna do the next two days?"

What we did, in fact, was have the best time. When the high stakes of everything to do with Gold faded, when the disappointment of losing Jennifer and Anthony passed, as it did by the end of breakfast, after I'd told her the Jennifer skinny-dip story ("Are you *sure* it was her?" "Abso-fucking-lutely!"), we were left with the delicious, rare reality that we were two old friends who had two whole days together in paradise, without the duties of spouses, children, or work, to do with whatever we wanted.

And we did things. We walked the rococo rooms and grounds of the Ringling Museum, snapping endless pictures of each other in front of the insane miniaturist circus that took up three thousand square feet of space inside. It was the kind of trippy oddity we'd have gotten stoned to go visit in high school, but we didn't—or, well, if Nat was hitting her edibles, she was doing it furtively—and yet we still found it weird, managed the same jokes we'd have made in high school about the whole thing coming alive late in the night to murder and terrorize the townsfolk of Sarasota, a karmic horror-movie act of revenge for decades of cruelty to circusfolk.

We spent hours in the late afternoon on the beach of Siesta Key, alternately swimming and napping on that cool, blindingly white sand, watched the psychedelic sunset, ate tacos on the way back to the hotel, even rallied that night after showers and went out to a charmingly awful gay bar, danced stupidly with some local drag queens to ABBA and Lady Gaga. The next day, we bought bag lunches and hiked through Myakka River State Park, its swamps and infinite shades of saturated green, fearsome clusters of gators sunbathing by riverbanks, peaceably alongside spoonbills and limpkins, their beaks outsize and strange. We rented bikes and spent two hours on the Legacy Trail, the extravagance of immense warmth and sun on our bodies that had been shouldering their way through a New England winter.

The present caught up to the past. It was a phenomenon I'd noted on a few prior occasions, spending an unusually large and luxurious amount of time with someone you've not seen in a very long time. At first, you are blinded by your old iteration of them, looking for it in everything they say and do, desperate to connect those dots between then and now, that reassurance that there is a through-line, that nothing really changes. And then slowly, maybe even reluctantly, you give way to the realization that this is, in fact, the new iteration, the one that reflects years of events you were not privy to. And your lens alters to accommodate this, to see someone who is in fact a hybrid of the person you knew and the one you're only just getting to know. This shift with Nat occurred in listening to her talk, in dribs and drabs over two days, about her kids—what she loved about them, where they were difficult, things she'd had to do for them, things she still struggled with despite having tried everything. I'd never thought deeply about how her life had been ballasted with responsibility the past fifteen years, about how the pot-smoking and the magisterial vinyl album collection—which to me had always symbolized Youthful Nat in her infinite musical erudition and expansive freedoms—now coexisted alongside the banal, hunkered-down Nat that filled out school health forms, attended parent-teacher conferences, puzzled over family budgets to make them accommodate extracurricular expenses. When Otis was badly sick when he was eight years old, shaking with fever, she'd curled up with him in the blankets, holding him, while she played live Grateful Dead sets to soothe him—Fillmore East 1970, Capitol Theater 1971, Nassau Coliseum 1990—narrating the backstories of the songs to him until he fell asleep, even if briefly and intermittently. That was the use of the Dead in her life now.

I looked at her with a kind of new respect, even awe. *You're incredible*, I wanted to say, yet it seemed like such a strange thing to say, so fraught with the risk of seeming to condescend, that I did not. She was narrating the details of her current life freely to me now, offhandedly, in a way that suggested maybe she didn't usually have such a sounding board, and I found it was nice to merely listen without offering much commentary or counsel. It was also heaven to be freed from thinking of what awaited my own life once I arrived home.

Her revelation about her and Gold, still so fresh, continued to weigh on me. So much so that, at our final dinner—by the pool at the resort because we were tired of researching places to go, and because the meal would go on Anthony's house tab—I ventured: "I hope you don't mind that I can't stop thinking about you and Gold. I'm not sure how outraged at him I'm supposed to be."

Her eyes widened slightly, as though she were briefly startled to find I was revisiting the topic.

"You wanna know something?" she finally said. "I spent so many years feeling like I should be outraged, especially when I'd read things or see things on the news or *Oprah* or whatever. But I never managed to feel really outraged. So finally I went to a therapist and she said, 'Do you think you really don't feel outrage? Because if you don't, it's okay. Or do you think you're not allowing yourself to feel outrage, maybe because you think you're partly responsible for something you were really too young to make an adult choice about?'"

"Hmm," I said.

"And the minute she said that, I started bawling, Tip! Like—the floodgates. And then I *was* in touch with my anger. Like, she gave me permission. So I get what a huge violation he pulled, like I said the other day. I get that it was on him, not me, not to let it happen."

"Yeah."

"But then I think about other things and I just can't sustain the outrage. It's confusing, believe me."

"Like what?"

"Just talking with him about music. While we were listening to music. Debating with him about the Beatles versus the Stones. Hearing about his time in the East Village in the summer of '68. Books he gave me." She paused. "He was the first grown-up in my life who I felt equal to, and who treated me like a grown-up. And he made me feel like my grown-up life had finally begun."

It was strange to think that when I was in college, after we'd parted, when I was having what I considered the first truly sophisticated and adult conversations in my life, she was having her own version of that—with Gold, no less.

"But like I said," she continued, "I get it now. And you wanna know something really fucked up?"

"It gets more fucked up?"

She laughed, but only shortly. "A part of me was happy to see him like that the other day," she said. "Not happy for Janet, but happy—for me, I guess. Kind of grimly happy. It felt—very just. That's fucked up, right?"

"No," I said. "I had those thoughts, too, believe me. But I also felt badly for him and wished we could see flashes of the old Gold, especially after he was such a sardonic little bitch on the tape."

"I know! He used to be very much that way with me. Uncensored. He cracked me up."

"And if he'd actually remembered us, and had been happy to see us—touched—that would've been nice. Despite what we had to say to him. Because, from the tape, we obviously meant something to him. I had to admit that choked me up."

"Yeah," she said. "Me too."

"Overall," I asked, "are you glad you saw him?"

She considered. "I'm glad *we* saw him. I wouldn't have done it alone."

"Same."

We both became quiet again, staring at the blue and white tremors in the pool water. I was contemplating another dip when she said, "I was thinking about something else last night."

"What's that?"

"I wanna ask Aaron if he wants to cut the polyamory when I get back. Even just for a while."

"Oh, yeah?" I twisted my head her way. "I thought you said that's what was making it work this time."

"I did." She was staring straight ahead, eyes hidden behind sunglasses. "But I want to know what it feels like to not have an out. To see if I can live with that. *Breathe* into it." She paused, then laughed. "I'm not saying I know I can! Just—I wanna try it."

"How do think he's gonna take it, now that you've turned him on to the northern New England swingers' community?"

"Unless he's *really* gotten to like it, maybe he'll be open to a shift in gears. He said he did it for me in the first place, after all."

"That's a mensch, Nat," I remarked drily.

She folded her arms across her bathing suit, mock-boss-style. "Or maybe I've just got him pussy-whipped."

We both cracked up.

Then she regarded me, reached over, and smacked my arm. "And you're gonna work things out with Marcus, too. I know it."

Just hearing his name deflated me somewhat; I'd enjoyed putting thoughts of my own life on hold. I just grimaced, said nothing.

"Tip." Her tone was more serious now. "You need to go back to your meetings, or therapy, or whatever will help you not go off the rails again."

"I know," I said sourly.

She shook her head, laughed lightly, frustrated with me. "Honestly, why don't you just commit to weed and nothing else? The worst thing is you'll be a little bit lazier. And so what? That's good sometimes."

I laughed. “You kill me.”

“Look,” she continued, emphatically. And this time, she shifted in her chaise until she was fully facing me, propped up on one elbow, and then she grabbed my chin and tilted it her way. “I want you around for the next fifty years. I need you, okay? You’re a thread for me.”

I met her stare. “You’re a thread for me, too. And I need you, too.”

I think I’d forgotten as much the past few years of being out of touch. But she’d reminded me. So I was glad I said it.

THIRTEEN

On the train from Logan, and in the cab home from the train station, I looked out at the grim mess of filthy snowbanks and slush that was Providence in mid-February, the pastels of the Gulf Coast supplanted by a gunmetal sky, angry with the threat of more snow, and the browns of old brick mills. I'd not wanted to let go of Nat at Logan as we shared a long hug goodbye, found it almost unbearable to wave at Aaron and watch him drive her away from me. Loneliness flooded through me, then intensified as I approached Providence, shrugging into myself in the parka I'd gladly abandoned the past four days. The loneliness crested as I stared up at the dark windows of our second-floor home, kicked my shoes against the bottom step to remove the slush in the dim back stairwell—torn apart by the renovators, covered with sawdust—collected the mail, ascended with my bags, entered, flicked on the light.

Marcus, characteristically, had left the apartment immaculate—no left-behind coffee cup with a brown ring around the inside, no rank leftovers in the fridge. The bathroom was clean, the bed was neatly made, the dishes were done and stored away. The mail that had accumulated for me before he decamped he'd left trimly stacked on the coffee table. There was a noticeable gap on the side of the closet where his shirts and pants hung, about a half dozen hangers in a row, denuded.

My heart pounded. The desolation I'd felt the moment Nat drove away from me, which had not dissipated, now transmuted into something worse, a queasy hybrid of shame and dread, a black ball in my stomach. I'd meant to briskly unpack, assemble or at least order in some sort of dinner, pop open my laptop, and get a head start catching up on work emails before reappearing at the office the next morning. But instead, overcome, I left my bags in the foyer, took off my shoes, and walked straight into the dark bedroom, curling up on the bed in a fetal position, eventually pulled the blanket up over me. The house itself, the prospect of getting up and functioning in it, scared me.

My phone buzzed in my pocket. I pulled it out. It was a text to all of us from Anthony.

> *My lovelies—that was not as long as I would've liked but it was still amazing. I feel different—younger! Do all of you? Will you come to NY in the spring or summer?*

Then another text: *And look what I forgot to send you!*

Then the photo of the four of us gathered around Gold on his modest front steps, a shadow of Janet, the picture taker, falling across us due to the late-morning sun. Our awkward, obligatory smiles and Gold's vacant, cross expression, a look that asked Janet, *Exactly what the hell is going on here?* Gold's white curls fringing the bottom of his Red Sox cap. Gold's knobby exposed knees and curiously small feet in flip-flops. Gold's polo shirt hanging on his concave, old man's torso. Gold's handsomeness in his acerbic, dark eyes still intact.

The funk I'd already been suffused in spilled over into the photo. We'd gone to Florida thinking we'd zap him. However loftily Jennifer wanted to put it, that business about restorative justice, however gently we'd intended to go about it, we were still planning to ambush him, after all. But he'd ended up punking *us*, inadvertently, with his inability to even register who we were, let alone why we'd come. What had felt good in the moment, as Janet had kindly thought it might—speaking our truths to his uncomprehending face—now felt ridiculous to me. There was no real filament between the then and the now. Gold's entire archive of experience, of memory, had evacuated his body even before his body expired. The same would happen to us someday. What, *what*, conferred any meaning or importance on one's life, once the raw excitement of youth passed? I was forty-two and living in an endless diminuendo, chasing ghosts. I hated myself for feeling that way, especially after the tremendous gift of the trip—the literal gift from Anthony, its sheer expensiveness, and the gift of reunion it contained—but I could not help it.

I fell asleep like that, far too early, inevitably waking around dawn in my damp and rumpled clothes, lying there, unable to go back to sleep, eventually rising, reminded of the house's emptiness and neatness. I stared out the window while the coffee brewed; the day looked clear and the sky was that raw blue on top with those bruised pinks and oranges below where the sun was creeping forth. I showered but still had hours before work. I ended up standing in front of the bookcase with my coffee, thinking about all the books, exactly when and where I had read them, the ones I'd never cracked or all but forgotten versus the ones that marked some turning point in my life, that had stabbed me with the desire to write something as good, as lasting, as consequential—a little flag you stick in the ground against your own obsolescence.

There was the big fat paperback collection of Whitman I had worked from in high school in putting my presentation together, its spine creased from a long tenure having been stretched back in service. I pulled it down, sat, flipped to the pages of "Song of Myself," the dog-eared and smudged pages, marked up in pencil with my high-school handwriting, those funny traces of cursive you carry over from elementary school and incorporate into your everyday scrawl.

> The living sleep for their time, the dead sleep for their time,
> The old husband sleeps by his wife and the young husband
>   sleeps by his wife;
> And these tend inward to me, and I tend outward to them,
> And such as it is to be of these more or less I am,
> And of these one and all I weave the song of myself.

I looked where I had marked my emphases and my breaks—notations that Gold had taught us and insisted we apply with every piece. I read the lines over. *And these tend inward to me, and I tend outward to them.* How on earth could I have known where to put stresses and breaks when I couldn't even understand what I was saying? Reading the poem, I recollected now in a sharp stab, had been like swimming around in a lush bath of words and images, a universe of new ideas. It hadn't mattered that I didn't understand every line; it had just felt so good, like plunging headfirst into my own future, sweet with the promise of vastness, Gold helping me get there. What had happened?

I went into the office early, when it was still empty, turned on all the lights, and brewed more coffee in the kitchen. Powered up my computer and set to those emails, a fresh queue whose unopened secrets had the power to focus me, set me aright, and track me back into the small but stabilizing duties of my life. I was well into the work of catching up when coworkers started filing in between nine and ten, the inevitable recounting to them of my little hiatus—framed as just a short midwinter reunion among high-school friends, nothing more. Variations on *That's so nice that you guys still do that!* And *I'm not in touch with anyone from high school!* Stepping out for a short lunch with my two work besties, a frame of normalcy holding at bay the dark chill of the night before, which still crept at my edges. Night was coming again, in a matter of hours. Dread called.

Marcus hadn't texted or called, though he had to know I was back. An old binary rebloomed in my head, sharpening my shame: virtuous, clean-intentioned, well-adjusted Marcus, the cancer nurse, the model of forbearance, his life upended by his delinquent, fucked-up boyfriend, the middling career writer, still struggling with substances at the tragic age of forty-two. Marcus's chorus of devoted colleagues, half of them telling him to move on, he deserved better, the other half rooting for us, asking Marcus if he knew if I had read *this* life-changing self-help book, looked into *that* kind of transformative therapy. It was that half, the half that felt for me and showed benevolence, that really gouged my self-loathing; I agreed with the damning, unsentimental half. He did deserve better.

I could not bring myself to reach out to him first.

I'd grimly fixed to go straight to a twelve-step meeting after work—the penance, the punishment, the atonement. You enter a room of people, among the handful of other recidivists there, the ones like you who have also not sufficiently whittled down their egos, who have "taken back their will" by once again picking up that bottle, that prescription you should have flushed down the toilet but never did, that rolled-up bill, that glass pipe. And you make your face and tone sheepish, and the nonrecidivists hug you, say "keep coming back" and "you're right where you need to be," while their eyes signal what you can clearly read, which is their own gratitude that you showed up today, not so much for your own rehabilitation but because in you they are reminded of the abjectness and shame their own successful renunciation of self-will has allowed them to leave behind. And you are expected, when the time comes, to raise your hand and say, "I have one day back"—or maybe two, three, or four as the case may be, however long shame kept you from walking back in that room after your fall from the light.

At which point you will be applauded, your back will be rubbed by those nearest to you, you will be the recipient of those smiles reading *there but for the grace of God go I*, you will be invited to walk to the front of the room and accept the white plastic coin, about the size of a silver dollar, that embodies your redoubled commitment to purging your own unruly, childish will, your appetite for escape via self-destruction, from your body. Certainly, afterward, you will be urged to come along for that burger or pizza, that round of coffees or Diet Cokes, where certain well-meaning nonrecidivists will make a point of sitting next to you and telling you the invaluable new lessons *they* learned after their last relapse, ten or fifteen or thirty years ago. And you will be sent home with hugs and new numbers in your phone and every intention to fulfill your nightly confessional to your sainted sponsor, who feigns a lack of injury that you have not called for three months and a stance of "I'm just happy you're ready to surrender your will again."

And you will resolve daily to check all the boxes that add up to a successful renunciation of one's will, knowing deep down that your heart is not in this particular path toward happiness, until the day you stop and take back your will (i.e. that bottle, those pills, that glass pipe) as though you were suddenly rising to break the surface of the water and gulping wildly, ecstatically, for air.

Well. It's not really fair of me to use the *you*. Because all that might well work for somebody else, not set them up for that vicious merry-go-round, and if it does, more power to them. Truly.

It's me it doesn't work for. And I realized, definitively, that I needed to find some other path, even though I didn't know what it was, even as I suspected it meant digging into the bowels of the university health plan to find out exactly whom they would let me see, and how much they would pay, and how much I would be stuck paying. So that's why I didn't go to the meeting after work that night. That, and because it was a meeting held on campus that was full of students and faculty, all of them with that particular rumpled, offhand hauteur that was the school's signature, and because, as a campus staffer so marginal I did not even work on the actual campus, I'd always felt like a poor relation there anyway, an interloper, an adjacent at best. All the more so when the meetings were attended by Siobhan O., one of the star faculty of their graduate writing program. In fact whose last, lushly lauded work of "autofiction," whatever the hell that meant, was based on the very trajectory that had brought her into the meetings. She had spun gold from her abjection. I had merely kept falling back into it, a casualty rather than a conqueror.

So I would not go to the meeting. But, I vowed, I would *not* go to the gay bar downtown, though the gravitational pull was mighty. Yet I could not go back to the apartment, with its tidy, empty, silent rooms whispering my failure, the loneliness my wreckage caused.

That very bad feeling, burning from the pit of my stomach, engulfed me. So badly I wanted to be back in that blue-striped tent with Nat and Anthony and Jennifer, facing the Gulf. That evening had flooded my heart, *harmonized me*, as Jennifer had said, and finally now I understood why. It was because we'd known one another as babies—because teenagers are babies, only shallowly responsible for their choices—and because the blue-striped tent returned us to that state of innocence, of wide-eyed appetite, yet finally with the wherewithal to insulate ourselves, and one another, from the world's cruelties we'd not seen coming twenty-five years ago. I'd had an inkling that I was no longer a punching bag, that I'd truly become a grown-up, that I had some agency and dignity.

But that feeling, like quicksilver, had slipped away, and I felt raw again. Not just literally raw, in the face, from the damp cold of Providence that evening with the last bit of light in the February sky, but raw as in exposed, too tired to self-preserve, looking to be played with and abused, because that feeling was comforting in its familiarity, to go numb and get it over with. Anthony back in his luxury loft with Alexis, Jennifer in her pretty house with her loving husband and children, even Nat in her rented three-bedroom with her new man and her kids—they all seemed far away now, deserving of their dreams in a way I couldn't relate to.

I about-faced and headed down toward India Point Park, walking onto its lawns, between the trees, just as the last bit of daylight slipped away behind the smokestacks on the other side of the river. In the dark, the lamps not on yet, I walked the path that wound alongside the river. I was attuned for trouble now, I knew it—it was a kind of inevitable feeling, a gas that fills your brain, easier to give into than fight—and I also knew that if I didn't find it here, I'd find it elsewhere tonight, because there were places downtown where I would not be alone in my desire to stay up all night, where what I was looking for after a few drinks would surface easily. *Come on, nighttime,* I thought, my heart pounding. *Fuck me up.*

Well ahead on the path, I discerned in the gloom a figure that I knew to be another guy, head down, hands thrust into the pockets of his parka. Cruising happened here in warmer weather, I well knew, but in these raw months I almost always found myself alone on the pathway at night, when I fled down here with that after-dinner gasping-for-air feeling.

We both slowed, spying each other, then both proceeded. And when we were perhaps ten feet from each other, I saw that it was Marcus.

Mortification seized me. He must have known I was out looking for trouble. To look him in the face was too painful, so I turned and stalked in the other direction. But I heard his steps coming after me, and in a moment, he grabbed me by the arm and turned me around to face him.

"You weren't at home, so I thought I might find you here," he said.

"You came home?" I asked.

He nodded. "I'm not giving up. I love you too much."

I sobbed. It was all too much—the moment itself, the trip to Sarasota, the entire past. "I love you, too," I said. "But you should give up. I'm too weak to do this." Then I said what a little voice deep inside had always told me, what I feared I'd never come back from if I said it out loud. "I'm broken."

He embraced me. "You're not," he said into my ear. "You think you are, but you're not. And I know you're not, because I see you every day. I see parts of you that you can't see."

I sobbed deeper into the shoulder of his puffy coat. "I'm never getting past this."

He extricated himself, took me by both arms. "Listen to me," he said. "You're not out there alone anymore, Thomas. I'm here to protect you. But you *have* to protect me, too." He pulled me back in close just as a horn moaned from a low, dark barge bearing slowly down the river. "Let's protect each other. Can you see it that way?"

Could I? I'd only ever considered myself someone needing, and lacking, protection—from boys who locked me in small places, from bad habits that felt like good ideas, from my wicked mind. To see myself as someone else's protector—source of strength, father figure, shelter—was a new thought. A strange new thought that still held the contours of something I'd never realized I deeply wanted, needed, to be. An adult. A man.

People can change. Anthony—of all people—had said that on the beach a few nights before. If Anthony could believe that—

"I can try," I said.

Marcus removed his gloves, carefully wiped tears from my face. "Let's go home," he said.

"Actually—will you walk me to a meeting? Up on campus. I can still catch the second half. I know I need more than that, but right now—I have to put these feelings somewhere."

"Let's go."

"Can you sit with me in it, then we'll go home? Make dinner?"

"Yep."

A tremendous cold gust of wind came off the river, hit us both so hard that we leaned rightward slightly. Something unknotted and quieted in my stomach. It felt akin to that moment of the first sip of the cocktail, the inhalation of the first fat white line, the joining of one's lips to a stranger's in a late-night bar—that exquisite relief, that release, that dissolution of the self and utter surrender to the moment. But in this instance it was only prompted by the feeling of his arm around me, against the wind. It was terror rushing out and gratitude rushing in.

I put my own arm around him and we walked against the gusts from the river, out of the park.

Acknowledgments

Special thanks to Susan Golomb, Mariah Stovall, and Madeline Ticknor at Writers House; and Patrick Nolan, Annika Karody, Brian Tart, Andrea Schulz, Kate Stark, Lindsay Prevette, Mary Stone, Jason Ramirez, Colin Webber, Claire Vaccaro, Eric Wechter, Lauren Monaco, and Andy Dudley at Viking. I am so lucky to have such great agent and publisher teams.

Friends and readers who helped me make this book better are Kevin Hertzog, Alyssa Kelly, Virginia Vitzthum, Maggie Malina, Ben Feldman, Diana Scholl, Kate Steinberg, Rhea Mokund Beck, Dana Irvis, and Keli Tianga; and my mother, Noreen, and brother, Dan Murphy. So much thanks to all of you for your insight and your suggestions.

Others I'd like to thank for support while writing *Speech Team* are Marlon Meneses, Olivia Straw, Mike Ackil, Mike McCabe, Jerome Ellison Murphy, Wellington Love, and Cara Buckley.

Though we are far from a utopia when it comes to how kids who are "different"—by race, sexuality, gender, or physical or mental ability—are treated as they grow up, we've come a long way from my 1970s childhood and 1980s adolescence. This didn't just happen. Many people and groups worked hard against the status quo to make it less acceptable for children and adults alike to mistreat young people solely because of aspects of their identity, and often those people included, bravely, the mistreated young people themselves. So I'd like to also thank all those people as well, even as we acknowledge that this struggle continues.